DIRTY WAR

DIRTY JUSTICE BOOK TWO

N. E. HENDERSON

Editor: Ellie McLove
Beta Reader: Tesha Cupak
Proofreader: Charisse Hankins
Cover Design © Shanoff Designs
Cover Photo © Sara Eirew

DEDICATION

To anyone that's loved someone others
thought was wrong. Love is love!

CHAPTER ONE

Beep.

    Beep.

    Beep.

What is that incessant sound? Whatever it is, it needs to stop now!

Beep.

Beep.

Beep.

Oh, dear God, someone make it stop.

But it doesn't. It's a continuous repeat of annoyance that's echoing inside my head. *What the hell is it?*

Making myself hone in on the noise, I realize exactly what that sound is. I've heard it plenty of times before when I've had to come to the hospital to interview victims and criminals.

"Baby, please wake up."

Drago. He's here, but where? His voice nicks at my heart. I've never heard him sound so distraught, if that's even the right word for it. It's more than agitated and crazy. He sounds a little desperate in the way he's begging.

"Why isn't she waking up?" His voice cracks. "It's been hours dammit!"

Something, or someone, squeezes my hand in a tight grip, but I can't seem to gather myself enough to respond. What's wrong with me?

"Mr. Acerbi, I wish I had a better answer for you. The only thing I can tell you is that she'll wake up when she's ready. Be patient. These things can take time." The man's voice is soft, patient—but lacking concern for D's state of mind.

"Some doctor you are."

That's what I'm saying . . .

It's with that thought that all of the events from before hit me at once, smacking me in the face. *Gabriel.* Shit, I want to cry and I'm not the crying type. That son of a bitch took him! And I didn't protect him like I was supposed to. Some fucking parent I'll be one day. I let Drago's son be taken by a ruthless drug lord that's capable of just about anything, and just as unpredictable.

The pain that rips through the center of my chest hurts so badly, making me wish for darkness to overtake me again. I don't want to face this. I don't want to be the one that let them both down. Let myself down even.

I'd never forgive me if I were in his shoes.

"What the fuck is happening?" Drago demands, his voice taking on a panic I wouldn't have thought possible with the strength he outwardly projects. "Why is the monitor making those sounds?"

"Her heart rate has increased. It's accelerating rapidly."

"Why? Do something!" D demands.

There is a fast, scraping sound to my right as if a chair was shoved backward.

I open my eyes, and I'm hit with a bright fluorescent light hanging above me, blinding me. I wince, squeezing my eyelids as tight as possible.

Trying again, I open them, only slower this time, blinking and allowing my sight to come into focus. It's then I realize I'm lying in a hospital bed just as I thought when I first heard that telltale beeping noise of a heart monitor. Rolling my head to the left, strands of my hair pull, tearing from my scalp, but I need to find him.

Scanning my eyes everywhere, I finally roll my head the other way, finally locating him. Our hands are clasped together and he squeezes once again, only this time I'm able to return the affection.

Drago stands tall on the other side of the bedrail, looking down at me. His forehead is puckered with his brows knitted together. D's eyes appear nearly pitch black but rimmed red with worry. It bites at my chest, gnawing deep inside.

"Bri, baby?" His voice sounds broken and so unlike him.

Does he know that sweet boy is his son? *No.* My mind shuts that thought down. If he did, he wouldn't be here with me. He'd be out searching every hole for his boy just like I want to do now. We have to find him. The urgency pounds into my head, hammering over and over. Gabe has to be okay. He has to.

"Are you okay?"

My thoughts are lodged in my throat. Mike had to have gotten that Amber Alert out by now. He had to have. But how long has it been?

D sits down in a plastic chair that had been pulled close to the bed. The grief-stricken look that mars his face makes me want to crawl under the covers rather than face the man I've been keeping a huge secret from. I'm not weak, I remind myself, steeling my back on the thin mattress I'm lying on.

I stare at our clutched hands. Both of his are wrapped around mine, holding them close to his lips like he's in prayer.

"Gabe," I croak out.

"Stop worrying about that kid and worry about you," he forces out, confirming he's still in the dark about his son. "Are you okay?"

D doesn't give me a chance to answer. Instead, he turns his face away from me, looking toward my feet.

"Is she okay? Is she going to be okay?"

My eyes follow the direction of his voice, landing on a tall, dark-skinned man dressed in a white coat who's standing at the foot of my bed. My gaze zeroes in on the name threaded through the fabric in cursive script: Marcus Thornton, MD. He's good-looking, late thirties I'm guessing, and even in my medically drug-induced hazy vision, I can see he's well-built underneath his clothes.

He reminds me of someone—but who? I don't know and it's not something I care to waste my time examining. Gabe is my priority.

"Welcome back, Miss Andrews, or Detective Andrews, if you prefer," he greets me. "I'm Dr. Thornton. I'm the trauma surgeon that treated your injuries upon arrival a few hours ago."

A few hours ago? How long ago was it? How long has that fucker had my baby? *Dammit!*

Everyone is right. I'm already too attached, and I have been damn near from the beginning. I know he isn't mine. I know I cannot keep him long-term. But that fact doesn't stop me from caring about him, from loving him. It's impossible not to.

"Bri. You can call me Bri—or Brianna," I croak out, my mouth dry as bone. I've never cared for the formalities or the titles.

"I prefer Miss Andrews or Detective Andrews."

Then why the hell did he even ask? Whatever. I don't care. All I care about is finding the little boy that was depending on me for his safety.

The cold, sterile environment of a hospital that until this moment has never bothered me, coats my skin, and starts to seep deep into my pores as it wafts up my nose, making my stomach churn with nausea.

I want out of this bed. I want out of this plain, off-white room. I want out of this hospital.

I have to get out of here if I'm going to find Diaz and his men that stormed into my home, shot me, and took what wasn't theirs to take.

"How do you feel, Miss Andrews?"

My eyes flicker up to the doctor's dark brown ones. He's emotionless, and I suppose you have to be when you see the things they do on a daily basis. I know that better than most people. I have to turn off a lot when I'm on the job. If I didn't, I wouldn't have lasted a week as a cop. You can't wear your heart on your sleeve. That doesn't mean I don't have sympathy or empathy, because I do. It simply means I have to look at everything with a clear head in order to make the right decisions.

I also know I haven't had a clear head since Gabriel and Drago both entered my life. If I had, maybe he wouldn't have gotten taken.

"Fine," I tell him. "When will I be released?"

"Not tonight," he says, almost with a hint of amusement that I don't care for.

Well, I don't know anyone that wants to stay in a hospital longer than necessary. It's not like people vacation here.

"What do you mean not tonight? Didn't I say I feel fine?"

"Bri." Drago draws out my name, but I don't bother to look in his direction or acknowledge I heard him. My eyes stay locked with the doctor's, waiting on an explanation as to why he thinks I need to be here instead of out in the city, searching for the missing boy *I* failed to protect.

I don't feel any pain so I must not have been injured that bad, but then I catch something in the physician's eyes and facial features that make my stomach drop while dread washes over me from head to toe. *Oh, God, is it Gabe?* If that motherfucker hurt him I swear to God I'll kill him—consequences be damned.

"Perhaps your friend would step out to the waiting room and we can—"

"I'm not fucking leaving. How many times do I have to say that, doc?"

I squeeze D's hand, making sure he knows he's not taking even an inch away from me. I'm a strong woman. I know I am, but the feeling in the pit of my stomach is scaring the shit out of me right now. And if this does have to do with Gabriel, shouldn't Drago be present?

A moment ago, I was prepared to leave here so I could find the man that put me in this bed and place him behind bars. But now . . . I'm not sure if I'm going to even get that chance.

Was Gabriel already found? Did something worse happen?

My mind races like it never has before. I'm starting to feel slightly crazy, so I need Drago here with me, beside me.

"Are you sure, Miss?"

A growl rips from Drago's mouth.

"Yes," I bite out at the ridiculousness of his mannerism. If it is about Gabe, then Drago definitely should be here. If it's about me, then just tell me and let me get out of here so I can do my damn job.

"Very well." The doctor sighs and it's then I recognize the hint of sympathy in his eyes. "You have a concussion from hitting your head. Your ribs are severely bruised, and I'm surprised none of them were broken by the numerous blows your body took. You were very lucky there." He nods. "But you'll be in a lot of pain once the morphine wears off. You do have a button to push should the pain get too unbearable though."

His head dips, nodding to my side, and it's then I look down. Lying next to my free hand is a white plastic device with a red button on top. I pick it up, but I don't press it. Other than stiffness and grogginess, I feel okay, so why the cloak and dagger nonsense about D leaving while he speaks to me? I know now even if he knew something about Gabriel, he wouldn't be the one to tell me.

There would be no reason for him to.

So what is it then?

This, what I'm feeling now, with the drugs in my system, is nothing like the pain that sliced through me when Diaz shot me, or when—

"I'm sorry I have to inform you of this, but you miscarried your baby."

CHAPTER TWO

'm frozen where I lay. I can't move, and I can't look away from the man standing in front of me. His eyes betray him. Dr. Thornton's face is forced into what appears to be empathy, but his dark gaze doesn't translate what he's trying to make his face say. Maybe it's like seasoned officers; maybe he's seen so much trauma he's desensitized to all of it—the violence, the tragedy, the loss . . .

A miscarriage? I was pregnant? No way. I couldn't have been. He has it wrong. Why on earth would he think I had a miscarriage?

"What?" Drago's question comes out as a whisper, as if asking himself. It snaps me out of my internal realization of what I was just told. It's then I finally take a breath, inhaling a gulp of air.

"I'm sorry." My head shakes slowly from side to side, still unable to wrap my brain around it. "I what?"

"So, I take it you weren't aware of your pregnancy then?" His eyebrows lift high on his forehead as if finding it hard to believe. Well, I'm finding it hard to believe he thinks I was pregnant.

It's now I realize where I've seen him before. He's Jase Teller's stand-by medical physician at MMA fights. I've been to a handful with Nikki and he's always there. That knowledge seems irreverent now.

Pregnant.

"I'm not." I can't be. There's no way. He definitely has the wrong patient—the wrong information.

"I assure you, Miss Andrews, you were pregnant. We did not do a D&C while you were unconscious, or while we removed the shrapnel from the bullet that grazed your leg. It's a surgical procedure, which can be performed to prevent hemorrhaging and infection, but since you were only seven weeks along, it doesn't have to be done. Your body can naturally abort it. However—"

Seven weeks . . .

"Naturally?" What the fuck does he even mean by that? Didn't he already say I've miscarried?

My heart suddenly stops, or that's what it feels like. I feel it the moment it happens—I've lost the . . . Oh, God. I lost another baby. The full force of everything that has happened today hits me like a sledgehammer to my head and a shot through my chest.

"Yes," he continues in his clinical manner like this realization isn't breaking my heart, isn't shattering me into a million pieces. "A woman's body, in most cases, will naturally expel the fetal tissue. What I was going to say is that some women elect to have the procedure anyway for emotional reasons, so they can go ahead and begin the healing process—both physically and mentally."

I gasp for air again, not realizing I wasn't breathing.

Gabriel is missing. I let a monster steal Drago's son. And in an attempt to save one, I lost another I didn't even know I had in my care. *I allowed one life be kidnapped while another was murdered.*

No!

This can't be real.

This can't be happening.

My chest feels like the weight of an elephant is squatting down on me, with no chance of it moving off. I'm suffocating; that's what this feels like.

"Bri!" Drago yells my name, the force of his voice washing over my frozen face.

"Calm down, Miss Andrews, please, you'll only cause your body more harm."

My injuries? Who gives a fuck about my injuries? They are nothing compared to what I've lost today—what was taken from me.

"No . . . no . . . no . . ." I continue repeating the words over and over, shaking my head. This isn't happening. None of this can be real. It's a nightmare, not my reality. I'm going to wake up and all of this will wash away. I'm going to wake up and Gabriel will be tucked safely in his crib, sleeping with his monkey. He's just in the other room. Wake up dammit!

"Bri." My name is called through clenched teeth. Drago's hands tighten around the one he's still holding, squeezing in an attempt to reach me. "Baby, please slow your breathing down."

His palm starts to run up and down the length of my arm.

I'm on the verge of hyperventilating. I know I am. I've seen it plenty of times on the job. But right now, it's me, and my heart is jackhammering so hard, threatening to rip out of my chest. I can't turn it off. I don't know how to compartmentalize this. It's impossible. How do people survive this type of thing? This is unchartered territory for me and it's completely unraveling me.

"Miss Andrews, you are going to have to calm down, or I'll have to give you something to relax you."

His words have an effect on me—or my body; I don't know which. I know I don't want to be given more medication. I don't want to be sedated. I know that's what they do to patients that have suffered traumatic events and can't control their mental state. That will not be me. I won't let my emotions take center stage. I may have lost one life today, but there is still a chance another can be saved—no matter how small of a chance that is, I'll take it. He needs me. And maybe I *need* him too.

I pull in a deep, cleansing breath, expanding my lungs to full capacity before exhaling slowly. There are tears behind my eyes, stinging and threatening to spill, but I won't allow them. Not now. Not here. And not in front of Drago or this physician.

I'm stronger than this, both mentally and physically. I'm a woman that will not break, not right now at least. I have never shown weakness. I'm not about to start now. I will hold my shit together for as long as I have to.

"If this is too mentally taxing on you, Miss Andrews, just say the word and I'll give you something to allow you to rest. It's what you need the most."

What I need the most? How dare he? He doesn't know a damn

thing about what I need the most. The two things I need the most are gone. The first, the thing I didn't even think I wanted, at least not right not, is gone forever. The second, Gabriel, I may never find because every hour that passes makes it less likely..

All the "what ifs" start to plague my mind. The painful thoughts are distracting, but I push them deep into my subconscious where I can deal with them when the time is right. When I'm alone and have Gabe back in my arms, safe.

I. Will. Not. Break.

"No," I bite out, letting my word lace with as much venom as I can muster. I do not need drugs. I control my emotions. *But do I really?* I'm hanging on to the little bit of control I have in me so that I can get out of here and find my little guy. "I don't want more drugs." I take another deep breath, feeling physical discomfort for the first time since waking up. Taking so much air in causes an ache on my right side, just under my breast, shooting downward. I do my best to work through it, squeezing D's fingers until the pain releases its hold on me.

"Baby," he soothes.

"I don't understand," I finally say. "We've used protection every time. How—"

Drago cuts me off. "Not . . . every time."

CHAPTER THREE

N ot . . . *every time.*

His voice is raw; like a confession.

Turning my head, I look at him as if he's grown two heads.

"What do you mean, 'not every time'?"

"I'll leave the two of you alone. If you need anything at all just buzz for the nurse." Dr. Thornton clears his throat before he leaves, but I gain my wits enough to stop him from reaching the door.

"Wait." I pull my hand from between D's, turning my attention back toward the doctor. "When will I be discharged?"

"I'm sorry?" His head rears back as if he didn't hear me correctly.

"What can you do to rush the paperwork along so I can get out of here?"

"Detective Andrews." He addresses me as a cop instead of a patient. "You were shot tonight. You have a mild concussion. You've had a miscarriage. If you were thinking clearly, you'd know we aren't going to release you, at least not tonight. I want to keep you at least twenty-four hours for observation."

"That doesn't work for me." I shove the pain to my heart at his mention of my miscarriage—that I don't fully understand—away for now. "I need to get out of here. There was a baby kidnapped that I—"

"Bri!" Drago says from my right, but I ignore him, staring down the physician that's keeping me from being the cop I am first. "Stop this," he continues. "Stop with this kid. He isn't yours. Let your department or whoever find him. You could have been killed. I could have lost you."

"Stop what?" I yell at him, instantly regretting my outburst as shooting pain rips across my abdomen the very moment my muscles clench together in frustration.

I grab my middle, jerking my body up in the bed; the pain catching me off guard is momentarily unbearable. It's like nothing I've ever experienced before; so intense.

Drago's hand is instantly on my back, rubbing, attempting to soothe me, but there is no amount of comfort that can make the reality of this go away. This brief, yet painful, setback doesn't change a single thing. I still have to find Drago's son—my sweet boy.

"Baby," D's voice is strained.

"Brianna!" My head snaps up, looking behind the doctor. My father stands in the doorway, his dress shirt missing his tie and unbuttoned at the collar. His dark, disheveled hair is grayer than I've ever seen. It's almost enough to make me pause in my demand to leave—almost.

"Dad?" I groan from the ache that hasn't fully died down.

He rushes around the doctor, coming to my bedside, pulling my head to his chest in a hug. It's shocking, initially. I don't remember the last time we've embraced. He used to hug me when I was little, but it wasn't often, and then when my mom died he became more distant with Jackson and me.

"I'll leave you all alone for now," Dr. Thornton tells us. "But Miss Andrews, you aren't leaving this hospital tonight, so please try to get some rest." He leaves before I'm able to gain my wits to dispute his authority. He may be the physician treating me, but I still have a choice if I stay in this bed or not.

"Dad?" I pull back a little, making him ease up on the pressure his palm has against the back of my head, and I look up. "What are you doing here?"

"I called him." I hear Mike's voice from behind my father.

"Why is he here?" my father barks. Glancing upward, I see my dad looking over my head, eyeing Drago with so much disdain showing in his blue eyes. *Great.* Now I have this to deal with.

"I'd like to know the same," Mike chimes in at the foot of my bed.

"You were shot!" My dad's voice rises. "Did he have anything to do with it?" he asks me. "Are you the reason my daughter could have died today?" He redirects his questioning to Drago before I'm able to get a word out.

"Dad—" I start, but Mike intercepts.

"Is he, Bri?"

I pull away from my dad, facing a man that for the past couple of years has always seemed more of a father figure than the man that hasn't removed his hand from my back. "Why was he at your apartment? Why is he here acting a little too acquainted with the detective that's investigating him?"

"What?" My father goes still next to me, eyeing Mike, trying to work out what he's just revealed.

"Can we discuss that later? What news do you have on Gabriel?"

"Bri," Drago says in warning.

"No, Bri. Let's not, because Tom is out in the waiting room. What do you think he's going to ask the minute he knows you're awake and alert? So, tell me now and then get your shit together before he gets in here and starts interrogating you."

"Do not talk to her that way," Drago seethes. "She's been through enough tonight. Whatever *shit* you or anyone else wants to know, can wait."

"I'm sorry, but I don't believe I was addressing you. And no!" Mike holds up his hand, palm facing Drago. "This cannot wait. Her fucking job is on the line here."

Drago stands, the force making the chair he was just sitting scrape across the floor. My hand juts out, wrapping around his wrist, allowing my nails to dig into the skin where the tail of his dragon tattoo sits.

"D, sit back down."

"Brianna," my father says, placing his hand on the railing next to me. "Please tell me you aren't mixed-up in something with an

Acerbi."

Ignoring my father, I pull on Drago, finally gaining his attention. His head swings down, and his dark, tired eyes land on me. I silently plead through our locked stare. I don't need him doing anything reckless or stupid. It'll only make matters worse. There is more on the line than just my job. In fact, that's the least of my worries. That realization surprises me. I love my job and the work I do. I don't want to lose it, but there is a life that matters more than a paycheck ever could.

"D, why don't you take a walk. Take a breather." I glance up at my dad. "You, too. I'd like to speak to Mike alone."

Drago slides his fingers through mine, lacing them and squeezes. I turn my head back up to see the determination on this face.

"Bri, if you think I'm walking out of this room on my own accord after the bomb that doctor dropped, then you don't know me as well as I thought you did. The only way I'm leaving your side is if I'm physically forced out."

"That very well may be a possibility, Mr. Acerbi."

CHAPTER FOUR

A chill runs down my spine. My eyes snap toward the door, seeing Deputy Chief Thomas Ramirez standing there, eyes locked with the man I shouldn't be holding hands with. Drago tenses, his hand gripping mine a little too tight, but I try not to retract. Instead, I squeeze him back, not sure if I'm offering him support or trying to steal it for myself.

I knew this could happen. I knew I was risking my career. No one can say I wasn't. Those thoughts have plagued me since I woke up in his bed the morning after our first time together.

Seven weeks . . .

My thoughts go back to what the doctor told me. I was seven weeks along. It's been eight weeks since Gabriel has—had been placed in my care. I marked the calendar on my desk just a couple of days ago with a heart. I'm not even sure when I started doing it. I think it was when I stopped trying to reach Tom's contact for witness protection—when I should have pushed my boss on the fact that I still had him. It's my fault he's gone. It's my fault an innocent baby was taken. If I'd gotten through or found another way to contact Captain Williams, then Gabe would be safe. I was a fool to think I was the better person to take care of Drago's son.

I don't know one thing about babies. I couldn't even carry one to term.

No!

I won't chastise myself now. I won't think about him or her—it. I can't. I'll break and right now that is the last thing I can allow myself to do.

Not here, I tell myself for the hundredth time.

"Mr. Acerbi." Tom walks over the threshold. "Care to tell me why one of my detectives was shot by an associate of yours?"

"Unless you have a warrant, I have nothing to say to you," Drago informs him, his voice taking on a lethal tone I've never heard from him. It's eerily how he can flip and it come out so naturally.

"That could be arranged." Tom stops a foot from Mike. "But if you're innocent like Andrews keeps trying to persuade me to believe, then I'd think you would want to clear your name. After all, you're the only suspect I currently have that would have a reason to hurt my detective and kidnap that child?"

"What the fuck kind of bullshit are you trying to stretch these days, Ramirez? I'm the last person that would hurt Bri."

"Yet the first person that has a motive to take the boy."

"Tom," I say through gritted teeth.

Drago shakes his head, clearly not understanding my boss's

underhanded allegation. "Why is—"

"Oh." The chief cuts him off, looking right at me, wearing a smirk. "I figured with your up close and personal relationship with my detective, she must have told you how the boy plays into the investigation."

"What boy?" my father asks. I cut my eyes over to my dad, but I don't answer. This isn't the time or place. Tom knows that, so why is he acting like this, divulging things . . .

"Ramirez," Mike says, almost coming out like a warning. Mike's body is tense, rigid as he continues to stand at the foot of my bed, eyeing me with disappointment and pity. It pisses me off. I don't want anyone's pity; disappointment I can take and maybe it's even deserved. But pity? He can take that shit and shove it up his ass.

Having enough of Mike's stare, I scan the room until my eyes land on Tom. He raises an eyebrow, directing it at the more senior detective in the room, but Mike doesn't seem to give a damn what our boss thinks of his tone.

"Chief . . ." I take a deep breath, shaking my head. "This isn't the time or place for that. We should be focused on finding Sebastian Diaz, not accusing Drago of something he wasn't a part of."

"And you know he wasn't how?"

My jaw locks. The sound of Houston's voice brings out the rage that's been sitting just under the surface of my skin. Why is he even here?

"Leave my room," I bark, then turn my eyes back on the chief. "We can discuss this later, but not here, not with everyone in this room."

"I want to know how you possibly think I would take that kid?" Drago demands. My gut knots, needing all of this to stop.

"Because he's your son."

That son of a bitch. I want to go off on my boss so badly right now, but I know it won't do any good. It'll only hurt me in the long run, but it doesn't stop me from throwing venom at him through my blue eyes. I know I don't scare him, no one does, but—

My thoughts are cut short when I realize Drago's hand slides out of mine, leaving me cold and allowing a feeling of dread to sink in.

"Wow!" D says with a laugh, not believing Tom. He turns his gaze on me, his laughter dying the moment our eyes lock when he sees the truth I haven't been able to tell him—not even now. "Bri?"

My dad grabs my hand, squeezing me reassuringly, and if I weren't torn to pieces by the anger brewing behind those dark eyes I like so much, this might feel awkward. The man that has always been in charge and in control rolls off my father's tongue smoothly, effortless, his voice takes on the superiority I'm used to. "My daughter has been through a traumatic experience. It's time everyone leaves her room. Now."

Lance snickers, but I don't give him the satisfaction of reacting, nor do I even look in his direction. I ignore him as if he's not even here.

"That isn't possible," Drago says on a whisper.

"I'd like you to come down to the station for a formal interview, Mr. Acerbi. If you are so innocent, that shouldn't be a problem for you."

"Tom," I bite out. "He didn't shoot me. He didn't kidnap Gabriel. Diaz did. Diaz is the one you need to be looking for. What's the status on his location?"

"That's none of your concern anymore. Andrews," Tom steels himself, "I'm placing you on administrative leave, pending an internal investigation. I expect you in my office the day you're released from here. And whether IA deems any of your wrongdoings as criminal or not, I'll make it my personal mission to strip you of your badge and gun—for good."

CHAPTER FIVE

thought I was prepared for the consequences of my actions. But hearing Tom tell me he'll see that I'm fired one way or another before storming out of my room has me second-guessing myself. Now I'm not so sure anymore.

"Bri, explain." My gaze travels slowly up, meeting Drago's hard stare. "Because that kid isn't mine, so what the fuck?"

"He is, D." I all but breathe that confession out.

"Andrews," Mike barks. "Maybe you should keep your mouth closed on this before you get into deeper shit than you already are."

"With all due respect, Mike, I'm done playing by Ramirez's rules. I didn't believe in them when I was handed a case that made no sense, and I don't believe in them now that he's pulled this BS."

"Is your career bullshit?" he asks.

"Everything isn't black and white."

"You know, you sound just like them?" *The Dirty Blue.*

"Don't!" I'm not one of them. I'm not like Lance Houston, because I know that sorry motherfucker is a dirty cop. I think I've always known it. I'm not a member of The Dirty Blue, and I never will be.

Fuck him for even thinking it.

Mike closes his eyes, locking his jaw a second later. Upon opening them, they land back on me as he shakes his head. The disappointment is so clear in his light blue eyes.

"Do you need me to go with you when you meet with Ramirez?"

"No." I don't need him babying me. I don't need him fathering me. I'm a grown woman who made her own bed and I'm prepared to lie in it. I can own up to my actions. And I can damn sure walk into Tom's office, facing him at work. I won't hide. I won't let someone else assume responsibility for what is mine.

"Fine," he grits out. "Call me if you need anything and you better be prepared for IA to be there. You've pissed Tom off. He's going to be hell-bent on canning your ass." With those last words, he leaves, leaving me with only my dad and Drago.

"D," I whisper. "I don't know where to start to explain it all."

Somewhere along the way, I fucked up, and I'm not even talking about my job. I should never have gotten personal with Drago, but even as that thought comes to me, I know I never stood a chance keeping everything on a professional level. For whatever reason, I was drawn to him from the start and I should have laid it all out, telling him everything, not just pieces by leaving Gabriel out.

"How about the facts? That's a start." His tone is defensive and it's understandable, but knowing that doesn't stop the wedge that's seeping between us.

"Your case fell into my lap when a woman dropped Gabriel off at the police station the night I happened to be on-call. She made vague accusations and that's how it all started. She made claims that she and her baby weren't safe—from you."

His eyes are darting everywhere, so I'm not able to get a read on him.

"I'm not following," my father says.

"Dad." I look over. "Please stay out of this."

"So." Drago backs away from me. "You've had that kid in your care for"—his head shakes from side to side—"how long? And you've thought from the beginning he was mine, right?" He doesn't give me a chance to respond. "You should have told me from the first time we spoke. You should have said something, Bri."

"D," I call out, but he holds up his palm, stopping me as his head shakes again.

"This has fucked-up written all over it. He's not my kid, for the record." He takes another step away, making me swallow hard because I know what's coming. "I'm out."

"Drago," I try to stop him with my voice since I can't readily jump out of bed to go after him, but it falls on deaf ears. He leaves, exiting my room without looking back.

"What on earth have you gotten mixed up in?" my dad asks.

"Ahh!"

Fuck it all to hell. I might as well lay it all out for him. I need advice, and even if it's from him, I'll take it. At least I know he'll give it to me bluntly. That's something I've always known I could count on from him. He tells it like he thinks it, and he doesn't care whose feelings get hurt in the process. He has no filter or no fucks to give.

So, I tell him. I pour my heart out to my dad for the first time in my life.

WHEN I WAKE UP, THE HOSPITAL ROOM IS DIM. ONLY THE LIGHT IN THE bathroom shines through the crack in the door. When my father finally left, I cried for the first time, allowing myself to feel every emotion I kept hugged to my chest. They didn't stay trapped long once I let the floodgates lift.

I cried until I wore myself out. I thought the tears would've eventually stopped, but that "cry until you can't cry anymore" isn't real. They kept coming until I passed out from exhaustion. Even now, if I allowed myself, they'd want to breach the surface again.

I don't want to cry anymore. I don't want to feel this way anymore. I shouldn't feel this way to begin with and I don't understand why I do. My emotions don't make any sense to me. I'd understand them if I'd been connected with the baby I carried unknowingly for seven weeks.

How can you miss something you never knew you had? How can you want it back so badly when its existence wasn't known until it was no more? And Gabriel . . . my sweet Gabriel. He isn't even mine, but that doesn't stop me from wanting him back. The restless nights, the non-stop crying that first night, I'll take it. I'll take it with open arms if I can hold him again.

Blinking my thoughts away, I turn to face the other side of the room, only to wince at the on-site of pain that follows my movement. I can't even tell you if it's from my bruised ribs, being shot, or . . .

I stop my brain, steeling myself from fully thinking the one thought that could potentially break me. I will not cry again. I am stronger than this, and if I'm going to get out of here and locate Gabriel, I have to gather all the strength I have and not let the results of what happened to me weaken my drive.

When I open my eyes, easing onto my side the rest of the way, I see him—Drago.

He's lying on his back on the small couch next to the window, his arms folded behind his head with his eyes open, staring at the ceiling. I don't have to look up to know he's not interested in anything up there. He's thinking—maybe lost in thought, because he's deathly still.

It makes me nervous and this is a first for me around him. I've never experienced anxiety until this moment. Right now, my stomach is breaching my closed throat.

I don't know what to say, or do, so I watch him as he continues staring at the tiles on the ceiling.

He's beautiful even though his large body is hanging halfway off the hospital furniture. One leg is stretched over the end, his other bent with his foot planted on the floor. In any other circumstance, I might find amusement in how he doesn't fit. I'm not even sure why he came back after he stormed out. I doubt I would have if someone I had been fucking and carrying on a relationship with had kept me in the dark like I did him. Does it really matter that I wasn't allowed to divulge the information? In hindsight, now that I'll probably lose my job anyway, I still can't answer that. My conscience keeps flipping sides, torn between what was the right thing to do both personally and professionally.

"What happened?" After several minutes, the silence is broken.

"What do you mean?" I croak, my mouth dry as a bone.

"At your condo." He doesn't turn to look at me and it makes my stomach plummet. I want to see his eyes. Good or bad, I need to see them to know how he feels about me. I know I don't deserve his mercy. I wouldn't give it if the roles were reversed. I know that wholeheartedly. "I want to know every detail." His voice is strained, his jaw a block of steel as he forces them out.

I look over my shoulder, needing water if I'm going to relive it all again. It's not like I wasn't expecting this part. I'm surprised Tom didn't take my statement earlier, or have Mike do it. Now that I think back on it and my head is clearer it's very odd, actually.

Why didn't he? That's routine and the first thing you do if the victim is able to speak.

Spotting a plastic jug of water on the rolling table next to my bed, I turn back over, biting my bottom lip to stifle the pain that wants to be verbalized.

Before I'm able to reach for the cup and jug, Drago has rounded the bed, picking them both up, pouring the water for me.

"Thanks," I say, taking it and trying to lift myself up with my free hand.

"They have adjustable beds in hospitals for a reason," he says, retracting his hand and then proceeds to reach down to the side of the bed, pressing a button that begins to move the bed into a seated position.

"Thanks," I tell him again, taking a sip, the ice water shocking my system as I swallow the liquid down.

"You ready to spill yet?"

He's not being a jerk, but he is so standoffish that I'd rather welcome his anger right now.

Taking in a slow breath, I exhale even slower, focusing on his face and not the pain. I haven't hit the morphine button once, and I don't plan on it. The pain will pass. I'm healing, and this is just part of it.

Taking one last sip, I pass the cup back to him and launch into what happened and what Diaz told me, leaving out the part where he groped me and made sexual innuendos. They aren't important where D is concerned. He needs to worry about his son—not me.

"He said Gabriel is insurance to get you to start moving his drugs again."

Drago walks over to stand in front of the window, not saying anything more for several minutes. Light is just starting to break through the sky, telling me it's morning, probably around six o'clock or maybe a little before.

"If *you* know he's mine, where did you get my DNA from to test?"

"The morning after we first slept together," I confess. He turns, putting the back of his head against the wall, eyeing me. "When I used the bathroom, I saw your toothbrush sitting on the counter and got the idea to take it." His brows scrunch together in confusion. "I found an extra, unopened brush head in one of the bathroom drawers, so I put the new one on and took the one you'd been using."

"Had that always been part of the plan that night you showed up at the club? Try to seduce me and take my spit?"

I have to grit my teeth in order not to tell him to go fuck himself at that very thought.

"No," I finally force out when I know I have more control over my tongue. "I would never do something like that."

"No." He half-laughs. "But you'll let me fuck you, let me date you, all while knowing I somehow magically have a kid I knew nothing about. I must say, I'm not sure I believe he's mine."

"D, he is. I assure you." I ignore the hurt in my chest the way his tone feels like lashes against my skin.

"Seems convenient. Too convenient. LAPD would do anything, your boss would do anything, to find a shred of evidence that my family business isn't legit." He blows out a rush of air. "I don't put this past any of you to use an innocent child as some form of leverage."

"*We* didn't take Gabriel. Diaz did." I have to swallow, taking a calming breath before I finish. "I thought Gabriel being with me was the safest place for him, not with some stranger he didn't know and they didn't know him." But I was wrong. And if I could go back and re-do every time I didn't push Tom to get me in touch with his contact or every time I chose not to bring it to Mike's attention, I would. I knew he would have handled it had I said something—anything.

"If he's mine, who's his mother?"

Fuck. Should I tell him? I'm already in hot water so . . . I make a decision I know could cost me more than just my job.

"Chasity Carlisle."

His brows knit together and it's like he's scrutinizing me to see if I'm being honest. It makes me mad more than anything else.

"The Mayor's Chief of Staff's niece?"

I nod, thinking back to my first and only conversation with her. She doesn't seem like his type after I've gotten to know him. Then again, what do I really know?

"Hmph."

"What's that supposed to mean?"

He shrugs. "I've never fucked her, so tell me again how this kid is mine, *Detective*?"

My brows furrow, not understanding how that's possible nor liking the way he's back to calling me by a title rather than my name. Letting the latter go, I cock my head, thinking. Maybe he doesn't remember sleeping with Chasity. It's not a stretch after all. I don't remember the first time D and I slept together so . . .

"He's your son, D. I swear I'm not lying to you."

"With the exception of you, I've never fucked without a condom. And her?" He laughs.

"Wait. What?" He stills, closing his eyes. It's then I remember his comments from last night. *Not every time.* "When did we have sex without protection?" Obviously, it had to have been that first night, I think to myself, because I've been sober every other time we've been intimate. "D," I prompt when he doesn't say anything.

Opening his eyes, he turns, looking back out the window.

"Drago!" I call out, regretting the moment the words leave my mouth. "Shit," I whine.

My hand shakes uncontrollably and tears threaten to spill from the unexpected cramp. It's the worst I've experienced yet. I've always been lucky; my menstrual cycles have never been bad.

He's at my bedside within seconds, grabbing my hand. As quick as it struck, it's gone, relief taking over. When I look up, our eyes lock.

"I can't, Bri. Leave it for now." His eyes bore into mine, and for the first time, I see a vulnerability in them.

Clearly, he should understand my need to know what happened. Why would he have had sex with me without a condom? Sober, I would never consent to sex without the use of protection, and I would've thought that even in a drunken state I would be no different. Surely I would've had enough sense to demand he use one.

I'm about to tell him that when the overhead light flicks on, making me blink at the abrupt brightness.

I look at the door, seeing the doctor from last night entering.

"Good morning, Miss Andrews. How are you feeling today?" He looks worn out the closer he gets to my bedside.

"Better than yesterday." I lie. The pain is much worse than when I woke up yesterday, but I'm not telling him that. I plan on getting out of here today even if that means going against doctor's orders.

"I'm glad to hear that." His voice sounds genuine and being a physician I'm sure it is. I doubt he would be in this profession if he didn't enjoy helping patients get well.

"When do I get to leave?" No sense in beating around the bush.

"Bri," Drago says in warning—which I ignore.

"The bullet barely grazed my leg. The wound and my ribs will heal over time. And you said the other"—I fist the hand Drago isn't holding so tight my nails dig into my skin—"would handle itself naturally. So, when can I be discharged?"

Dr. Thornton—I read the name on his coat, now remembering it from last night—breathes out a long breath of air, looking at me and shaking his head. "Determined, aren't you?"

"No sense in running up a hospital bill when I'm sure there are other people in the ER that need this bed more than I do."

"Bri," Drago says again.

"I'd like the obstetrician to check you over this morning, talk to you about your options, and then if she clears you, you can be discharged later this afternoon."

Afternoon. Jesus.

CHAPTER SIX

slowly ascend the stairs, my feet heavy and dragging. Everything still hurts, but I welcome the pain. I need it. It'll fuel me like drugs can't—not for what I need. *Anger.*

After the trauma surgeon left this morning, I finally moved around and inspected my injuries for the first time. My body is wrecked. I'm not a vain person, but when I looked in the mirror, I cringed at the person looking back.

I'm black and blue from head to toe. I have a gash on my forehead just below my hairline on the right side. My abdomen looks like it was used as target practice, and well, I guess it was. Taking three shots at close range will do that to a person. It's only by the grace of God that I still had on that vest. The wound on my leg isn't near as bad as I had expected, so that's good, I guess. Fragments had to be dug out of my skin, but the bullet literally grazed me. Didn't stop it from hurting like a bitch when it happened though.

This is the first time I've been back to his house since our first night together; the night we had created something neither one of us knew about. And then it was gone before I could cherish it; protect him or her. That sounds cruel; it feels cruel. My job feels insignificant compared to the ache that continues to fester inside of me.

I halt, shutting my eyes while grabbing ahold of the railing and stealing a moment to breathe, so I can keep my emotions at bay. If I don't let my mind process it, I'm okay. I can deal much better.

I don't want to think about my miscarriage, so opening my eyes, I peek around as I stand in the middle of the stairwell, taking in my surroundings. Drago has family photos along the wall. His house feels like a home. It's warm and inviting. This is Drago's sanctuary, but it still makes me wonder if this is really him or if it's Mona, a longtime family friend and his housekeeper, trying to give this powerful man a comfortable place to lay his head at night.

I never gave it much thought—coming over to his house, and it's not like he invited me either. It was just more convenient for Drago to come over to my place with me caring for the baby.

My Gabriel.

I miss him so much, and I can't shut off my thoughts where he is concerned. He's out there somewhere and who knows what's happening to him, if he's scared, if he's being fed. Worry like nothing I've ever experienced before is seated on top of my chest and hasn't let up. And I know it won't until he's safe. Until he's back with me.

Please, God, please let him be found.

My throat closes up again. I've lost count how many times it's happened today.

I don't know how I'm going to locate him now that I've gotten myself suspended and have an internal investigation to deal with—but I must find a way.

My cell phone rings from the back pocket of the scrubs one of the nurses was kind enough to give me to go home in. I had been in that hospital way longer than I intended to be and I didn't want to wait for someone to bring me clothes to change into.

I sent Connie a text message this morning and got a response saying she wasn't allowed to have any communication with me until IA completes their assessment. *Fucking bullshit.*

The department wouldn't tell me who I could and couldn't speak to if the roles were reversed. Then again, maybe that's why I'm in this mess and she isn't.

Still bullshit in my mind.

Pulling out my phone, I look at the screen, seeing *Dad* displayed at the top of the screen. He's furious at me. But at this rate, who isn't? I haven't had time to call my brother yet, and I asked my dad not to tell him. I know he won't speak to Alana, so there is no fear of her finding out unless I tell her, but Jackson— that's another story. The fact that he isn't here can only mean my father either accepted my wishes, or my brother is out of town on business. I'm guessing the former since he hasn't called me— which surprises me because my father never bends to my will. Of course, I never bend to his either.

"Bri," Drago barks, making me turn, looking over my shoulder at him standing at the bottom of the staircase. Not that he's that far down. I've only made it up the seventh or eighth step in my slow trek up. "Why didn't you ask me to take you upstairs?"

"Because I can do it," I tell him. I'm not helpless. A bullet and a beat-up body won't stop me. Not today anyway. "And I didn't want to bother you any more than I already have. You could have taken me home like I asked, you know."

"Your condo is a crime scene, or do I need to remind you of that again?"

"No." I breathe out in frustration. "I could've gone home with my dad." That's why my dad is mad at me. I chose Drago over him. Well, that's how he sees it. Drago didn't exactly give me a choice. He was dead set on me leaving with him and instead of joining the Battle of the Alpha Male shouting match happening in my room, I conceded. Besides, D and I really need to have a serious talk with no other ears listening so . . .

Rather than respond to me, he places his hand on the rail then steps up, walking toward me until he's standing on the stair below me. God, he's handsome. With everything that's weighing on my mind, Drago's good looks shouldn't be one of them, but it always is when I look at him.

"Come on," he says, grabbing both of my hands, pulling them over his shoulders. "I'll take you upstairs. You need to rest."

Wrapping my arms around his shoulders, I cup the back of his neck firmly as he lifts me, being careful not to touch the leg that's banged-up underneath my clothes. I don't refuse him because I need his touch. I need to feel more of his skin than the few times he's held my hand in the last twenty-four hours. I need the contact more so now than I ever have before.

I need him, and I don't know that I deserve it, so I'm not voicing it out loud.

He's warm, and for the first time today heat seeps through my skin, coating me—on the surface at least.

I lay my forehead against the fabric covering his shoulder, breathing him in. His scent is light today with only a faint hint of burnt wood. It's more him rather than the cologne he usually wears. I doubt he put any on whenever he changed clothes from the ones he was wearing yesterday. He smells good though. I prefer him over a synthetic scent any day. There is something about his natural smell that appeals to me; it soothes and comforts me.

"Mmm," I hum, not meaning to.

"Am I hurting you?" he asks, loosening his grip, mistaking my sound of enjoyment for pain. I just shake my head without lifting it off him.

The lighting changes when he walks through the door of his bedroom. It's brighter inside his bedroom. My eyes are automatically drawn to the open drapes where the sun is shining through.

Drago's feet eat up the short distance to the bed where both of his dogs jump off to the carpeted floor and instantly they're dancing at his feet, obviously excited to see him.

I'm placed gently on top of the mattress at the head just before the pillow. His bed is neatly made with the covers already turned down. I can't help but wonder if he slept here last night after storming out of my hospital room or if he even slept at all . . .

"Come on, boys," he calls to the dogs, bringing me back to the present. As if to purposely disobey him, one jumps back on the mattress, coming up and plopping down behind my back rather abrasively at that.

"No," I interject. "They don't have to leave. This is their home, not mine," I tell him when the other one, not remembering what their names are, hops up, joining the other dog.

"Trust me, you don't want them in the bed with you. They'll trample all over you, vying for your attention."

"Maybe I could use the attention," I mutter.

Something darkens in D's eyes, but he quickly looks away, peering out the window as he cups the back of his neck, squeezing. Eventually he sighs, sounding every bit as exhausted as I know I am.

"Suit yourself, but if they get on your nerves, shoot me a text and I'll come get them out of here."

"D," I whisper, stopping him as he turns to leave. He doesn't turn back around to face me or look over his shoulder like he knows what's coming next. He's probably expecting it. He should anyway. "It's time to tell me when we had sex without a condom and why."

"Just rest for now. We'll talk later."

"Turn around," I say slowly so the words don't come out like an order even though that's exactly how I mean them.

Forcing out a breath, long and hard, he pivots, crossing his thick arms over his chest and taking a firm stance from across the room. Even though he looks every bit of the strong, dark man I saw in that first photo all those weeks ago, his eyes aren't the same. They aren't scary, but they are weary and maybe even a bit uncertain.

I wait a beat, expecting him to talk, but when he doesn't, it only amps up the irritation I don't have the energy or patience for.

"Just tell me." Even if I do know, I want to hear him tell me.

Drago's eyes have taken on a haunted look I've never witnessed before. If he's battling half of the emotions I am right now, this is gutting him too.

"That first night." His eyes finally meet mine, and there is more than just anguish flickering through them. There's guilt. I recognize it because it matches my own, but for a different reason.

"We had unprotected sex?" The one night I don't remember is the one night he didn't wear a condom and he's just now telling me this? Sure, it was already on my mind that it had to have been that night, but it still doesn't diminish the shock factor of hearing it out loud.

He nods, confirming what I already assumed.

I was drunk that night, so my guess is he was just as wasted and forgot to put a condom on.

Does he think I'd blame him for the pregnancy—or the loss neither of us has spoken about? I wouldn't. It's not his fault. Not the loss of the child neither one of us knew I was carrying. That fault lies with someone else, but I shove that thought away before it materializes fully.

"I'm just as responsible for that night as you are. All I'm asking for are the details since I only remember small fragments of what happened once we arrived here."

"Bri," he starts, but I cut off his objections. There is no way he's getting around this.

"I don't blame you. Jeez, D, just—"

"I blame me!" he yells, cutting off my words and startling me so much my body jolts. "Fuck," he says, seeing my reaction.

He blames himself? What the . . . Why?

The ache in the center of my chest deepens at the sight of him. It's clear this isn't something he wants to willingly address and it's affecting him emotionally. It's instinctual that I want to stand and go to him; offer him the comfort he was giving me when he was carrying me, but my body is fighting against me.

"I don't blame you," I offer with the hope of putting his guilty conscience at ease and rid his eyes of the self-loathing look that's staring back at me.

"You should. It is my fault. All of it." He shakes his head, closing his eyes.

Letting my feet fall to the floor, I stand, shaking off the wince that breaks from my lips when I take my first step toward him. Closing the distance between us, I place my hands over his forearms, wrapping my fingers around his hot skin and look up.

"We both drank a lot. We screwed up and had unprotected sex once. It's not like you did it purposely."

"You think we just fucked once that night?" He shakes his head, stepping away from me and almost out of the door. "I was hell-bent on fucking you out of my system. Once wasn't going to cut it. And . . ."

"And what?" I prompt when it doesn't seem like he's going to finish.

"And,"—his voice cracks—"I was drunk but not so much that a

condom never crossed my mind."

"I'm sorry, what?" I straighten my spine, ignoring the pain it causes to my abdomen.

"I was already in a pissed-off mood that night, so when you showed up it only added fuel to the fire. I didn't know you, B, not really. Not like I do now. All I saw was another cop that thought I was the same dirty drug lord your people see my father as."

"Are you saying he's not?"

"No." His head moves from side to side. "He's a lot worse than the police could ever imagine."

"Still doesn't explain why you fucked me without a condom."

"I had it in my mind that you thought I was dirty. Another dirty Acerbi a cop wanted to lock up."

Dirty.

Is that why he keeps using that term? He thought I saw him like his father—a dirty rotten criminal. That is how I see his dad, but I've never once seen Drago like that. *Not until now.*

Everything I'm piecing together in my head still doesn't make sense.

"What does that have to do with us having sex without a condom?"

Why would he deliberately be that stupid? We're both nearly thirty years old.

"I wanted to make you as dirty as you thought I was."

I know the doctor said I have a head injury and I'm sure if it weren't for the drugs still lingering around in my system, I'd understand more clearly.

"I don't understand, D."

"I drank a lot that night, Bri, but I wasn't drunk enough to have forgotten to use a condom. I chose not to use any."

"Why?" My question comes out more like a whoosh of air than a word. "Why would you do that?"

"I just told you why."

Oh, he thinks that makes sense to me? It doesn't. I've never once done anything that should have given him that impression. I've always given him the benefit of the doubt. Hell, I've risked my career in doing so, and he never once divulged the details of that first night.

Fucking Christ. I don't know what to make of all of this.

I take a step back, disgusted with him for the first time. My expression must show it because the shock in his eyes makes him stumble back, hitting the doorframe.

"Was it your plan to get me pregnant then?"

"What? No," he whispers and I'm about tired of watching his head shake. "I don't plan on having kids—ever."

For some reason that comment feels like a slap in the face, making my empty stomach plummet to the floor.

"Really?" My words come out harsh. "Because lack of protection often leads to knocking a woman up, or is that not something you learned before now?"

"I figured you were on birth control."

"I'm not. Not that you ever asked." Birth control makes me sick, so I haven't taken it since my early twenties. "And forget about that; what about diseases?"

"I'm clean."

"And you somehow know my medical history then?" He just

stares at me, making it damn near impossible to tamp down my anger. "What in God's name made you think I see you the same as I see Vincent Acerbi? What have I ever done that led you to believe that?"

"Nothing."

"Then fucking help me out here. Why? Why the urge to make me *dirty* and have to fuck me out of your system?"

"It's not an excuse, Bri, but every local cop I've ever encountered has treated me like I'm just like *him* and I figured you were just like the rest of them. What I did was wrong. I knew it the second the thought of fucking you bareback came to my mind. It felt malicious when I bathed you afterward, and then fucked you again in the shower. I've known it was wrong from the beginning."

"Why haven't you come clean before now? You know me now. You've known me long enough to know how I feel. So why?" His head falls back against the wood of the doorjamb, looking up at the white ceiling above us, blinking repeatedly. "Drago!"

"Because when I woke up with you in my bed that next morning, all I wanted to do was keep you in it." His head rolls forward, our eyes locking again. "I never lied when I told you I liked you. And that has only morphed into something much more."

What the fuck am I supposed to do with all of this on top of everything else?

Jesus fucking Christ, this is fucked-up.

CHAPTER SEVEN

Two days have passed with no additional information on Gabriel's whereabouts. Statistics show if a child isn't located within the first forty-eight hours the chances of finding them are substantially lower.

My mind has been completely focused on him, so I won't allow other thoughts to break through. And since I've only spoken a couple of words here and there to Drago, my missing little angel consumes most of my thoughts.

I have to do something. I need to do something. I can't continue laying in Drago's bed *resting* like he keeps asking me to do. It's driving me mad. It would drive anyone mad I'd imagine, but me—I'm not used to resting. It feels like a lifetime ago that I've even had a good workout but I know I haven't recovered enough to get back to the gym. Which reminds me, I need to shoot Nikki a text message. Since it's the week of a holiday, she probably hasn't given it much thought that I've missed a workout this morning.

Thanksgiving.

It's usually a holiday I enjoy. I've only missed one Thanksgiving event at Jackson's house since becoming a police officer.

The mere thought of my brother and his family—my family— has me missing them. I know I won't be able to dodge my sister-in-law's calls much longer. There are only so many text messages she'll accept before she get suspicious. Not coming home is going to be a red flag to not only her, but my brother too.

I can't.

Right now, today, I don't feel thankful for a damn thing and I hate that I feel that way. I have my life when I shouldn't, yet, I can't bring myself to feel grateful while Gabriel is still missing and my baby . . .

I shut my eyes, closing them as tight as I can.

My phone rings, releasing me from the hellish thoughts that plague my mind.

"Hey, Dad," I say, holding my cell phone to my ear.

"How's my girl feeling?"

His girl? I'm momentarily stunned. He hasn't called me that since before my mom passed away. I don't know how to respond.

"Brianna?"

"As well as can be expected, I guess." I try my best to make my voice sound more like me, but I fail. I don't sound like the confident person I've always thought I was. I sound sad and I'm not so sure that's something I should be feeling.

Do I have that right?

He isn't mine. At some point Gabriel was going to leave me. I know this. It was only a matter of time before they transferred him out of my care. Sure, he was mine to keep safe and I failed, but he isn't my son. Yet, there is an ache in my chest I don't understand.

And the other *thing*? I didn't know about him or her until it was gone. Who misses something they really never had, or didn't know they had?

"I'm going to come see you today."

His statement pulls me back to our conversation.

"You want to come here?" I ask, scooting up in bed, resting the top of my back and head against the headboard.

"Yes. Why is that so hard to believe?" His tone sounds a bit hurt.

"I don't know if that's a good idea," I object.

Drago's already in a bad mood and they don't like each other as it is. My father showing up could add fuel to the fire, and that's something I don't need.

"I don't give a shit," he says in a matter of fact tone, making me scowl even if he can't see me. "He'll have to get over it. I'm laying eyes on my daughter today whether either one of you likes it or not."

"Dad . . ." I start to reason, but he says nothing. There is complete silence, making me bring the phone away from the side of my face.

The call is no longer connected. He hung up on me. What the hell is his problem? Doesn't he realize I have enough shit to deal with without adding him to the mix?

I blow out a breath of frustration.

Looking at the phone, I decide to call Mike again. I need an update. Fuck, I need an actual status to begin with before I can get an update.

I understand that getting involved with D on a personal level when he was my assignment was pushing boundaries I shouldn't have been pushing. But from the moment we met, everything was different. He affected me like no other person ever has. I was instantly drawn to him. There was a spark, and no matter how hard I tried it was going to light. It's like it was kindling before we ever met.

Even now, with the distance he's placed between us, I feel it. It's stronger the farther away he gets from me. But instead of it being a scorching feeling of excitement, it's a stinging burn of pain.

The phone goes to voicemail after only two rings, telling me he declined my call.

Heat washes over my chest, pissing me off. What the fuck? Mike has never declined a call from me.

While I'm staring at my phone in disbelief a text message comes through.

Mike: I told you when I knew something I'd call you.

Me: That was yesterday.

Mike: You need to let this go. That kid shouldn't have been in your custody.

Me: That's irrelevant at this point. He was taken, Mike. What the fuck is anyone doing to find him!?

Mike: I'm going to get my ass handed to me for discussing this shit with you.

Me: I don't fucking care, dammit!!! Gabe is more important than Tom bitching at you.

Mike: You need to take a step back. You are way too close to this when you shouldn't be. You are a cop. Or at least I thought you were until I entered your apartment Friday.

I throw my smartphone across the room in frustration. It's obvious he isn't going to tell me a damn thing. And the fact that he is questioning my capability to still be a good, by-the-book, police officer stings. I feel like I'm letting everyone around me down.

I slam my head backward, colliding with the wood of the headboard and regretting that move instantly. Pain slashes through my skull, making me wince. The cut above my eye throbs, protecting my fit of haste.

Two warm furry heads land on my stomach simultaneously, pulling my eyes down to see Hulk and Thor looking up at me with their weird dog eyes. Bull Terriers certainly have odd shaped heads. What I've learned about these two is they are either being lazy, laying on the bed or another piece of furniture, or they are going zero to sixty, spazzing out. Luckily for me, they are currently in a lazy state, which is the majority of the time—until they get excited.

I glance up, seeing Mona entering D's bedroom. The dogs jump off, leaving me. Cool air hits the warm spots they were both lying against, chilling me.

"Hi, honey. How are you this morning?"

She doesn't acknowledge the two beasts on the ground jumping up and down and doing crazy circles on the floor. A quick laugh bubbles out as I watch them, shaking my head. Drago's dogs have a lot of character.

"Restless," I say honestly. *And heartbroken,* I think, not willing myself to verbalize the thought.

I force a smile when she continues to stand there, holding a mop and a bucket with cleaning supplies.

"Well, if you need anything at all, you just tell me and I'll get it. Okay, honey?" Her smile is sincere and not at all sympathetic like everyone else's.

That's why I'm up here and not downstairs with Drago and his siblings. They all look at me like I'm going to break at any minute. They don't know me. I'm a lot stronger than I look. Sure, I haven't allowed myself to feel the things I know I should, but I really don't have the time to face them. I don't know what my department is doing to find Gabriel, if anything at all. I can only allow one person at a time in my heart and right now my focus needs to be on Gabe.

My sweet, sweet Gabe.

What if he's hungry right now?

What if he's lying in a dirty diaper?

Or what if he's cold or crying and there is no one there to comfort him? Nobody knows that he needs chest-to-chest contact to be able to get to sleep. What if—

"Bri, dear. Are you okay?"

I look up to see Mona standing next to the bed looking down with concern in her dark brown eyes.

"I . . ." What do I tell her? Drago hasn't mentioned Gabriel being his son. He doesn't want to discuss it. He's determined his son isn't his. And a part of me gets that, but I know for a fact he is Gabriel's father. And there is no amount of denial that will change that. "I need to speak to D."

"Oh." She takes a step away from me, giving me room to slide my leg off the bed. "Honey, I'll get him for you. You just rest."

Fuck resting.

My head shakes on its own accord, disagreeing with her. I'm over all of this resting. I don't want to see this bed, or any other, until I've worn myself out. Lying here longer isn't going to do that, so I stand. I haven't mentioned last night's incident in the bathroom to anyone. I'm not quite ready to talk about it. I barely allow myself the briefest thought of the baby I lost.

"I can go find him."

JOGGING DOWN THE STAIRS, I IGNORE THE PAIN PROTESTING THE JOLTS AS my right foot hits every step. I shouldn't be moving this quick, risking the chance of ripping my stitches. But right now, I don't care.

I'm done hiding away in his room. A room that's been vacant of *him*. He didn't come to bed last night or the night before, leaving a gaping hole in my chest. I won't lie to myself and pretend I don't miss the warmth of Drago's arms, because I undeniably do. I need them—I need him.

And doing what I'm about to do is certainly not going to bring me any closer to his embrace. That's something I need to start coming to terms with. I may never have the security I feel when I'm in his arms ever again, but I can't dwell on that. At least not right now.

Once I reach the bottom of the stairs, Luca's eyes pop up, landing on me from where he's lounging on the massive sectional couch in Drago's living room. Mia, his little girl, has her head laid in his lap. She's napping while her dad is watching TV.

Does he not have a job? It's Monday, midmorning.

Looking over, I see Caprice with a paperback book clutched in her hands and an intense look on her face. She's biting her lip something fierce, so it must be good. But she's far enough away that I can't read the title on the cover.

Noise coming from behind me makes me look over my shoulder, seeing the dogs race down the stairs. My eyes follow them as they run past me, jumping onto the couch and both plopping down at Mia's feet. One of them—I don't know which—lays down on top of the other one. D's dogs certainly have personality.

"Where's your brother?" I ask, directing my question to Luca.

"In his office probably."

I nod, looking around because I haven't exactly explored much of Drago's house, so I don't know which way to head. Luca must read that on my face.

"Down that hall"—he gestures to my right, toward the kitchen—"past the hall bathroom and laundry room, but before the garage. The door will be closed."

"Thanks," I offer behind me as I head in the direction Luca pointed me in.

D's house is big, but it's not as big as I originally thought. It's actually quite homey. The living area and kitchen make an open and airy room with a lot of natural light. His bedroom definitely exceeds the standard of any master suite I've ever seen. It's much larger. But what surprises me is that for a house this size it really doesn't have as much room as one would expect.

I'm guessing it's custom built, and well, why wouldn't it be? He's the son of a wealthy man and runs a company that, even after all of my investigating, seems to be legit. Drago mentioned he found discrepancies in his logs and I have to believe he wouldn't have divulged that information if he was the crooked one.

I still wish he had given me access to them. Maybe I could have helped him sort them out. And if I wasn't able to help, someone in the police department could have. Why D doesn't want to help me clear his name is beyond me, but like everything else, that isn't at the forefront of my mind right now.

Gabriel is. And finding him has to be my only priority right now.

Seeing only one closed door, I stop in front of the dark-stained wood.

Taking a deep breath, I raise my fist to knock, when the door flies open and I'm nearly barreled into.

I take a step back, stumbling as I try to avoid being run over.

"Fuck, Bri."

Drago's arm reaches out, wrapping around me and then he tugs me to him. Grabbing hold of his bicep with one hand, I fist the material of his T-shirt along his side with my other. When my eyes snap up to meet his gaze, I can't control the gasp of air that escapes my mouth any more than I can control the heat that rushes to the surface of my cheeks, flushing me.

For a moment, everything swirling around inside my head

washes away and only he is left, taking up every crevice of my brain.

Drago's eyes flick down to my parted lips, his eye dilate, the brown minimizing as the black overtakes as if seeing food—or prey. His tongue juts out, wetting the lips I've so badly missed that I can't suppress the whimper that releases.

I want him. I want him more than I've ever wanted him before.

His palm connects with the bare skin on the back of my leg just under where my cotton shorts stop. His touch is warm, soft, and gentle, just the way I remember. I had started to think the man I witnessed only a few weeks ago—the one that had made me swoon, seeing his son sleeping on his chest—was gone.

He's not, and whether he realizes it or not, he's showing me the guy I fell for is still here.

Slowly, his hand slides up, cupping and kneading my ass. I shudder as sparks pass through my body, lighting me up.

We're locked in a stare until the craving for more contact wins out. Unwrapping my hand, I slip it underneath the material of his shirt, flattening my hand against his heated abdomen. A rugged breath escapes Drago's lips, fanning my face as his eyes flutter closed.

"Bri . . ." he says my name on an exhale, making my insides dance with joy, knowing I still affect him the same way he affects me. I knew it was wrong to keep Gabriel's true identity from Drago, but I did it anyway, and there is no changing the past.

His head dips, lowering until his lips kiss the skin along my neck, nipping once and then he lightly sucks.

"Mmm." A moan slips out of my mouth as my body presses

forward, molding against his. "Dra—" I start, but I'm quickly cut off by the sound of his phone ringing.

He freezes against me as if only now realizing what is happening between us.

A curse flies from his mouth as he releases me, stepping away. Turning, he pulls his phone out of the pocket of his pants, answering it as he stalks back inside his office.

"What?" he barks into the phone as I follow him.

Looking around, taking in the space, I notice it's bigger than his office at the docks—and nicer too. His desk is positioned in the center of the room toward the back with a wide window behind it. The curtains span from the floor up to the ceiling and they are pulled open, allowing sunlight to naturally brighten the room rather than having the lights turned on. The lights really aren't needed.

There is a bookcase to my right and a leather couch with an unmade blanket at the end opposite a pillow, telling me this is where he's slept the last two nights since I've been here.

"I told you not to bother me with this shit, Rebecca. I'll be back when I'm back. Stop questioning me, goddammit."

I stop following him when he rounds his desk to stand behind one of the two guest chairs in front of him. Bending at the waist, I rest my elbows on the back of the chair.

D drops his smartphone on his desk. A billow of air steaming out of his mouth follows.

"What did you need?" he finally asks as he leans his denim-clad ass against the short filing cabinet in front of the window.

"Just wanted to talk."

"About?" He grips the edge of the wooden furniture. Lifting an eyebrow, I look at him. "Not this shit again, Bri."

"Hear me out. That's all I'm asking of you."

"Fine," he bites out. "Plead your case."

I look down, eyeing the gray fabric of the chair. Now that he's given me the green light to talk, I suddenly don't know where to start. I didn't give this much thought, which isn't like me.

"I need your help," I admit. Those words have never been easy for me. I've always ensured I could do things on my own. I never want to be weak or be perceived as such. But failing that little boy that counted on me? It proves I'm not as strong as I thought. I do need help.

"With?" he asks, skepticism evident in his eyes.

"Put me in contact with Diaz."

"Are you fucking crazy?" His eyebrows pull together.

"No. He took your . . ." I pause, reading the heat that flares across this face. He knows what I was about to say, and pissing him off isn't going to help me at this moment. "Sebastian took that little boy, D."

"Not my problem."

"All I'm asking is that you give me a phone number or whatever will get me in touch with him."

"He shot you. No!" He shakes his head. "The cops will find the boy. That's their job."

"And what if they aren't doing shit? He's just a baby, Drago." I add that last bit hoping to appeal to his softer, caring side that he's trying hard not to show.

"What do you want me to do? I'm not about to meddle in

LAPD shit, Bri. I have enough of your people constantly looking for the smallest morsel to pin on my family."

"He took Gabe for insurance to get you to bend to his ways. Whether you believe Gabriel is yours or not isn't the point. Diaz believes it and he plans to use him against you."

"So, what are you suggesting?"

"We play his game. You tell him you'll do whatever he wants. We—"

He cuts me off. "I'm going to pretend you did not just suggest that right now."

"I'm sorry." The words slip out. "You're going to pretend? An innocent person's life is on the line, dammit."

"And the cops will handle it. I'm not getting involved."

"He's your fucking son!" I shove the chair forward, getting pissed off.

"Would you keep your voice down before my family hears your nonsense?"

Nonsense? He thinks this is fucking nonsense? What in the hell is wrong with him?! Just when I think the man I fell for is back, he's gone just as quick as he returned to me. Maybe he never did return, and it was just my imagination making me believe he had.

"Why won't you believe me?"

"I want to, Bri." He looks up, taking in a deep breath. My eyes cut down, seeing his fingers draw in at his sides into fists.

"Then why can't you?"

Blowing out his breath, he drops his head, glaring at me.

"Because there is no record of you interviewing anyone the

night you said you did."

I draw back. "Excuse me?"

No record? That's impossible. Every interview and interrogation is not only video recorded but also voice recorded. Therefore, I know there's a record. Besides, I'm the one that pressed the voice and video button before I entered the room.

Wait a minute . . . How does he know there isn't a record of my conversation with Chasity Carlisle?

He must read the question on my face. "I have my sources."

"Your sources?" I question. He turns away from me, giving me his back as if dismissing me.

Fuck that!

Rounding his desk, I snag his elbow, yanking on him. "What sources, Drago? What are you keeping from me?"

His body barely moves. His muscular biceps flex as his head turns, looking down at me.

"Doesn't feel great, does it?" He doesn't give me time to process where he's going with this. "Sucks finding out someone is keeping something from you, doesn't it?"

Is he kidding me right now? His fucking feelings are hurt? Well, you know what? I don't give a fuck at the moment. He's a grown-ass man. He needs to start acting like it.

I'm sure learning you have a child you knew nothing about is a real kick to the gut. But when that kid—his kid—has been taken by one of the most dangerous criminals in the country, you don't act like a fucking kid yourself, kicking and screaming because someone kept you in the dark. You man the fuck up and deal with the here and now. There is plenty of time for him to deal with fatherhood after we've gotten Gabriel back safe and unharmed.

"Grow the fuck up!"

"Don't you see this for what it is?" He turns, facing me.

I step back, fearing if I don't get some distance from him I'm going to go for the one place I can hit and bring him to his knees in pain. If he thinks I'm above kicking a man between the legs, he'd be mistaken. Right now, he deserves worse than aching balls.

"I guess not. Enlighten me, *Acerbi*." I use his last name, hoping to tick him off and it works. His nostrils flare.

"You're right about the boy being used. And no, I don't want harm to come to him. But I'm not going to play Diaz's, or the cops', little games to trap me. I've worked too damn hard to make sure my father's lifestyle doesn't affect Luca or Caprice, and even Mia. I won't let anyone damage my family any more than my father has. I won't allow the fucking past to hurt them. And Diaz, your boss, or fuck, maybe both of them together are trying to do just that. One wants me to grant him a gateway to get his dope into this country. The other wants to pin something, anything, on me because he can't touch my father."

I'm not so tunnel-visioned that I don't understand where D is coming from. But to accuse my boss and my fellow law enforcement officers of plotting to set him up unlawfully, or even worse, working with a criminal to bring him down is too much of a stretch for me. I work with those people and have for years. Tom, although hard, has always done things by the book, that I know of.

The cops aren't the ones that kidnapped Gabriel. And it wasn't the cops that shot and tried to kill me. It was a man that will obviously do anything to get what he wants. And right now, he wants Drago.

"Did it ever cross your mind that your 'source' is wrong?" Maybe D's source is in bed with Diaz. I wonder if he ever thought of that.

"No!" he shouts, losing patience with me.

"Then why did Sebastian take him? Why did he take Gabriel, something he thinks you value most, to hold over your head?" I see the wheels turning in his head. He's thinking. He's considering the possibilities. "Why, Drago?"

Gabriel is his son. The first test wasn't wrong. And neither was the second one I had done independently that nobody but me knows about. Even if I just defended my fellow LEO's in my head, there's another side that falters to believe Tom is on the up-and-up this time. If I just knew why he was so adamant about finding criminal evidence on Drago then maybe I wouldn't be questioning my fellow badges.

But now isn't the time to tell D about the other test. He hasn't fully accepted the possibility that Gabriel is his son, and until he does, he won't listen to me. He won't believe me—and that hurts the most.

"Leave it!" he roars, confirming my thoughts.

"Am I interrupting?"

We both freeze. Drago's eyes going wide.

Oh, fuck. *Did she hear us?*

Her voice is sweet, a stark contrast to D's.

"No." Drago's voice is strained. "We're done here." His head rolls to the side, looking down at me to make sure his words are clear.

If he's not going to help me, then I'll have to figure something else out, because I am going to do whatever it takes to find Gabriel before it's too late. If Drago doesn't play his game or give Diaz what he wants, Gabriel will be of no use to him. With a man like Sebastian Diaz, there are logically two things he'll do: kill a baby or sell him. And neither are acceptable outcomes.

I train my eyes up, imploring them to show Drago just how disgusted I am with him at this moment. If something happens to Gabe and his father did nothing to prevent it or stop it, I don't think I'll ever be able to forgive him.

I turn, leaving hastily, brushing past his sister, Caprice, on the way out.

CHAPTER EIGHT

"Bri, wait up," Caprice calls after me.

I stop just before I reach the end of the hallway, turning to face her. My eyes automatically cut past her, eyeing the door I just stalked out of. He obviously has no plans of coming after me, fueling a fire that's kindling inside me.

"You and I really haven't had a chance to talk," she says quickly, sounding shy and unsure if she should approach me. She is different from Drago and Luca. Since D brought me home with him, I've kept myself tucked away in the bedroom over the weekend. I was still able to pick up on just how different she is from her brothers.

"Sorry about that, Caprice." I am genuinely regretful that I've ignored his family. They actually seem nice. Nothing like I first imagined when Tom assigned Lance and me to investigate D.

"You can call me CC," she offers in a sweet voice.

"Why do your brothers call you that?"

"Oh." She giggles, her face visibly brightening at the mention of Drago and Luca. "It's my initials. CC stands for Caprice Claire."

"Really?" It's my turn to smile, realizing we have something in common.

Her head cocks to the side, confused, when a bubble of laughter pops out of my mouth, releasing a little of the tension housed in my body.

"What's so funny?"

"Claire," I tell her. "That's my middle name too."

"Seriously?" She giggles like twenty-year-old girls do, warming my heart for the first time in days. Drago's sister is nice with genuine kindness in her disposition. I think I'm going to like her. She reminds me of my niece, Carrie. It's her girly personality.

For a second it makes me think about my family, reminding me once again that I'm missing the holidays with them. Guilt festers. I hate keeping Jackson and Alana in the dark when I know if the tables were turned and they were doing the same to me I'd be hurt—and pissed. But Jackson would flip his shit.

Remembering he had a tracking device on me, I knew if he learned of what happened last week it would push him from being the overprotective brother into psycho territory. And right now, I can't deal with that on top of everything else.

Still, when they do find out, because let's face it, I will eventually tell them, there will be hell to pay for. I'm just not telling them today, or tomorrow.

"Are you two hungry?"

I rest against the bar-style granite countertop, next to where

Caprice hops onto a stool.

"I'm always hungry for anything you're cooking, Mona," Caprice croons.

"Oh, shush it, child." Mona glances over her shoulder from where she's standing at the stove, shaking her head at Caprice.

"You know you're the best cook in the world."

Mona turns slightly, looking over at us, but her hand continues moving in circles as she stirs the contents of a pot. "She's still young. Her idea of good food is whatever she can scarf down while running between classes, so of course, whatever I cook is going to be better than that."

"Don't listen to her." Caprice pulls my attention over to her. "Her food is mouthwateringly amazing."

"You're in college?"

"Uh-huh," she confirms.

"Where at?"

"UCLA for now."

"Do you plan on transferring somewhere else later?" She's twenty, so she could be a freshman if she took time off after high school, or she could be several semesters along.

"After I make the big bad dragon happy."

"I'm sorry." I laugh, knowing she is referring to the meaning of Drago's name, so I guess it's some running joke.

"D is making me major in theater even though he knows I want to do finance."

"Those two are so drastically different." I can't help but point out the obvious. "If you want to study something else why would he force you to do something you don't want to do? And well, you are an adult after all. He can't *make* you do anything you don't want to do, CC."

"My brother"—she sighs, rolling her eyes—"means well. He wants me to do something I love, not something that's practical. And"—she laughs—"he can make me do whatever he wants. He knows all he has to do is look at me in that scary way of his, and I'll cave."

"Scary way?" The only time I've ever seen Drago look scary was in that photo I first saw him in. Other than that, he's never come across scary or intimidating to me. He certainly shouldn't act that way toward his sister.

"I'm saying it wrong. I just mean in that dad-like way of his. And since he's paying for my college, yeah, he can say so. But we compromised. I'm doing theater and when I finish, I get to go to graduate school. I want a master's in finance anyway. It's a win-win for both of us really. I get to love and enjoy theater while honing in my acting skills, and then I get to prove to him that I am serious about working for our family too, like he and Luca."

If she loves theater, then I guess this is different. For a minute I thought she meant D was making her do something he wanted and not something she wants.

"So, you want to work for D? And Luca, I didn't know he worked for your brother."

How do I not know this? I ran background checks on all of the employees on Acerbi Imports' payroll. Luca Acerbi wasn't listed. And besides, he's in his last year of college himself.

"Luca handles all the IT type stuff. D doesn't trust anyone else, so Luca has done it for the past two years. I guess since our dad up and took off to Italy." Her eyes cast down in thought. It's evident the mention of Vincent has her mood turning dark.

"I see," is all I say, hoping my voice brings her out from whatever it is she is thinking about right now. And luckily it does. She glances up, forcing a smile.

"I want to handle the finance side of things. The things Rebecca handles today," she says, bitterness in her tone.

"Is that distaste I detect?" I don't like that bitch either, but my guess, it's for a completely different reason than Drago's sister. Rebecca De Luca wants him, and that thought brings out a rage inside of me that I never knew existed until I met Drago Acerbi.

"Let's just say, I don't trust her. Therefore, by having a master's in finance, I'll trump her bachelor's in business. Plus, I'm blood, and I know if I push my brother, he'll eventually cave and let me come work for him."

Does she only want to work for D to get Rebecca out?

I raise an eyebrow way too curious to let that go and she must read the question on my face.

"I dislike her, but that's not the sole reason I want her out. I really do want to work alongside my brothers. I love them. They are my whole world. Getting to work with both of them every day would be awesome and fun. Acting comes easy for me. It always has. I've been doing it since I was little. Yes, I love doing it, but I want something that will challenge me. I want a career doing something that isn't easy."

"Okay." I laugh, sliding off the stool. "You've sold me. Excuse me, would you? I need to go to the bathroom."

Making an exit, I head back down the hall with every intention of going to pee, but then I see the door to D's office still open.

I hate arguing with him. So, even though I know I'm right and he's in the wrong when it comes to acknowledging his son, I go back to his office to apologize. I can't really fathom how hard all of this is. It's hard to imagine what is going through his head.

I stop just before coming in view, hearing Drago's deep voice.

"What are you saying?"

There's silence.

"It isn't possible, E. You know this."

This is the second time I've heard him refer to a person on the phone as a letter of the alphabet. Who could he be speaking to? I know him well enough to know he only calls those he likes, people he's close to, by the first letter of their name. So, who is this "E?"

"Fuck!" There is a bang, as if he's slammed his palm or something on his desk—or another hard surface area. I jump, but I don't peek around the doorframe. I don't want him to know I'm listening; well it's more like eavesdropping.

I feel a bit sleazy, but he's given me reason to doubt him and to not fully trust him anymore. I'm well aware of the fact that I'm not the only one who was keeping secrets in our relationship and I don't think he's a bad person. But from the beginning, I've always felt there was something he wasn't telling me, and that feeling hasn't gone away.

What if it's something that could lead me to the son he refuses to claim as his own?

What if by refusing to acknowledge Gabriel is his, Diaz does something Drago may later regret?

I can't bring myself to think of all the ways that monster could harm my sweet boy. I just can't. I can't fathom detrimental damage being done to such innocence. And all because of D's refusal to continue on with the business his father created.

Drugs.

Fucking drugs.

The sound of the doorbell ringing brings me out of my thoughts and not wanting to get caught listening in on Drago's conversation, I push off the wall, walking back the way I came with the intent of going back upstairs to use that bathroom instead of the one down here.

I'M ABOUT TO TAKE THE STAIRS WHEN I HEAR MONA'S SWEET VOICE FILTER IN through the opening in the parlor room.

"Can I help you?"

"I want to see Brianna." My father's demand stops me from ascending the steps in front of me.

"Someone is in trouble," Luca sings from the couch.

"Grown-ups can't get in trouble, Daddy." Mia giggles from where she is laying stretched out on the couch with her head in her dad's lap.

"Of course they can, sweet pea." He looks up, blinding me with a smile that's a mixture of delight and mischief.

For a half a second, I wonder why he isn't with this little girl's mother. Luca seems like a nice guy. His sister thinks the world of him and from the look on Mia's face, she does too.

"Then you're in trouble, Daddy."

"Grown-ups except for me," he amends, making me laugh. Luca is too cute for his own good.

"Especially you," Caprice says from where she's sitting, once again, reading a book.

"Daughter," my father calls from behind me, making me sigh before stepping to the side, taking him in.

"Dad?" I draw out, wondering why on earth he's here. I thought I was clear on the phone. "What are you doing here?"

"Is there somewhere we can talk?"

"Bri, dear, why don't you and your father walk out onto the terrace. It's such a lovely warm day out there. I'll bring drinks." Mona doesn't wait for a reply before turning and heading to the kitchen, I imagine.

The rose-colored blush gracing her cheeks doesn't go unnoticed. It's funny for all of two seconds, until I realize why. She finds my dad attractive.

"Bri," my dad calls out when I continue staring at the back of Mona's retreating form.

"Yeah. Sorry." I turn away from him, looking around. I didn't even know there was a terrace, so for a minute, I'm at a loss, not knowing where to go.

"Who are you?" Mia jumps off the couch, running up to my dad.

"Robert," he says curtly.

"Mia A-chair," she greets him, extending her small little arm. I snort a laugh and so does Luca when she pronounces her last name wrong. For a three-year-old though, she speaks really well.

70

"You forgot the 'be' Mia-bug," her dad tells her. Shaking his head, he looks at me. "Patio is through that door." He points to his left, over and behind the couch he's sitting on. There are floor to ceiling windows that line the wall behind him, but all of the blinds have been closed, making the room darker and more enjoyable to watch TV.

"Thanks," I tell him.

Once I'm through the door, the scenery is the first thing I notice. It's gorgeous out here. I wouldn't have realized we were on the second level of the house since it doesn't seem that way upon entering through the front.

Walking to the railing, I see a pool below, surrounded by lawn chairs and patio furniture with coverings over them. There is a patch of grass with a gate to my left. Inside is a big child play set that's much too big for Mia at her age now. There are toys scattered everywhere and the sight warms my heart. Drago obviously loves his niece if all of this is here just for her.

So why can't he open up to the thought of Gabriel?

Hearing a heavy sigh come from behind me, I turn, eyeing my father. He's standing by the door, dressed in his usual suit and tie. For a man in his mid-fifties he's fit, still has a head full of dark brown hair, and if you didn't know him, stunningly blue eyes that would make you want to trust him. If I look hard enough, I can see why Mona might be taken by him.

But if you know him, you know how cunning he really is. Robert Andrews, although not a bad person, can be very ruthless when he wants something. He isn't above using any means, money or emotions, to bend someone to his will.

Striding over, I take a seat in one of the many cushioned chairs scattered about on the large landing. My father, on the other hand, goes to stand next to the railing where I just left.

"You going to talk?" I prompt when he doesn't pipe up.

"Bri," he says too softly, not sounding like himself. "Come home with me."

"No, Dad," I argue.

"Please come home with me, sweetheart."

Why is this man using words like "please" and "sweetheart?" As odd as it is hearing them from his lips, it's also comforting that he's asking me to come stay with him. I haven't slept under my father's roof since the night before my high school graduation.

"You need to be around someone that can take care of you."

"I can take care of myself, Dad. I've been doing it for a long time."

"Don't get smart. You know what I mean." His eyebrows furrow together. "You've gone through a lot these past few days," he continues. "You need to be with your family. And I'm your family, not these people."

"I said no."

"If you aren't going to leave with me, then at least go stay at Jackson's for a few weeks. It'll do you good to get away from LA."

"Dad, have you forgotten I have Gabriel to find? I can't leave LA. I'm not going to leave Los Angeles unless it's to go after the person that shot me and kidnapped Drago's son."

"Have you forgotten you were placed on administrative leave?" He doesn't give me the chance to speak, continuing before I can open my mouth. "You aren't allowed to go after anyone. And you damn sure don't need to put yourself in more danger. Which is exactly what you are doing by being here."

"I'm not in danger here." Maybe that isn't entirely true. Diaz wants Drago, after all.

He raises an eyebrow. "That was a dumb remark coming from you."

"I'm not leaving LA until Gabe has been found, or unless I have to leave to find him."

"You'll get fired!" my father shouts at me.

"I don't care!" I say equally as loud as him.

"Jesus, Brianna. Just fucking come home with me."

"Why are you pushing this? It's not like you."

He turns away from me, bracing his raised arm against the thick wooden column, looking out toward the ocean. It's beautiful out here and I could never imagine living anywhere that wasn't close to water. But right here, right now, it's not the scenery I care to enjoy. I can't allow myself joy when I don't know what's happening to Gabe. I should have taken my duties more seriously. I should have expected something like this to happen when I knew Drago was involved with Diaz. Even if it's not of his own doing or free will, he's still involved to a degree. He may not be pushing his dope or giving Sebastian the means to bring it into the States, but being who he is and the family he was born in, his involvement still exists.

If I'm honest, it probably always will. At least while Vincent is alive.

"Your mother was strong—until she wasn't."

His somber words bring me out of my thoughts.

My mother?

What does my mother have to do with the topic of where I sleep at night?

"What are you talking about, Dad?"

"You think I don't know you." He turns, facing me, pressing his backside into the railing. "I do. You are my daughter whether you like it or not, and I do know you better than you think. I know you are strong. You are the most strong-willed person I know. You want people to see you as a strong woman and they do. But unlike your mother, you're avoiding dealing with your miscarriage when you shouldn't."

"Unlike my mother?"

What the hell is he talking about?

"She had three miscarriages." His statement washes over me, shocking me. "Two between the time you and Jackson were born, and then there was the last one." He exhales on a heavy sigh. "She avoided the first two. Refused to talk about them and then the last . . ." He trails off, turning away from me, looking back out toward the sea. With his house tucked away in the hills, you can see the ocean in the distance and a few of the other homes around here.

"Mom had—" I can't even finish the sentence. It's a word I haven't spoken out loud yet.

"I was mad at her when she got pregnant with you. I knew she was going to lose you too, but when she didn't, I finally felt like I could breathe again. But then she wanted another and I said no. I put my foot down and refused her, but she went behind my back and stopped taking her birth control." He shakes his head slowly from side to side, remembering what seems to be a dark time for him and my mother. "I should have known she would, but I was busy. I let her worry about you kids, the house, the bills. I made the money and she had free rein to spend it however she wanted so long as we were all taken care of." He stops, breathing in the fresh coastal air and pushing it out with a heavy sigh.

"I'm getting away from the point I'm trying to make. The last miscarriage consumed her and I was too angry and hurt to take care of my wife like I should have. She died of a broken heart, but it was brought on by consuming too many pills. Pills she thought she was taking to control her depression. Only she wasn't taking them as prescribed. She was abusing her medication and I was never around to notice."

"Dad," I whisper, standing and going straight to him.

"I don't want"—his voice cracks as he wraps his arms around me, hugging me to his front—"I won't let what happened to her, happen to my baby girl."

"It won't."

"I need you to face what happened, but do so the right way, sweetheart. I want you to talk about it and deal with your feelings."

"I haven't processed them yet."

"Exactly. Which is why I want you to stay with me."

"You're going to have to compromise on this." I don't have the luxury of time to deal with anything that isn't helping to find Gabriel. Telling him that though, probably won't do any good. Hell, telling that to anyone, especially D, doesn't seem to be doing any better either.

"I don't compromise on anything. Even you know that."

"I have to find Gabriel." It is what it is. Why can't anyone understand this? He's an innocent life that got caught up in something that isn't his doing.

"That boy isn't your responsibility."

"Yes, he is!" I step back, looking up so that my father sees my eyes. "He was in my care. He was taken from my home."

"He shouldn't—"

"Stop." I hold up my hand, backing away even more. "We're going to have to agree to disagree on that one. I'm going to find him or at least ensure someone at the department finds him, whether you like it or not. This is not up for negotiation. In fact, this topic is done."

"Brianna."

"Connie sent me a message earlier. I can go back home when I'm ready. My condo was released."

"You are coming home with me, goddammit."

"She said no, Robert." We both turn, seeing Drago standing in the doorway. "How many ways does she need to tell you the same thing?"

"Stay out of this, Acerbi."

"This is my house, so that's not going to happen." His words are full of authority. It's rare anyone takes that sort of tone with my father. Not even Jackson does.

"Dad," I say, turning my body halfway between him and Drago. "We're done. Thank you for telling me about Mom, and I did hear every word. But I'm still not leaving with you. And as far as Jackson is concerned, I'd rather my brother and his family not know about this. I don't want to put them at risk because of my involvement."

He looks down at me before sighing. Then he takes a step forward, placing his warm palms on my cheeks, his breath drifts across my face. "You know, you are a lot like me too. When you have your mind set on something of absolute importance you don't compromise either."

My eyes cut to the side, thinking. He's right about that. I like things my way. Is that so wrong? In this case, I know it's not.

"I won't say a word to your brother, but you will keep me informed. I have to know you're safe. And that is not up for discussion. I don't give a damn that you're twenty-nine. You'll always be my baby." He pauses, letting it all sink in. "Got it?"

"Yeah, I got it," I agree because I know how I feel about Gabriel when he's not even mine. For once, I think I might understand where my dad is coming from.

He leans forward, kissing the top of my head.

"I love you, Dad," I tell him just as he releases me to leave.

After my dad left this morning, Drago and I stayed in a locked stare, standing out on his covered patio, not speaking a single word. He finally stalked off, presumably to his office. But in the few minutes our eyes were locked, so much passed through us. Heat, want, disdain, anger, sorrow, and something else, something stronger, I think, but I honestly can't be sure if he hates me right now or if he just feels guilty for Diaz trying to end my life . . . or if he's trying to lock down feelings he doesn't want me to see.

I've been wracking my brain all day on what I need to do; where I should even start.

I tried calling Ms. Lincoln, but her son answered her phone, politely asking me not to call his mother ever again. I really can't blame him. She wasn't injured, thank God. But she was scared for her life while Sebastian had her tied up to one of her dining room chairs with a handkerchief around her mouth to muffle her screams for help.

I feel terrible that happened because of me. All because I enlisted her help, caring for Gabriel. It should have never happened. She should never have been involved—which is another reason I don't want the rest of my family knowing anything about what's happened.

My dad thinks there's a chance of me going into a deep depression over the loss of my baby. But if something were to ever happen to Jackson or Alana or one of the kids because of me, that's when he would have cause for worry.

I'll eventually deal with the things I've shut off, and I'll be fine. *At least I hope I will.*

I pick up my smartphone, turning it so that the screen lights up, showing no new notifications or any missed calls or text messages. Every time I look at the screen, my heart dies a little more inside because the hope of Gabe being okay dwindles.

"Will you please stop checking your phone while we're eating?" Drago asks in a not-so-polite kind of way.

It was more of an order than not, and it successfully pisses me off. He knows what I'm doing. He knows why I'm doing it. So why the fuck is he making a big deal of it?

"No," I say in a strained voice, holding back an outburst that would be rude to display in front of his family. And with Luca's daughter at the table, I won't, no matter how much Drago deserves streams of profanity thrown at him. He's being unreasonable.

"A word," he bites out as he stands, his chair sliding across the floor, echoing his displeased expression.

Like I give a damn in this moment.

He knows I have one thing on my mind and one thing only, yet he insisted I join them all for dinner. Mona cooked a wonderful meal that smells divine, but my appetite is nonexistent. If I force it, it would only mean I'll end up in the bathroom puking it all up later.

Following him out of the formal dining room, and then through the living room, he bypasses the stairwell, turning and heading down the hall to his office if I'd have to guess.

I'm right. He turns the knob on the closed door, opening it and disappearing inside as I'm still trailing, slowing my pace the closer I get. Dread develops in the pit of my stomach. Whatever this is, it isn't going to end well for either of us.

That much I know.

When I walk in, I close the door, leaning against it and staying as far away from him as possible. He's standing in front of his desk, his ass propped against the edge, looking at me with his arms crossed over his large chest.

I want nothing more than to go to him, climb up his body and lose myself in his touch. He has the ability to make me forget as well as he can make me remember things. Turning everything off, forgetting everything that's happened—even for a little while—

would be welcoming. And he's right there. The problem is, I can't allow that. Every minute, every second I spend not focused on Gabriel is every second I lose what little hope I have left.

"Say whatever it is you have to say and get it over with." There's no reason to beat around the bush.

"Goddammit, Brianna."

"Oh, so I'm Brianna, now?"

His face reddens as his jaw turns to steel.

Good, I think, feeling a moment of triumph, knowing that I got under his skin. Even if it was only for a second.

"You were almost killed," he barks. Unfolding his long arms, they fall to his sides. As if trying to hit his point home, he smacks the top of his desk with his palm. "You almost died because of me. Do you get that?"

"I was there, so yeah, I'm pretty sure it was crystal fucking clear."

"This isn't the time to be a fucking smart-ass."

"Well, hallelujah, you do have the capability of getting something right," I retort.

"If you aren't going to eat, then take your ass upstairs and get some rest, but first, hand over that phone." His arm rises, palm held out, waiting for me.

I stand there dumbfounded, not believing the words that fell out of his mouth just now. I almost want to laugh, because now he's spit out the stupidest shit I've ever heard.

"I'm waiting."

"And you'll be waiting until the end of time." I'm not going to hand over my phone like I'm some teenager getting grounded by her daddy.

"You need to take a step back from all this shit, Bri." His hands go to his hips. "You might be alive, thank God, but our baby isn't. It was murdered just like you were supposed to be."

I have to lock my jaw in order to hold myself upright. I'm not ready for this conversation. Not today. Probably not tomorrow either, but that doesn't stop him from continuing.

"And my—" His voice cuts off abruptly with Drago taking a breath while shaking his head. My head leans to the side, stretching the muscle in my neck as my eyes squint at him. Was he about to say, *my son*? Was he about to acknowledge Gabe as his? "That boy was stolen, fucking kidnapped right under my nose. If you had—"

"If I'd what?" I demand, realizing exactly what he's thinking. I've thought it too in the last three days. It's a thought that will not go away no matter how hard I try to pretend it isn't so.

It was my fault.

"If you would have told me about him, I would have known to protect him. I wouldn't have let him get taken by a goddamn drug lord."

My stomach plummets to the floor and something deeper sinks into my chest. It hurts. I knew he blamed me. I've seen it mocking me, silently yelling at me through his eyes for days.

"You don't think I have regrets." I throw my hands up. "I had a job to do. I couldn't tell you no matter how much I wanted to. I would have lost my job if I'd broken protocol." It ate at me keeping the truth from him. And now that my job is hanging in the balance, maybe he's right. Maybe if I'd revealed the truth about Gabriel then maybe he wouldn't have been at my place, and maybe he wouldn't have been taken to be used as a pawn in Diaz's plan.

"Fuck protocol. It's a job, Bri. It doesn't come before us. Before what you think is the truth," he yells.

"What the fuck does that mean? What I *think is the truth*? I'm not following here."

"You've thought from the beginning that boy was mine."

"He is your son," I retort, cutting anything else he was going to say off.

"No, you think he is. There is a difference, and if you'd—"

"What the fuck!" I yell. "Don't be a dick right now. He's. Your. Son."

"Enough of this fucking shit already. He's not. Whatever, whoever, made you believe he was, is playing you for a fool. Can't you see that?"

"No." My eyes widen as my head shakes from side to side. "If there is one thing I do know for sure, it's that Gabriel is your flesh and blood. It's your DNA he shares with that cunt bitch of a mother of his."

"I never fucked her. It isn't possible."

"You got drunk when you decided to fuck me without a condom. Maybe you got drunk and fucked her too."

His mouth opens, showing me perfectly shaped teeth as he grits them like a dog does right before a growl escapes its chops.

"I might have had a lot more to drink that night than I normally do, but I still remember every moment I was inside you—unlike you," he jabs back, throwing in my face once again the night I can't remember; the night we created the baby we lost.

"You'll have to acknowledge him eventually, D. Whether it's today, tomorrow, or next fucking week. He is yours. Learn to accept it and help me get him back."

"I'm done with this." His head glides from side to side. "We aren't doing this anymore. It's done, Bri."

"It's not done until he's safely home with us."

"No," he barks out in the harshest tone I've ever heard come past his lips. "This"—he points between us—"is done. I'll have Luca take you to your dad's. Robert was right. You should stay with him. Or better yet, go to your brother's and get away from all of this."

I'm momentarily stunned. I don't know what to say or do. He just broke up with me like it's nothing. Like we're nothing.

"Fuck. You."

I turn around, pulling the door open with so much force it hits the wall as I storm out of Drago's home office.

CHAPTER NINE

Does he really think I'd go running to my *daddy*? I swear, it's like he doesn't even know me. And hell, maybe he doesn't. We've only known each other just over two months and it's not like we've spent every moment together. Relationship growth takes time and commitment—which apparently he wasn't up for.

"Where . . . to?" Luca asks from the driver's seat of his Tahoe. He couldn't hide the awkwardness from his tone even if he wanted to.

"Head toward Pacific Palisades. I live in a condo off Temescal Canyon."

"D said I was—"

"D can kiss my ass!"

"Bad word! Bad word! Bad word!" Mia chants from behind me. "You in trouble, Beee." She giggles, making the ache in my chest lessen momentarily.

"It's Bri," Luca corrects.

"That's what I said, Daddy." Her words come out like a pout, but I don't turn around in my seat to check.

"Sorry," I tell him.

"Not like she hasn't heard worse," he admits, his voice coming out resigned.

"What's that mean?" I ask, curious about his change in demeanor.

Rolling his head sideways, he looks at me as he slows at the end of Drago's driveway. "Not a convo for little ears."

I nod, understanding he doesn't want to talk about it in front of his daughter. Luca just gained a little more of my respect with this answer. It shows what type of father and person he is.

"Mia's mom's condo is on the way. Do you mind if I drop her off first?"

"Not at all."

"No home!" Mia whines. "Stay with you."

"Sorry, Mia-bug." Luca's eyes glance up, looking at her through the rearview mirror. "But you get to go see Nana and Pop. That's exciting, right?"

Luca isn't excited. That's very apparent in his tone and the way his forearms strain every time he tightens his hands around the steering wheel.

I wonder what their story is?

It's a fifteen-minute drive before he pulls off the highway, and then another five until he's turning into a high-rise condominium complex that screams luxury from the outside. Each building, or tower rather, is designed with panoramic views.

"Her mom sure lives in a nice place," I can't help but comment. If Luca is twenty-two, how old is Mia's mother? Maybe the girl still lives at home with her parents. Then I remember his comment about Mia going to her grandparents', and since his mom is no longer living and his dad is out of the country, that can only mean she's going to her maternal grandparents'. That must mean this is Mia's mother's residence.

A dry laugh escapes his lips. "You should see the inside."

"Do you live here too?" I ask as Luca pulls into a vacant parking spot.

"Nope." Luca unbuckles his seatbelt, leaving the ignition running. "Okay, kiddo. You ready?"

"No." She pouts from behind me.

"I'll be back in a few minutes."

As he totes Mia away, my cell phone makes a sound, telling me someone has sent me a text message, so I reach down, pulling it from my purse.

Tom: My office tomorrow, Andrews.

Fuck!

Guess it's time to face whatever music waits for me. Not like I can avoid him forever. I should have gone in today, but I didn't want to deal with the chief or Internal Affairs that'll surely be waiting on me when I get there tomorrow.

Me: Any particular time?

Tom: 9am.

Me: Yes, sir.

Closing out of my text messaging app, I tap on the photos app, pulling up my albums and go to my Favorites folder. Tapping on the last one I took, I see a picture of Drago that I took while he was asleep in my bed last week. He looks at ease when he's sleeping. He's at his sexiest when he's sacked out.

I may be mad at him for ending us, and doing it the way he did, but I miss him more than I'm hurt.

Sliding my finger right, I see a photo of Gabriel I snapped while getting him ready for bed one night.

My finger presses the button on my phone, making my screen go black. I have to shut my eyes, squeezing them tight or I'll choke up.

He's gone.

He's in danger and I have no idea how to find him or where to even start.

For the first time in my life, I feel helpless. And it's a feeling I hate with every fiber of my being.

I jump, my eyes popping open, startled when the door flies open. I relax when I realize it's Luca hopping into the SUV.

"You okay?" he asks.

"Yeah. Of course." I sigh. "Why wouldn't I be?"

His eyebrows climb up his forehead, but he doesn't say a word.

"So, I take it you and Mia's mom aren't a thing anymore?" I ask when he pulls his seatbelt over his body, clipping it into the lock.

He sighs, long and hard, before grabbing the gear and pulling it into reverse.

"We never really were *a thing*. We just fucked around here and there." He smashes on the brake, and then switches the gear into drive, leaving.

"Oh."

"London is a bitch. I love my daughter. I wouldn't change anything in the world—unless I could change who her mother is. But since that isn't possible, I'm stuck putting up with London's shit."

"She that bad?"

"She's a stuck-up, self-entitled whore"—his head swings my way—"with a coke problem. I hate leaving my daughter with her. But I have no choice."

"If she has a drug problem why not go after full custody?"

"My last name is Acerbi. The judge would think I'm the reason for her drug addiction. I can't risk losing my little girl. And London is smart. She knows my weakness. She knows how to use Mia against me to get whatever she wants."

"Damn, that sucks. I'm sorry."

"I don't really want to talk about my never-ending problems. So, tell me what's really going on with you and my brother?"

Way to flip the conversation.

"What did D tell you?"

"Not the truth. That much is obvious, so I want to hear it from you."

That's not going to happen. I won't lie to Luca. He doesn't deserve that, but I can't tell him what's going on either. One, it should come from Drago; definitely not me. And if I'm worried about my own family finding out the details of my involvement with Drago, and that it could potentially put them in harm's way, that's even more of a reason why D's family shouldn't know either. They are even closer to the source than mine.

Then again, maybe they're already involved—being as they share the same last name.

Maybe it doesn't matter if I tell him or don't tell him.

Still . . . This isn't something that he should learn from me. It's up to Drago to tell him about Gabe.

"Luca—" I start, but I'm quickly cut off.

"My brother likes you a lot. He wouldn't have dumped you like he did if something big hadn't have happened."

"Thanks for pointing that out," I chime in.

"How did you get shot? Did it somehow involve my brother?"

Oh, jeez. He needs to drive faster. I'm not getting into this with him. I'm going to have to shut this down.

"Luca, you need to ask him all of this."

"He's made it clear he isn't going to tell me."

"Well then, neither am I." And I leave it at that. The rest of the drive is spent in awkward silence.

CHAPTER TEN

I don't know how much longer I can go without an ounce of sleep. It's useless to even get in bed, so I didn't after I got home yesterday. I showered and changed the dressings on my wound. Then I worked up the courage to knock on Ms. Lincoln's door, only no one ever answered. I assumed she wasn't home. Maybe her son took her back with him. Maybe that's where she was when I tried calling her the other day.

I wish I could at least tell her how sorry I am for getting her caught up in my mess.

I'm a cop. I should have anticipated something like this. I allowed myself to get too attached and it blinded me to all of the possibilities that could have happened and did happen.

Parking my car in the parking garage next to city hall, I lean forward against the steering wheel, pulling in a deep breath. I'm exhausted, yet I can't make myself rest no matter how hard I try.

I'm on autopilot and it's only a matter of time before I crash.

My cell phone sounds, making me groan.

Relaxing back into the seat, I snatch it up from the cup holder.

Nikki: When the fuck were you planning on telling me you were shot?

How the hell does she—fucking media. That's how. It has to be. Why didn't I think of that sooner?

Nikki: I had to find out from Jason. Bitch, you better be okay.

Me: I'm fine, but I won't be in this week and probably not next week either.

Until I find Gabe, working out is of no concern to me.

I drop my phone, letting it fall into my lap, staring at the concrete cinder block wall I'm parked in front of.

If I don't get Gabriel back, I don't know if I'll ever return to the *me* I was before he was taken. I'm not concerned with the flesh wound on my leg. It'll heal, and I'm sure I'll be fine in a few weeks to return to normal activity. But right now, everything can fuck right off until he's safe.

Another chime sounds, breaking me from my thoughts. I pick my cell phone back up, looking at the message.

Nikki: Fine doesn't cut it. Are you still in the hospital? How bad?

Me: Not bad at all. I'm lucky, and I'm already home.

Nikki: Vague much?

Me: It's too much to get into over text. I'll tell you when I return.

Nikki: Take care of yourself and if you need ANYTHING, let me know.

That's sweet of her to offer. She's never come off as anything but hard, so for a second, I start to choke up. We aren't that close of friends, so maybe talking to her might be easier . . .

But as that thought trails off, I know all I'm doing by staying in my car this long is delaying the inevitable. It's time to face my chief. Another message comes through, but I decide it can wait. Without checking it, I toss my phone into my purse then step out of the car.

Normally, I'd take the stairs to the ground level, but I've exerted my body so much as it is in the last twenty-four hours that I've ripped a couple of the stitches on my wound, so I make myself take the elevator.

Stepping out of the parking garage, I stare at the building across the street wondering what fate has in store for me.

Only one way to find out.

I halt just before stepping off the sidewalk as a black SUV stops abruptly in front of my path. The lock on the door pops and the window rolls down.

"Get in."

I start to reach for the weapon that should be secured at my hip, but then I realize it's not there. I left my badge and police issued gun at home. It feels awkward being without it. Ever since I became a cop, they've been a part of who I am. And I don't want to lose my job.

Fighting the urge to curse, I take a cautious step backward.

"I'm waiting, Detective." He leans back into his seat. He's turned sideways, looking at me with one long, chocolate-colored arm stretched out across the steering wheel. His dark eyes look bored, but I'm not about to make a move toward him. I don't even know him.

"Who are you? What do you want?"

"Get in and I'll explain."

"I don't think so." I tip my chin. "You can explain while I'm out here."

Rolling his eyes, he shakes his head while reaching into the neck of his plain black T-shirt. A badge attached to a chain pops out.

Okay, so he's a cop. A federal agent at that. Then again, it's not like a badge can't be faked.

"Jesus, lady. Are you going to get in or just stand there?"

"Stand here until you tell me what you want."

"We're on the same side, Detective. I'm going to be your saving grace. Now"—he drops his badge, allowing it to hang on the outside of his shirt—"please get in the fucking vehicle. We need to talk."

"I'm about to be late for a meeting, agent."

"Special agent," he corrects in the same mocking tone I used. "It won't take long, and trust me, you'll want what I'm offering." He smiles as if going for good measure.

Isn't he sure of himself. He certainly looks the part of confidence rolled into authority. Reminds me of Drago in a way.

Going against my better judgment, I step forward, open the door, and slide into the passenger side seat.

"Okay, I'm in."

"Do you think you could close the door?"

"Do I look that stupid?" For all I know, I am. He could be

someone Sebastian sent to finish the job he started.

"Well, you did get yourself shot inside your own home only a couple of days ago, so . . ."

"Talk," I bite out. "Or I'm gone."

He reaches forward, grabbing something off the top of his dashboard. He tosses it at me and I quickly realize it's his credentials. Opening it, I look down. DEA special agent Eric Alders.

"What's a DEA agent want with me?"

"Baby, I'm your new best friend."

"I'm not your baby."

He just laughs, ticking me off.

"Do you actually have something you want to tell me or is this some game?"

"I'm here to help you." His demeanor turns serious. "I have another gift for you."

Another?

The photos.

"It was you." The realization falls from my lips.

Ms. Lincoln said the man that left them was tall, dark, and hot. The man sitting next to me checks off each one of those descriptions.

"What was me?" he asks, even though it's clear he knows what I'm talking about. Eric was the guy that left that envelope with those photos inside it with my neighbor.

What's the DEA doing involved? Did Ramirez keep this from me? Did Houston? My mind spins, wondering everything at once.

"They were a gift."

"Explain."

"You're demanding for a cop that's about to walk inside that building over there and most likely get grilled by Internal Affairs. How are you going to explain your personal involvement with Acerbi? I'm curious."

"Why don't you explain your involvement in all of this first?"

"I've been working the Acerbi case far too long to let LAPD come in and fuck up all of my hard work. Not when I'm close to nailing that son of a bitch."

"Drago?" My gut clenches at the thought.

"No." His eyes dance dramatically as his head shakes from side to side. "Vincent Acerbi is the criminal, not his kids."

"D's dad isn't here. Hasn't been in the States in two years."

"Fuck," he draws out. "So, you did get personal with the very man you were tasked with pinning a crime on."

"Fuck you," I fire back at him. "Don't accuse me of setting up Drago for something he didn't do."

"You need to learn right now not to put words in my mouth, sweetheart. I don't like it and I won't put up with it."

"You're a pompous ass! And don't call me sweetheart, *sweetheart*," I mock, raising one of my eyebrows in challenge.

"Well, I'm your partner, so to speak, so you're going to have to get used to my pompous ass."

He tosses a file into my lap.

"What's this?" I ask, flipping the file open to one sheet of paper.

"A document." I raise an eyebrow at him, beckoning him to explain further. "It's pre-dated, obviously, and it basically says you've been working with the Department of Drug Enforcement Administration. An official NDA of sorts, saying you weren't allowed to tell anyone, including your superiors, about your involvement with my investigation of Vincent Acerbi." His dark eyes cast down to the paper in my hand. "You just need to sign it to make it legal."

"Why would I do that?"

"To save your ass." His eyebrows turn inward. "To save your badge, Andrews." He removes a pen from the breast pocket of his T-shirt, holding it out in front of me. "You want to keep it, right? You want to get IA off your ass before they start digging around and find validation that you were, in fact, fucking a man you were supposed to be investigating?"

"Why do you care? What does me keeping my badge have to do with you or the DEA's interest in Acerbi?"

"You don't worry about that. Just sign the piece of paper and we'll both go hand it to your boss. I'm looking forward to seeing the look on his face actually."

"I'm not signing shit until you tell me what's in this for you and the DEA."

"I want to wrap-up a case I've been working on for far too long. I want to put the man who is responsible for countless murders and trafficking more drugs than you will ever see in your lifetime into our country, behind bars. Even if he deserves far worse than prison." His tone is bitter, angry. Personal. "And I want your help in taking down the dirty cops that help keep him and men like him out of prison."

"Which cops are dirty?"

"That's still to be determined, but I have a good idea who they are. Sign the paper, so we can get this on the way, Bri. I can call you Bri, right?"

There is something about him that strikes me as good. He's mouthy for a guy. But for whatever reason, I think I might be able to trust him and work with him.

"No. We aren't friends."

"Oh, yes we are, Bri."

I take the pen he stretches out in front of me.

Entering the elevator, I turn and place my back against the back wall, clutching my purse with both hands in front of me.

"So, we're just planning on walking in there and expecting the deputy chief to accept that falsified document?" I eye the file folder clutched in his hand.

He presses the button that will take me up to my dreaded fate.

"Only you and I know it's falsified," he whispers as if this isn't a big deal, which in hindsight it is, and I can't fathom why I'm even going along with it. Other than the fact I don't want Internal Affairs to recommend I need to be let go.

Eric sidles up next to me as we ascend.

Just the thought of getting fired almost brings tears to my eyes. Pulling in a deep breath of air, I blow it back out in a steady stream, calming my emotions and nerves—or at least trying to. I shouldn't have had that extra-large coffee with an extra shot of espresso in it on the drive here. The caffeine has only amped me up with jitters I don't need right now.

I can do this.

I can walk into Tom's office with a straight face and lie to my boss.

Fuck, I'm going to Hell for this.

"With the look you have on your face, Ramirez will have an opening to question this." He holds up his hand. "Get your shit together, Detective. Confidence. You need it, and if you don't have it, fake it." He smiles, his face softening. "You can start with tipping those lips up. Yeah?"

His hip knocks lightly into mine.

"Son of a fuck." I slam my palm against the wooden panel to my back. Pain shoots up my side and down my leg so fast and unexpected.

"Jesus, Andrews," Eric sounds off. "What the hell is your problem now?"

My jaw snaps shut, locking down on the pain until it passes.

"You asshole," I bark at him. "This is the leg Diaz shot, fuckwad." I point to the thigh he bumped into.

"Oh shit!" His voice does a one-eighty. "I didn't mean to hurt you, Bri. I forgot you were shot. You're walking and moving normally. I figured you must not have been injured too badly."

"It's fine."

"I'm sorry," he continues. "I normally don't assume shit like that."

"I'm fine," I assure him.

The elevator comes to a soft halt, so I take one last deep breath.

Eric is right. I do need to conjure up every ounce of confidence I have. The best method for someone believing you is if you believe it yourself, and although it is a lie, this is my life, my job, and my career on the line. I need to do whatever it takes to ensure I have one when all of this is said and done.

"Lead the way." Eric steps out, waiting for me to exit.

Steeling myself, I look Eric in the eyes, giving myself one last mental pep talk.

I can and will do this.

I have to if I'm going to give myself every opportunity to get Gabriel back unharmed and safe where I need him to be. Even if that means he gets fostered with someone other than me. Nothing matters at this moment other than doing what it takes to ensure I have the means to locate him.

I still don't know why I'm being called into the department today, but if the internal investigation hasn't been completed and I'm stuck on admin leave, then finding Gabe will be way more difficult without PD help. It'll be like my hands are shackled with no key to get free. That is unless what Eric fed me out in his vehicle earlier was the truth and not bullshit, then he can and will help me find Gabriel. He has the resources to do so.

There's no doubt in my mind that I have to do this. I have to lie through my teeth. Is it wrong? Sure. But what other choice do I really have? Not accepting Eric's "get-out-of-jail-free" card would mean I'm giving up. I don't give up. I'm not a quitter, not even if it means I get inducted into the Dirty Blue.

They say the path to Hell is paved with good intentions. Maybe that's true. Maybe it isn't. All I know is if this helps me get one step closer to finding that innocent little boy, then I guess I'm on the next train to Hell.

"Let's do this."

"Now that's the right attitude to have, Detective." He snickers. "Or soon-to-be Special Agent."

"Doesn't it take months of interviewing just to get a chance at becoming part of the DEA?"

"What the fuck do you think you've been doing for the past two months?"

I walk past him, down the quiet hall until I see Tom's office door come into view. Becky, his assistant, has her spectacle-framed eyes glued to the computer screen in front of her.

She doesn't look up when I stop in front of her until she hears my voice.

"Tom is expecting me," I inform her.

"Detective." She jumps, smiling awkwardly. She obviously knows why I'm here and why wouldn't she?

"Hey, Becky."

Eric's large frame stops behind me. Becky's eyes glance up and over my head, seeing him. Warm air fans the back of my head when he lets out an amused laugh.

Eric and I might have gotten off on the wrong foot when he demanded I get inside his SUV half an hour ago, and I can't say we're on the path to friendship yet, because I don't know him, but even I can admit he's a looker. Like my neighbor said, he has a dreamy appearance. But he's a cop. And there is something about fellow badges that I've never been physically attracted to.

"I thought only you were meeting with the chief and Detective

Summers? He didn't tell me anyone was accompanying you."

Ah, hell. *Justin Summers?* That man has a reputation that precedes him—and not in a good way. As much as cops don't like IA, even I know they are necessary; a check and balance on policies. But Justin Summers?

Eric leans forward, his mouth stopping behind my ear. "You're tensing up. Relax. Summers won't be a problem."

"Easy for you to say."

"No, Bri," he corrects. "Not easy for me. My ass is on the line, same as yours," he whisper-yells.

"Can we head on in, Becky?" I say a little louder than necessary.

"Let me take you." She scoots her chair backward, stands, and then walks over to Tom's door, knocking. After a beat, she pivots around. "You both may go in now."

"Thanks," I say, sliding past her to enter Tom's office.

He's seated behind his desk, forearms stretched across the center, looking every bit in-charge until his mask slips the second Eric enters behind me.

Glancing over, I see whom I'm guessing is the Internal Affairs detective. He's seated in a relaxed position at the end of the leather couch in Tom's office. He sits up, taking me in as I do him. Detective Summers is dressed in a dark gray suit with a light blue shirt that makes his striking blue eyes pop. The jacket is tight along his biceps, showcasing exactly what's beneath the material. His blond hair is cut short in the back and styled longer on the top. The trimmed goatee and beard make him appear older, but I'm betting we are about the same age.

He's not at all how I've imagined him. And very easy on the

eyes.

"Andrews," Tom greets, standing. I look away, giving my boss my full attention as Eric comes to stand beside me. "I don't recall telling you to bring a guest."

"Sir," I start, but I'm silenced when Eric places his hand on my forearm. I turn my head, questioning him with my stare.

"I don't plan on being here long, Chief," Eric tells him.

"Alders, why do I get the feeling you're here to fuck up my cut and dry case?" Detective Summers stands, crossing his arms over his chest, staring at Eric.

"Nothing's ever cut and dry, J. You know that."

My eyes snap up to Eric's and then over to Detective Summers, noting the silent conversation they both seem to be having. Eric referred to him as "J" rather than Justin or addressing him formally. In the time I've known Drago, he too refers to those close to him by their first initial. Eric's a lot like D when I think about it. Or at least I get that feeling. Perhaps when and if I get to know Eric more, that'll change.

"Fair enough," Detective Summers says, then his eyes glide over, landing on mine. "Justin Summers." He walks forward, then stretches his hand out toward me. "IA, but I'm going to assume you know that already."

"Brianna Andrews." I slide my hand into his, squeezing. His palm is warm and gentle. Looking up, I can't help but scrutinize his gaze. He's doing the same to me, only it's not my eyes he's checking out. It's my mouth. There's a hint of approval behind the sparkle in his blue eyes. "I'd say it's a pleasure, but we both know it's not."

A low chuckle escapes his lips as his eyes flick back to mine.

"No. I guess it wouldn't be if I were in your shoes."

"Summers," Ramirez calls out, earning all of our attention. "You know this man? Please, fill me in then."

"Sir, I do," Summers responds.

"No need." Eric holds up his hand to Summers then pulls out the chain from under his T-shirt, letting it fall to his chest, revealing his badge. "Special Agent Eric Alders."

Tom's features visibly change; anger washes over his face.

"What reason would the DEA be in my office and with my detective, nonetheless?"

Eric flips the file folder up, slapping it against my arm to take, which I do and then step forward, handing it over to the deputy chief.

Tom's eyes watch mine the entire time. He seems reluctant to take it at first, but finally, he pulls it out of my hand.

"What's this?"

"Open it, sir."

Looking down, he flips it open, taking the sheet of paper out and then places the file on his desk. His eyes scrunch together as he reads. And when his face reddens, something inside me relaxes a margin.

He's buying it.

"What the hell is this, Andrews?"

Tom shoves the legal-size document in Summers' direction. I watch him take it, reading it so diligently that I tilt my face, observing him. His eyes move from side to side and I'm struck with amazement for some odd reason. He's thorough and not rushing himself to finish.

Taking two steps back, he sits back down on the couch. Once he's finished, he pauses, looking off to the side. He's digesting it and then his eyes snap to mine. For several pregnant pauses, I think he's going to call bullshit. But he doesn't. He doesn't even speak. Just watches as I watch him—until Ramirez's voice booms.

"Well, fucking explain."

"Sir," I say calmly. "It's pretty self-explanatory. Alders and I have been working together for some time now, almost the start of my investigation."

"I approached Detective Andrews," Eric butts in. "I had already been eyeing her as a potential candidate for the DEA. When I learned of LAPD's interest in Acerbi, I knew it was a sign."

"A fucking sign?" Tom questions. "How would you have even known anything about my interests?"

"That's really here nor there other than I'm good at my job."

"You're telling me." Tom pierces me with his stare. "You colluding with a suspect was all an act?" He shakes his head. "Sorry, but I don't buy that. That miscreant knocked you up, and I'm supposed to believe it was all a little act to get close to him?"

How the hell does he know that?

That was never discussed with anyone other than the physician, Drago, and my dad. D's family doesn't even know. And I can't imagine my father divulging that piece of information after everything he told me about my mom. So how does Tom know?

Eric's hand comes to rest on my back, bracing me, which helps to steady my frame. In my distracted thoughts, I hadn't realized I'd taken a step back.

"Oftentimes, when immersed under deep cover, a cop has to do and act ways they wouldn't normally. She was faced with blowing her cover or going along with something she normally wouldn't. You know this, Ramirez, so what's the real issue here? You don't like being kept in the dark when your detective is vying for a spot with a federal agency—or is it something else? Don't want the feds taking over *your* case on Acerbi?" Eric's laugh is sardonic. "Although, it was never your case to begin with. I've been working Acerbi for far too long to give him to the local PD."

"My issue is that—"

Summers cuts him off. "All of this is legal and binding. I've known Alders for a long time, Chief. He does everything by the book. Maybe off-handed, but still straight-up and by the law." Summers stands. Taking a long step forward, he passes the document to me. "Detective Andrews, I still have to complete a full investigation of your actions. Normally, something of this nature would make Alders' case a conflict of interest, but taking what he's told us into consideration, I'll sign off on you consulting with Alders on his case. You'll remain on administrative leave until your physician has released you, though. There is no way around that, Detective."

"Actually, I have a follow-up tomorrow," I tell him, remembering my discharge orders for the first time since leaving the hospital.

"Good." Eric claps his hands. "I submitted a request to you just this morning, Chief, asking that Andrews be allowed to continue working alongside me on this case."

"Get me a copy of her release and then she can consult *only*,

Alders until my internal investigation is complete." Summers faces me, looking down at me, but when he opens his mouth to say something, he's cut off by Ramirez.

"Summers, you can't—"

The deputy chief is cut off once again. "With all due respect, sir, I can." His voice is firm, silently commanding acceptance. "It appears Detective Andrews is playing an important role in Special Agent Alders' case. I will be forwarding my latest update to the Chief of Police as well."

Tom steels his jaw, breathing in long and hard, before releasing it all while drilling holes into me with his dark blue eyes.

"And if I refuse to allow her?" Tom directs his question to Eric.

"I'll be forced to take my request to my director." Eric lets out a dry laugh, while Summers bites his lip in order to contain his.

"I'll inform Detective Bristols that you'll be on assignment with another agency for the time being," Tom grits out. "Now get out of my office—both of you."

"I'll see them both out, Chief. Until next time," Summers remarks, before making an exit.

Eric and I follow behind him. I have to quicken my pace to keep up with their long strides. Once at the elevator, Summers turns, facing us.

"Earning yourself another enemy, Alders? Hell, soon you'll have as many as I do."

Eric shrugs his shoulders. "All in a day's work." He laughs. "It's the fun part of my job."

"Wish I saw it that way." Summers' gaze flicks down to mine. "If you're gonna fuck a suspect, at least make him wear a rubber."

He pauses. "Tell me Ramirez was wrong and you aren't carrying an Acerbi?"

"What the fuck?" I burst out. "What if I were?"

"Bri," Eric scolds, grabbing me by my bicep.

"Well, you either are, or you aren't. Which is it?"

"Drop it, J. This isn't the place." Eric pulls on my arm, practically dragging me inside the elevator. "Let's go." His voice takes on the authority he eluded when he pulled up to the curb earlier.

I have to bite the inside of my cheek in order to control the tears that are climbing to the surface.

Summers doesn't enter the elevator, which is probably a good thing for the both of us. My emotions hit me square in the face. I wasn't expecting them to feel like another shot to my already abused body.

As soon as the door closes, I turn, facing Eric. "How does everyone know?" I demand.

"Know what?" He looks puzzled.

"What do you mean what?" I toss my arm out, stretching it to the closed elevator door. "How does my boss and IA know I was pregnant? You heard him just then."

"Wait, he was serious?" Eric takes a step away from me. "I didn't know you were," he whispers as his head tilts and his eyes flicker down. Suddenly they snap back to mine. "Was?" he questions.

"I had a miscarriage Friday." Fuck. The pain that lashes through me takes my breath away momentarily. Maybe my dad is right. Maybe I do need to face these feelings now rather than later.

"Was it Drago's?"

"Yes," I answer honestly, and doing so makes me realize how much I miss him.

I lean back, bracing myself against the wall while the elevator descends, and for a minute, I wonder what D is doing right now and where he is. Is he thinking of me? Of the baby we lost? Or of the son that's missing?

Gabriel. I close my eyes, remembering the last moment I saw him. He was so tuckered out from the trip to the zoo. Maybe if I hadn't taken him, I would have been home and better prepared for them. Maybe they wouldn't have gone to my neighbor's, tying her up and scaring her. Maybe—

"Andrews." My eyes pop open, seeing Eric standing halfway inside the elevator and halfway out, holding the door open.

I push off the wall, walking out and passing him. Once outside, I pause and wait for him to catch up. He's next to me in seconds.

"I've gotta head over to my office. Why don't I call you tomorrow after your check-up? What time is it at?"

"Nine."

He nods and starts to walk off, but I spring forward, pulling on his arm, stopping him.

"I know why I did that. Why did you? What's in this for you?" I'm too curious not to ask.

"Rectifying a wrong." Without any more of an explanation, he pulls away, leaving me standing in front of the police headquarters, watching him.

CHAPTER ELEVEN

ectifying a wrong.

I'm still wondering what the hell that even means a day later.

I'm not sure about Special Agent Eric Alders yet. What could possibly be in this for him? Am I grateful he basically came to my rescue? Yes, of course. But I'm not sure why he did other than he says he doesn't want local law enforcement to screw up his case.

Something tells me that isn't the real reason he doesn't want LAPD involved. There's more to why Eric feels the need to rectify a wrong.

"Brianna Andrews?"

I snap my head up as a tall, slender blonde, wearing a doctor's coat walks in the room. "I'm Dr. Sanders." She extends her hand in front of me, which I accept, shaking her hand all while wondering where my gynecologist is—because this isn't her.

"Yes," I draw out, confused.

"I'm so sorry," she says, reading the expression on my face. "No one told you Renee had a family emergency, did they?"

"No," I confirm. "I hope everything with Dr. Monroe is okay."

The way she cringe-smiles tells me it's not. I feel bad for whatever is going on. Dr. Monroe has been my gynecologist since I moved to LA eight years ago. I hope it's not one of her kids. She's had three in the eight years I've been a patient at this clinic.

"This is Suzanne," she tells me when the same older woman who roomed me ten minutes ago enters the room, shutting the door behind her. "She'll be assisting me today. So, the notes on the appointment show you are following up on a miscarriage from last week. Is that right?"

"Yes."

"And you took a gunshot wound to the leg as well?"

"Yes," I repeat.

"You've been through an ordeal." Empathy shines in her eyes. "I'm so sorry, Miss Andrews. How are you feeling today?"

"I've been better," I say for the lack of knowing what else to say. My physical wounds are nothing compared to the state of my emotions. I think I've done a good job keeping them suppressed. The only time I've given in has been while showering under the spray of hot water, which is very difficult to do when you can't get one of your legs wet. But I figure if I can't feel the tears, then I don't have to fully acknowledge them in my mind.

"Can I take a look at the wound first?"

"Of course."

I lay back on the exam table as she snatches a pair of latex gloves from the box attached to the wall and proceeds with the exam. She's quick but thorough. I already like how this is going, even if she isn't my regular gynecologist.

"Looks good." She releases the sheet, letting it cover the bottom half of my body again. "You're doing an excellent job keeping your leg clean and bandaged. I don't see any need for wound management, but do you have a primary care physician that you can follow up with to make sure it continues healing as it should?"

"Not really. I only see Dr. Monroe for my yearly. If I'm sick, I just go to an urgent care clinic."

"I recommend all my patients have a routine physician like a family medicine doctor or an internist. If you would like me to refer you, I will."

"I'll look into it," I say to appease her. One yearly visit is enough for me. It's not like I get sick that often and I can take care of my leg myself. I don't have time to go see another doctor right now. I have other things that matter more, like finding the motherfucker that did this to me in the first place.

"Okay." She nods. "Let's discuss the miscarriage. How are you doing emotionally and physically?"

I sit back up, waiting for her to take a seat on the rolling chair positioned in front of a computer screen.

"The cramps are a lot worse than normal periods, but the ER doctor warned me about that. Otherwise, I think I'm fine. The guy who did this though . . ." I trail off, not wanting to run my mouth. I'm a cop. I can't just throw idle threats around. But I can't deny the thoughts of revenge floating around in my head. They are there. They've taken up residence and I don't see them leaving anytime soon. At least not until Diaz and his men are dealt with—one way or another.

I look over at her when she doesn't say anything. She's facing her computer, typing in quick successions to log in. Once she's finished, she turns on the stool, facing me.

"Being that you miscarried so early in your pregnancy, it might not have had anything to do with the trauma you experienced. Twenty percent of all pregnancies end in miscarriages. The fetus just may not have developed normally."

Is this woman for real right now?

"I know I must sound clinical. I just want you to know that what happened to you might not have been the reason why you lost the fetus. I'm sorry if the ER physician didn't explain that to you."

No. What I think right now is she's a bitch. But I keep my tongue in my mouth, not voicing that bitter thought.

"I've had numerous patients enter into depression after a miscarriage. It's quite common. And patients who find a reason to blame themselves or others have a harder time overcoming these things than women who know there wasn't anything they could have done to stop it. Miscarriages are more common than most people think."

I don't blame myself per se. I blame Sebastian Diaz and his men. Had I known I was pregnant, I might have done things differently. Then again, at the time, Gabriel's life was at risk, and even now I know I would have done everything in my power to keep him from being taken. But I don't tell her any of this. It's not a conversation I care to get into with anyone, especially not her, someone I don't know.

"I see in the system there is a note that you didn't choose a D&C while at the hospital," she goes on to say. "Is that something you want to consider now if your body hasn't passed it?"

"I don't think there is a need. I'm pretty sure I passed everything over the weekend. I stopped bleeding yesterday."

"You mentioned your cramps were worse than normal cycle cramps. How are they now?"

Fucking excruciating. I'm not used to heavy periods or cramping at all. I don't have the symptoms many other women talk about. I usually bleed for three to four days and then it's over. Other than my periods being a nuisance, I can't really complain. This time though . . .

"Yeah, they were, but I haven't had any today."

"In that case, I'd like to do an ultrasound to confirm your uterus is clear. Otherwise, you risk infection or even hemorrhaging."

"Whatever gets this over with."

"Lie back again, please." She stands from her stool. "Have you ever had an ultrasound before?"

"No." I shake my head.

"Then this may be a bit uncomfortable." She pulls out an instrument I'd forgotten about. It looks like a long dildo, but I remember it from when I went to one of my sister-in-law's ultrasounds early in her pregnancy with Caleb. I remember thinking just that—it's got to be uncomfortable.

When she inserts the thing, it's more awkward feeling than anything. When she's finished, I relax my back onto the exam table and I'm momentarily relieved. That is until I read her face.

"Is everything okay?"

"Yes. Everything is fine, Miss Andrews." I hear the "but" in her voice before her mouth opens again. "The miscarriage isn't complete as you had originally thought. So, let's discuss options."

"The ER doc said it would naturally pass."

She turns, handing off the wand to the nurse in the room before turning back to face me.

"It usually does within two weeks. We can still schedule a procedure if you'd like, or I can give you a pill that will help your uterus push it out."

"So, my options are surgery or medication?"

I scoot away from the edge of the table, and then sit up, covering my legs with the sheet in my lap, thinking. Frankly, I don't like either of the options in front of me. I don't want to go under anesthesia. I hate taking any type of medication. For one, I tend to react to most medicines, so I avoid them if it's not an antibiotic.

"No. You can still give it time to complete." She rolls away from me. "But I don't recommend that method. Like I said earlier, there is a higher risk of infection and hemorrhaging."

Yeah, but how likely are either of those things, I think to myself.

"I really don't want to have surgery."

"It's nothing like what's going on in your head, I can assure you. You aren't put under anesthesia. The procedure itself is rather quick. Usually takes ten to fifteen minutes max."

"So, I could do it now and it would be over?"

"Well," she hesitates. "You wouldn't be able to drive yourself home. You would be heavily medicated; therefore you would need a driver and I'd have to place an order so the medicine could be ordered. We would need to schedule it for another day, but I'm sure we could do it as early as next Monday. With it being a holiday, the clinic is closed tomorrow and Friday."

I'd forgotten about Thanksgiving.

Shit. I'm not going to be able to avoid my family. I'm surprised Alana hasn't called me in the last couple of days now that I think about it. The last text from her was on Monday asking when I was coming up, but I never responded. It's weird that she hasn't called me.

"Miss Andrews?" My head snaps up. "Would you like me to have the nurse schedule you for early next week?"

"No. I still don't think I want to do it. Can I just wait or," I pause, dropping my eyes and look down at my lap. "I guess I could do the pill if it'll work faster than the natural way," I tell her, looking back up.

I need this finished so that my focus from here on out can be finding Drago's son. Now that Eric has gotten IA and my boss off my back, I can do my job and find Diaz. And I will find him one way or another. I can't waste any opportunities or have any other setbacks.

"I'm glad you decided on that option. And yes, the medication should speed up the process."

"Will I be able to return to work right away?" I ask the question even though I know I'm still on administrative leave.

"I don't see why you couldn't return to work on Monday, but

it will be light duty for one more week. Your leg wound is healing nicely, but it's not completely healed. I don't want you to chance getting into any predicament that could possibly reopen the wound, which could lead to an infection."

"Why not tomorrow?"

"Well, I assumed you would want to take the rest of the week to rest, and with the holiday—"

"No. I'm good. I really need to get back to work as soon as possible."

"Well, I do recommend getting more rest, and if you need to speak to someone regarding the emotional side of healing, I can certainly refer you to a great therapist who specializes in cases like yours."

"I'm good."

"You may think you're good, Miss Andrews, but just think about it. Talking things out can do wonders for your mind. Trust me. I know."

I nod, even though I don't agree with her. I hate psych evaluations and I already know I'm going to be forced to undergo one from the department due to being shot, even if I wasn't on duty.

But at least I'm able to leave the clinic with the release form signed and dated.

PARKING, I TURN OFF MY CAR AND GO TO GET OUT WHEN MY CELL PHONE chimes with an incoming text message. Grabbing my smartphone from the center console, I peek at the screen as I open the door to step out.

Drago: You see a doc yet?"

My heart slams into my chest at the sight of his name alone. Fuck, I miss him. But I'm still mad too, so when I reply, I can't help but come off that way.

Me: What business is that of yours?

Drago: None other than I just want to know you're okay.

Me: I'm fine.

I don't know why I'm being a bitch about it. Texting me shows he still cares, but after the way he treated me, I won't give in to my desire that still wants him so badly. I won't beg for him to come back to me. And I won't give him insight on my health either. He made his decision and I made mine. My focus is on doing whatever it takes to find *his* son.

Nothing else matters right now.

Nothing else can matter.

My phone rings. The caller ID displays a California phone number I don't recognize. Normally, I'd let it go to voicemail, but it could be Diaz or someone else with information I need.

"Hello."

"Doc sign the release forms yet?"

Eric.

"I'm good to return to work if that's what you are asking."

"No. I asked if the medical release form has been signed. I have to have it turned in to your HR department and IA before I let you tag along with me."

Let me tag along?

What the fuck?!

"What happened to me being your new partner?"

"I already have a partner."

"Yeah? Then why do you need me?"

"Who says I need you?" He laughs, and I hear the sarcasm behind his words. "Seems to me, you're the one that needs me."

"Seems to me you just called to fuck with me."

"Nope. I just need the form so that you can *consult*."

"I have them. Can I give them to you in the morning?"

"In the morning? Are you crazy? I'm not working tomorrow. It's Thanksgiving."

"A baby was kidnapped, or have you forgotten that? Who the fuck cares about thanks-fucking-giving?"

The world—and all the bad shit in it—doesn't stop because of a damn holiday. And the thing is, I know before Gabriel was taken I thought the same way, and not just at holiday times. When my day was over, I left work at the office. Work and my personal life have always been separate—until Gabe came along and changed all that. Now I don't know where he is or where to start.

"Me. I care. And just so we're clear, Andrews, my case has nothing to do with that kid Diaz took from you. That's PD. It's on them to find that boy. Tomorrow, I'll be with family. Maybe you should think about doing the same." He pauses, but before I'm able to get a word in, he starts up again, making my jaw lock. "If you're in town on Friday, we'll get together and figure out how the two of us are going to work together. I really do think you have potential to become one of us."

"Go fuck yourself." I hang up.

Stopping at the exterior door at the front of my building, I bang out the four-digit access code, and then yank on the door, pulling it open with so much force that I regret it and instantly drop to my knees in pain. Doubling over, I grab my stomach, rocking back and forth.

Mother of Jesus.

My abdomen clenches tight, not letting up. Tears spring to my eyes unexpectedly, and it's then I realize I'm not breathing.

Placing my palm on the concrete ground, I exhale and then breathe deeply. I repeat the process a couple of times until the cramps pass and I'm able to stand. Reaching down slowly, I grab my purse and the pharmacy bag I dropped when I went to the ground.

Breathing in again, I take a lungful of air and push it back out through my mouth before finally stepping over the threshold and heading to the elevator.

Eric can shove his NDA up his ass if he thinks I'm helping him bring Drago or his family down. There are more important things than a badge to me and they are all wrapped up in that little boy I miss so much.

I never knew it was possible to fall in love this quick, if that is what I feel. I'm pretty sure I love Gabriel with every part of my soul.

How is that even possible? He's not mine. I didn't even have him that long but—

"Bri, dear?" My head snaps up, seeing the elevator has stopped on my floor. "How are you? Are you okay?" Ms. Lincoln walks forward, away from her apartment door. "I haven't heard a word and I've been so worried."

"Ms. Lincoln," I half gasp. "Oh, my God. How are you?" I snap myself out of the moment I had been having, and spring forward, jumping out of the elevator and stopping in front of her. "I am so sorry for what happened. You must hate me." Hell, I hate me for what happened to her, but that doesn't keep me from leaning forward and wrapping her in a tight embrace.

"Bri," she chastises. "Honey, I could never hate you. But I'm so confused. What on earth happened?" Her eyes look around me. "And where is our Gabriel?"

My heart sinks.

"Some really bad people took him," I admit.

"What?!" Her hands fly to her mouth, covering it. "No," she cries.

"I'm on it," I lie. "I'll find him. I swear it." My words sound convincing. I just wish I could believe them. I know logically that might not happen. He's been missing nearly a week and I'm not so sure anyone is actively searching for his whereabouts.

"Why did they want our little Gabe? He's just a baby." Her eyes flick to the side and then back to mine rapidly. "Oh, Bri, I know you said he was part of a case, but I never imagined . . ." She trails off, shaking her head in disbelief.

"Are you really okay?" I ask, moving the conversation away from Gabriel. Much more talk of him and I'm liable to lose what little bit of control over my emotions I have. "They didn't hurt you, did they?"

"I'm all right. Still shaken up a bit, but I'm doing good. They only tied me up and asked a lot of questions." Her eyebrows turn inward and stress lines creases her forehead. "But I didn't tell them one thing," she goes on to say.

"I'm glad to hear, but I'm still sorry it happened. I never meant—"

"You stop right now. This wasn't your fault, Bri."

But it was and I'd rather her acknowledge it than try to appease me. I brought this into my home. For the first time, I brought work home with me and I kept him. I could have pushed the chief, made him locate his contact and hand Gabriel over. But I never wanted that to happen. After that first long weekend, I was attached. That sweet little boy entered my life so unexpectedly, and without knowing it, I gave him my heart.

Shit. I'm going to lose it right here in front of her.

"Mom."

We both look behind her, seeing a tall, husky man leaving her apartment. Looking down, I see a large, rolling suitcase parked next to his leg.

"Oh, Howard, come here. You have to meet my neighbor, Bri."

Our eyes lock, and I watch as his expression visibly changes, hardening. He must have been the man that answered her phone when I tried calling her a couple of days ago.

"Mom, we really need to get going so we don't miss the flight."

"We have plenty of time, Son. The flight doesn't leave for another five hours," she huffs. "Plenty of time for you to say a quick 'hello' to this nice young lady."

"Hi." He walks forward, extending his long arm. "I'm Howard. Her son," he deadpans.

"A rude son at that." Ms. Lincoln follows up before turning

back to me. "I'm sorry, Bri. He usually isn't like this."

"It's okay," I assure her.

"I usually don't have a mother taken hostage in her own home."

"I truly am sorry," I say to my neighbor once again.

"I told you to stop that." She grasps my hand, squeezing, and then pats it. "Howard wants me to stay with him and his family for a couple of weeks. I'm doing it to make him happy, but I'll be back, you hear me? And I want our little Gabriel here when I am."

I nod, feeling my throat close. I shouldn't make her promises I may not be able to keep, but if I don't believe it myself, then I'll never be able to convince anyone else. And if I can't do that, I'm not sure my department will work as hard.

Being as he's Drago's son, he already has a dark mark on him that shouldn't be there. It shouldn't matter the DNA one possesses or the last name they bear no more than the color of one's skin or the religion a person follows. A person's life is valuable no matter what.

"I think it's a great idea, actually. Being with your family will do you some good. Don't you have grandbabies you haven't seen in a while?"

"I do. And I am looking forward to spending time with my little ones."

I lean in, pulling her in for a quick hug. She wraps both of her arms around me, squeezing as hard as she can. For an older woman, she certainly has great strength within her—mentally and physically.

Stepping back, I nod to her son, who doesn't return the gesture.

"Have a good time," I tell her. Then I step around and unlock my door, going inside.

After chucking my purse onto the couch, I walk into the kitchen and reach up over my stove, opening the cabinet. I pause, looking up at the whiskey bottle sitting there, and I wonder how long it would take to lose myself in the alcohol and forget everything that has transpired in the last six days.

Fuck it, I tell myself as I push up on my tippy toes, grabbing the bottle.

It's the expensive bottle Alana gave me for my birthday months ago that I've only ever drunk a few sips from. But if I'm going to get myself drunk, might as well do it on the good stuff.

Pulling the corked cap off, there's a hard knock on my door, making me jump. I sigh, eyeing the bottle.

Who the hell could that be?

I set the cap on the counter next to the whiskey, and then turn, walking back out of the kitchen and to the door. Not caring to look through the peephole, I twist the handle and yank, pulling the door open.

"What do you want?" I ask Eric.

"You hung up on me."

"Yeah. So?" I turn, giving my back to him and leave him standing there. He can come in or he can fuck off. I really don't care. I walk back into my kitchen to finish my task.

The sound of the door closing confirms he came in, but I don't face him or even acknowledge his presence. He pissed me off. He doesn't deserve my attention.

My case has nothing to do with that kid Diaz took from you. That's PD. It's on them to find that boy.

Yep. Still pissed off over that comment.

"I don't like being hung up on."

I look over my shoulder, seeing him through the opening over the kitchen sink, and for good measure, I shrug my shoulders, then turn back around to face the whiskey. Suddenly, it doesn't look so appealing. I can't focus all my energy on locating Diaz if I'm getting drunk.

"Now that's the way to apologize. I'll take two fingers since I have to drive home."

I cork the bottle and then push it to the back of the counter. Without replying, I push past him, walking out of the kitchen.

"What the hell?" he calls after me.

What the hell? Irritation slams into me so fast I pivot, with the intention of chewing his ass out for being another asshole cop wanting to push off a hard case because he doesn't want to deal with it. But that isn't what happens.

My lower abdomen clenches up, tightening to such an excruciating degree that I feel a repeat from half an hour ago is coming on. My teeth snap together, locking my jaw so I don't scream out in pain, but I swear to God if he wasn't here, that's exactly what I'd do. I need to scream. I want to scream. Fuck me! This hurts like nothing I've ever felt before.

My eyes shut, bracing for the impact my body is about to encounter with the hardwood floor. Yet, it never comes. I land on the ground, but I don't hit the floor. Eric wraps his large arm around my middle and I end up sitting in his lap. My stomach still feels the hard land, but not as bad as it could have been if he wasn't here to catch me, taking the brunt of the fall to the ground himself.

"What the fuck?" His hot breath coats the inside of my ear, making me squirm and tingle at the same time. "I thought you said your doctor released you?"

I relax against his hard chest. For a minuscule moment, he feels familiar; like Drago. And for that brief second, I let my mind pretend he is.

"Bri," he says, his voice softer. "Are you okay?"

"She did. I am fine, it's just—"

"It's just what? This doesn't look like you're fine. You're definitely not fine, Bri."

"I am fine. But apparently my miscarriage isn't completely done like I thought, so I have to go through the motions until it is." I take a deep breath as the last of the cramps pass. Then I look over my shoulder, seeing everything I don't want to see. Not now. Not ever. "Don't look at me like that."

Pity. I don't want fucking pity, but that's exactly what's looking back at me through those deep dark eyes of his.

"How did you get here so fast anyway?" I ask, changing the subject. He had to have been in the area to get here so quickly.

"Field office isn't far from here. I was wrapping up some documentation before I was going to head to the airport to pick up my parents."

"They don't live here?"

"Nah. They're currently in Virginia, which is usually where my sister and I go, but Dad has some business to do out here."

"What does he do?"

One of his eyebrows lift. "Getting personal for someone I've only known for a day, Detective." He smiles down at me, showing off his perfectly pearl-white teeth. From this angle, he's certainly more attractive when he smiles. He looks more boyish and carefree when his dimple on his right cheek displays. "Let's get you up. Yeah?"

I nod, then Eric pushes off the floor, standing us both up. He steadies me before removing his hand.

"Thank you," I say genuinely, not as ticked off at him as I was earlier.

"You have a hot backside. I'd be an asshole if I had let you land on it." He laughs, but his words trigger a memory.

Hot piece of ass.

I look down at the floor, glancing off to my left. While thinking, I bite my lip.

Where did I hear that?

"It was a joke, Detective. I mean, you do have a nice ass, I can't deny that, but I didn't mean it in a douchebag kind of way."

I hold up my hand, silencing him.

Badge.

That badge was right about one thing. You certainly are one hot piece of ass.

Diaz.

"Are you going to let me in on whatever is going through that head of yours?" He takes a step back, and I watch his feet retreat away from me. "You aren't easy to read like most people."

"I remembered something."

"Well, tell a brother already."

My eyes flick up, finding him staring curiously back at me.

"Before Diaz shot me, he said, *that badge was right about one thing. You certainly are one hot piece of ass.*" My entire body shoots off chills, going down my spine as realization dawns. "Eric, he was talking about a cop."

Eric doesn't say a word. He just stares at me with a blank face.

"Did you not hear me?"

"I heard you." He follows up with a nod, but the skin between his eyebrows crease with a hard line.

"This means there's a cop working for Diaz."

"No. It doesn't mean that—not without proof anyway. But it is likely." He moves to sit in my recliner, propping his leg on his knee and then leans back, resting both of his arms on top of the soft armrests. "It's been rumored there was an inside man working for Vincent Acerbi. So maybe Diaz has one, or that person is one and the same. Who knows." He shrugs his shoulders.

"Well, I for one want to know." I take a seat on my couch closest to Eric, placing my legs under my butt to get comfortable. "That person—if they exist—is probably who told Diaz I had Gabriel. That dirty fucking cop is probably the reason Drago's son is God knows where and the reason I lost—" I stop myself from saying the word baby. I can't yet.

"Don't you find it the least bit strange that a girl walked in saying that kid was Acerbi's? Not only that, but leaves the boy, who later gets kidnapped by the same man that has been trying to get Acerbi onto his payroll for years?"

"Years?" I question, thankful he doesn't give me that same sympathetic look he did earlier.

His question makes me wonder what all he knows about

Drago. Sure, he says he's been working to build a case against D's father, so he would have investigated Vincent's children heavily too. That is if he's worth a damn as a DEA agent.

"At this point, I probably know Drago Acerbi better than he knows himself. That, Detective, is how long I've been at this. Drago isn't dirty like his dad. But Diaz? That motherfucker is hell-bent on getting his dope into LA by means of an Acerbi."

"Yes," I admit. "The whole thing is bizarre. It's even more questionable now that Gabe is gone. I've had a lot of time to flip everything over in my head and"—I shake my head—"nothing adds up. I shouldn't have had D's son. He should have been in protective custody the whole time."

"So why are you so sure that boy is Acerbi's? If you think all of this is fucked-up, not by the book any way you look at it, then why do you still think that kid is his? Did it not cross your mind that those results could have been tampered with? And now that you believe there is a dirty cop involved?"

"Of course, I've thought about it. At least in the beginning, I had my doubts. That's why I had an independent test that no one except me knew about. Gabriel is Drago's son. That is the one fact about all of this I am sure of."

His head cocks to the side as he looks at me as if I've grown two heads.

"You are sure, aren't you?" His words are more realization than a question.

"I am positive. I just wish D would believe me."

"All right, Detective." He pushes up, standing.

"All right, what?"

"My case just took a turn," he tells me with the most serious expression I've seen on him yet. "I still want Vincent Acerbi behind bars, but I'll put that on the back burner for now—until we find that kid."

"Why the sudden change?" I can't help but ask. He was adamant earlier that locating Gabe was on the police department, not him.

"Diaz is equally as ruthless as Vincent. And taking down that son of a bitch might just get me a step closer to my end goal." He rounds the chair he was just sitting in, heading for the door. "We start tomorrow. Be ready at seven. I'll pick you up."

"I thought you wanted your *holiday*. Wasn't that what you were bitching about earlier on the phone?"

"Just be glad that kid of yours is more important to find right now." He pulls the door open. "Oh-seven-hundred, be ready to roll. This stays on the down-low, you got that? You are still on leave."

I nod, agreeing.

Without another word, he steps over the threshold, pulling the door closed behind him and leaving me speechless. Sure, I should be grateful he's going to help me locate Diaz, but what is he really up to? What's the motive I wonder?

That thought plagues me for hours and hours. I'm still at a loss as to why he now wants to help me. But those nagging thoughts soon vanish when the medication takes hold of me and I'm in the worst pain I've ever experienced in my life. Regret that I didn't have that procedure done while I was in the hospital soon becomes my reality and this isn't something I'd wish on my worst enemy. I wouldn't wish this on anyone.

CHAPTER TWELVE

Since Thursday morning, I've spent every minute of daylight with Eric. In those four days, I've come to the conclusion that he's annoying as hell. Every ounce of attraction I thought I had for him has evaporated. At this point, he's the proverbial thorn in my side.

I have also come to learn he's a damn good agent. A clever agent.

"It's done." He places his smartphone on the table. "See"— that megawatt smile of his makes an appearance—"easy. Just like I told you it would be."

Eric takes a sip of his steaming cup of coffee. He just contacted the cellular carrier of Lance's cell phone after emailing them an approved document outlining the DEA's request to wiretap a device. It's a common tactic of any federal agency that has probable cause. And since Lance is the only person I suspect of being Diaz's inside man, Eric spun a few details in our favor and got his director to approve the request.

The DEA director, not his SAIC—Special Agent in Charge— his superior. The fucking director of the DEA. I'm impressed that Eric knows him personally and was able to pull strings so quickly. I've met the Chief of Police for the city of Los Angeles a handful of times. He swore me in when I became an officer and I've seen him from afar when he's made multiple speeches. I got to speak to him when I had my last interview, but I couldn't call him up on a whim.

"Not bad," I tell him, leaning back into the quaint booth in the back of the coffee shop. It's late in the morning, so the bustle from the early morning crowd is long gone, the regulars that use the coffee shop as an office and the college students milling about. All wearing headphones or earbuds and focused on whatever it is they are all doing on their laptops or tablets.

"I got pull, Andrews." He snorts out a laugh and it's cute, making me laugh too. It's now I realize this is the first time I've found joy in well over a week. A pang of guilt hits me, slapping me across the face. I shouldn't be experiencing joy of any sort. Gabriel is missing, and my baby is gone.

I've clung to that hope every second of every day since I woke up in that hospital bed.

"Hey," Eric calls, his voice turning concerned. "I was joking. What's got you sad all of a sudden? I thought you would be thrilled we're making headway and we're going to nail those cocksuckers to the fucking wall."

I snap my gaze to his.

"I am. Just—"

God. I'm not a weak person, but lately, that's all I feel—weak.

"Just what, Bri?"

"Nothing." I sit up, picking up my less than hot coffee, taking a sip. I always order mine at kid's temp. I'm not much of a sipper, and I'm too impatient to wait for it to cool down.

"Didn't look like nothing?"

Before I can come up with another excuse, I hear a voice that has me flicking my eyes to the person standing in front of the barista at the checkout counter.

"This is wrong," she complains. "I ordered skim milk. This"— she pushes her coffee, shoving it across the counter toward the kid standing behind it—"is not skim milk."

"Ma'am," the barista says calmly. "I assure you it's correct. I made it myself."

"Well," she says condescendingly. "You made it wrong." She crosses her arms over her chest, looking at him like he disgusts her. I feel bad for the young boy. He can't be more than eighteen or nineteen-years-old. He doesn't need this bitch giving him so much grief. It's just coffee. Even if it is wrong, that's no way to act or treat him or anyone for that matter.

"What a bitch," I whisper under my breath.

Eric looks over his shoulder and I swear I hear a grumble fall out of his mouth. He quickly turns back around, downing the rest of his coffee like it's a double shot of whiskey he's throwing back.

"Not a fan of your boyfriend's future wife?" Eric asks.

"D is not my boyfriend," I mumble. *Anymore that is*. Then it hits me what he said. My eyes snap to his. "Wait. What?"

"Your boy's future misses." He jerks his head toward Rebecca De Luca without looking away from me. "The bitch over there at the counter."

"She's not Drago's future anything," I snap, not caring about the sudden venom in my voice.

"That shit has been planned for ages, Detective."

"What the hell does that mean?"

"He's Vincent Acerbi's son." Eric laughs, but it's pissing me off. I don't find anything coming out of his mouth funny at all. "Don't you get that he's supposed to fall into line—eventually?"

"D doesn't want anything to do with his father. Or his father's corrupt legacy."

"Maybe not today." Eric eyes me, gauging my reaction I imagine. "But how long before he does what his father demands of him—what's expected of him? How long before he starts pedaling Diaz's dope?"

"Never," I bite out with so much conviction I nip the side of my cheek with my teeth.

"How sure are you?"

"I know him."

"Are you sure?" he questions, making me second-guess myself. A part of me hates him for it. "What happens when he finds out that kid really is his? What do you think he'll do to get his own flesh and blood back?"

"Anything and everything, I hope." And I mean that. I do hope he'll do any means necessary to get his son back unharmed. "But he doesn't believe Gabriel is his." I sit up, suddenly ready to be out of this coffeehouse and away from the man sitting across from me. "So this is a moot point, isn't it?"

"I don't know, Bri. Because I can tell you if it were me and it were my son that sick psycho motherfucker had, I'd put a bullet in his head."

And something tells me D would do the same.

.

CHAPTER THIRTEEN

My eyes grow heavy as I listen to the last audio file from Lance's cellular device.

I've listened to all of his calls and I've gone through all of his text messages since Eric gave me access two days ago. Yet, nothing has stuck out. I wonder if Eric had any luck with his email or getting approval to access the chief's device.

Eric said he could get it, but it would take a little longer and a couple of chains higher to get a sign-off.

The thought of Tom being dirty doesn't settle in my stomach right. Sure, he's hell-bent on getting any scrap of dirt on Drago, but I can't see him being the one to bow down to Diaz and do his dirty work.

I shake my head, grabbing the corner of my laptop, I move it off my lap, placing it on the coffee table.

Since Detective Summers hasn't completed his report, I'm still on administrative leave, which is getting on my nerves more and more as each day passes. Being stuck at home, these walls seem to be closing in on me. To say I'm restless is an understatement.

Eric, on the other hand, would rather me work from home though. I'm sick of this resting bullshit. I'd rather be framed into a tiny cubicle at his field office than here, lounging on my couch. At least then I'd feel like I was doing something productive. His field office is only a five-minute drive from my condo. I could probably walk there and get the much-needed exercise I've been missing.

My phone chimes with an incoming text, so I swing my bare legs off the couch while snatching my smartphone off the end table, pulling it from the charging cord.

Nikki: What gives? I haven't seen you in 2 weeks. You're making me think you really aren't okay.

Me: Just because I'm out of commission for a few weeks doesn't mean I'm not okay. I am, really. I have a case that I'm working on though, so I'm busier than usual.

Nikki: Anything to do with that missing kid that's been all over the news?

Before I can reply, there is a knock on the door. Hopping up, I toss my phone behind me, letting it fall to the couch.

Pulling the door open, I gasp involuntarily. Not because I'm seeing him for the first time in far too long, but because everything hits me all at once.

His beautiful, sexy face that now has more than a five o'clock shadow gracing it.

The scent that is Drago—salt water and dust. He must have been pulling long hours at his warehouse today. The smell surrounds me even though I just opened the door.

And those fucking eyes. Why do I love staring up at them so much? Who knew a set of brown irises would be my undoing. Gabriel shares the same dark gaze as his father. I realized that not long before he was stolen from me.

Maybe that's why I fell so hard and so fast for Drago. Maybe it had to do with his son already owning a piece of my heart.

Seeing Drago hurts on too many home fronts. The longing to reach out and touch him is almost unbearable. We have this pull that I still don't understand. It's been there from the beginning and it's only gotten stronger the closer we get.

"You said you were fine," he barks, making me take a step back. "You aren't fine, Bri." His brows furrow together. "You lied to me."

I let out a frustrated sigh, dropping my hand from the doorknob and crossing my arms. It's a protection barrier I feel I need.

"I am fine, D."

Why does he even care? He pretty much kicked me out of his house. Maybe not by force, but it still had the same effect. He wanted me gone. He wanted us over. "What are you doing here?"

"You look stressed, " he pauses, taking me in. "And something else." His head cocks to the side. He's analyzing me, and this time, I hate it. I hate that he can read me so well when I can't read him. It pisses me off.

"Well, you look like you don't have a care in the world."

He doesn't actually. I know I'm stressed, and I see my stress mirrored in Drago's appearance. He hasn't shaved; even his hair is longer. His white T-shirt is wrinkled, and his jeans look like they've been worn all week.

Has he even showered? Maybe that's why the smell of the ocean is more prominent on him today than it has ever been before.

"I care about a lot of things. More than you'll ever know."

"What do you want?!" I stress, not biting on his words. If he cared so much, he wouldn't have tossed me out. He wouldn't have dismissed Gabriel like that little guy's life means nothing when it means everything to me.

Resolve washes over me. I can't be with someone or want someone that doesn't want *him*.

"You know what? I don't give a shit."

Stepping back again, I wrap my hand around the door and then slam it shut.

"Go fuck yourself, Acerbi!" I yell at the closed door loud enough for him to hear.

"Bri," he says just as equally loud, but his comes out as a growl.

I stand there, the resolve I just felt moments ago wearing by the second.

Why can't I turn my feelings off for him? Why are they so strong? It's like a rope tightening around my heart.

Silence lingers between us, and then with a hard thud, I know he's just walked away after slamming his hand against my door.

I finally let out a breath I didn't know I'd been holding.

Looking up at the ceiling, I blink away the unshed tears I don't want to fall. Falling tears mean there's more I need to face that I can't right now. I can't deal with my shit. I have to find Diaz and I have to rescue Gabe.

Soft rapping on my door pulls me from my clouded mind. Can he take a hint? I don't want to talk to him. I don't want the see him.

Yanking the door back open, I go to tell him to fuck off, but I stop just before the words fall from my lips.

"Alana."

"You have three seconds to tell me what the hell is going on?"

She crosses her arms over the green vintage wrap dress she's wearing. The plunging neckline enhances her cleavage.

My sister-in-law has always had a thing for vintage style clothing. She doesn't wear them often, but when she does, stunning doesn't come close to describe her. Her blonde, pixie haircut is longer than it's been in a while. For the last five years, she kept her hair short, only leaving the top with longer layers that you can still comb your fingers through.

"Thanksgiving. I know, I'm sorry."

"Sorry doesn't cut it or even put a dent in explaining what the fuck is going on. Robert says you're working an intense case and forgot." Her hands go to her hips. She's fuming. "Maybe I could buy that, except you aren't answering your phone."

For a second, I smile on the inside. She revealed my dad hasn't told them anything and he's even covering for me. For some reason, it warms me, even if it is all a lie. He did exactly what I asked. Robert Andrews bent to me rather than the other way around.

"I know," I start, feeling like the world's shittiest person. "But—"

She cuts me off, not allowing me to make another excuse.

"Jack may buy it, but I don't. Not for a second, Brianna."

My brother will believe almost anything my father tells him, so I'm not surprised he took my father at face value. Other than his wife, Jackson has never collided with the man like I have.

"If Jackson isn't worried, then why are you?"

"Because I know you." She crosses her arms again, waiting for me to break. And like that, the tears I haven't allowed myself to shed spill over, showering down my cheeks like waterfalls.

I'm yanked into a hug as Alana wraps her arms around, squeezing. I melt against my sister-in-law, bawling into the center of her chest.

"Bri, babe, what is it?" Her strong, assertive voice turns tender.

How do I tell her I lost a baby I didn't even know I was carrying? If it had been Alana, I'm certain she would have known the minute she conceived. Me? I was fucking clueless. I didn't get to experience the shock or the joy or the panic. My baby was gone before it was ever loved.

Shudder after shudder rips through me. It's worse than any of the stomach cramps I've experienced over the last two weeks.

Two weeks. My baby has been gone for nearly two weeks. Two weeks tomorrow to be exact. Two weeks tomorrow that I haven't held Gabriel in my arms. *Gabriel.*

This isn't fair.

"Bri," Alana calls out my name. "Please tell me what happened?"

I've never heard her beg before and it's a sobering realization. I've kept her and my brother in the dark too long. Guilt suddenly hammers down on me.

"Honey, let's go inside."

I breathe in her scent, letting the remnants of her perfume calm me. She smells of a light floral scent. I try to inhale it all in, needing her.

It works and I'm able to step back, allowing her arms to fall away from me.

I nod, taking another step backward and into my condo. She eyes me wearily for a beat before finally passing me, walking inside. Shutting the door, I turn around, placing my back against the wood while pulling in a deep breath air. Upon exhale, I push off and round the recliner and coffee table to sit next to her on the couch.

"I called you all day on Thanksgiving and every day since. Why haven't you answered any of my calls or my texts, Bri?"

I look down into my lap. How do I answer that and where do I start? There is so much to tell and none of it wants to leave my mouth.

"You're worrying me. Do we need wine for this conversation?"

"You didn't give me a heads up that you were coming. I don't have any wine." I sniffle, wiping at my nose with my long sleeve T-shirt.

"How could I?" she deadpans. "I haven't spoken to you in forever."

"I know," I start, feeling more guilt pile on top of me. "I'm sorry," I say, apologizing once again. There aren't any other words that could fix missing Thanksgiving with my family.

"Just tell me what's going on." She sighs. "This isn't like you. Is it a case? That kid you were caring for? What's happened that's obviously gotten you out of sorts?"

I look up, inhaling a breath to give me the strength to say the words I need to get out. When I ready, I drop my head, looking into her green eyes.

"I lost—" I suck in air, and it's like pulling in tiny shards of glass, each piece nicking at my insides. "I had a miscarriage."

CHAPTER FOURTEEN

"Oh my God!" Her eyes widen as her hand slowly goes to her mouth, covering her lips. "What? I—"

She grabs me by both of my biceps, pulling me back to her chest.

The tears are instant, coating my cheeks once again and I cry, letting it all flow out again. I bawl like I've never bawled before. Alana holds me, not letting up on her grip until I pull away. She's reluctant to let me go, but does eventually, her hands slipping from me as I sit back up.

"Why didn't you want to tell me? I would have been here the second I knew." Her voice cracks.

"Please don't take this the wrong way, but I had enough to deal with without you and Jackson flipping your shit over me getting shot."

"Wait a minute." She takes in a ragged breath. "What!? What

do you mean you were shot? You were shot, and no one told us? No one called us?"

Her eyes flip with multiple emotions and it claws at my chest. The guilt starts to choke me, suffocating me.

"When? Are you okay?" She scans me up and down, landing on my leg. My shorts have risen high enough in my seated position that she can see the bandage. It's still healing, and I've taken proper care of it so that it's mending well. Itches like a bitch, but I try to ignore the need to claw at my skin. That wound from the shot is the least of my problems.

"It really wasn't bad," I start but quickly shut up. Her eyes light with fire.

"Not bad?" Her face colors red. "Any gunshot is bad, Brianna!" My name comes off her tongue like a curse.

"That's where you're wrong. So wrong." The tears coat my cheeks again. I'd take another bullet in a second if it meant never losing Gabriel, or my baby, or even D. I want all three back. I want what was taken from me.

"This is why you don't need to be working the gangs and drug unit, or whatever it's called, narcotics." She slides away from me, throwing her head back against the headrest on the couch. I watch her blink rapidly, knowing she's trying to shove back her own tears. Alana and I are alike in that way. Neither of us are quick to cry over things.

I've always had the attitude of "what's the point," it's not like you can always control the situation, and if bad things are going to happen, then it's just life. It's the cards you were dealt. That is until it happened to me.

Another round of tears cascade down my cheeks. The control I once thought I possessed is gone as my emotions swamp me, taking center stage.

I might as well tell her everything. I've gotten this far. There is no reason to hide anything else, and for the first time, coming clean feels like the right thing to do. It's what I should have done weeks ago.

"There's more."

Her head rolls to the side, looking at me with dread in her green eyes. But just like a big sister, the mother-type that she is, my savior—she listens to every word that pours out about Gabriel being Drago's son. I tell her about keeping that fact from him until my stupid boss had to open his mouth and be the one to disclose that information, which resulted in D not believing a word that comes out of my mouth. I could accept that if it weren't for his son. Gabe deserves at least one parent to love him and want him. But Drago can't, or won't accept that he created a person.

Before he and I slept together, I wouldn't have believed it was possible not to remember the act of sex with another person. Now I know it's possible, so for him to say it's impossible that he had sex with Chasity Carlisle is laughable. It's obvious it happened. Gabriel is proof of that.

"How does he not believe Gabe is his? If you have a paternity test proving it, then why does he not believe it? Does he not remember fucking the source?"

"He claims he's never had sex with Gabe's mother." My stomach sours calling her his mom. She isn't. If she were, she would have never handed him over to me or anyone else.

Alana coughs out a laugh. "Just like a man," she deadpans, shaking her head. Her loose blonde strands swing, making me take notice of her hair once again. It's longer than usual and she isn't wearing as much product as she normally does, if any at all. Her hair, her makeup, and her attire are always pristine. Not that anything is lacking. Her dress covers her body like a glove, hugging her in all the right places. But she's less made up than her usual, and I like it. It makes her look younger without the heavy makeup or the tresses that are never out of place.

I miss this Alana.

For the first time in a long time, I'm homesick for my family. And now I want my brother's arms. He's always been my protector, even when I didn't need it. Thoughts from a couple of months ago creep to the front of my mind.

I take care of what's mine.

I was so mad at him for putting a tracker on me without me knowing it. I should have known when he gave me that car he would have installed something like a GPS that would keep him informed of my whereabouts. That's just like Jackson.

I'm no longer mad. In fact, I'm grateful. He just wanted to make sure he knew where I was when I wasn't close by.

With Gabriel missing and I have no idea where he could be, I understand my brother's need to know where everyone he loves is.

After I finish filling her in on my sordid mess, I'm ready for a change of subject.

"Why are you in LA?"

I wipe the remnants of my tears on my shirt, hoping she didn't fly down here simply because I didn't show up for a holiday dinner.

"I had a last-minute change of location for a business meeting, so it was the perfect opportunity to find out what was going on with you." Her eyes turn soft. "Bri, why didn't you call me? Why keep us in the dark when you needed family?"

"I had Dad," I explain.

"Since when are you and Robert so close?" Her tone is accusatory. It really bothers me that my father doesn't like my brother's wife.

"You act like I hate him."

"He's never been there for you like Jackson and me. Why would you share that with him and not us?"

"Mike called him, so when he showed up at the hospital, I didn't really have a choice. And—" I pause, the words feeling foreign.

"And what?" she barks.

"Maybe Dad isn't as bad as we make him out to be." My dad wanted to step in and take care of me after I was released from the hospital. He begged me to come home with him. Robert Andrews doesn't beg anyone, but he did for me.

"Maybe you still have a concussion from hitting your head."

It's then she stills. I watch her look around, eyeing everything visible in my condo from her spot on the couch. It hits me, she has just realized I was shot in here. This is where everything went down.

"You need to come home with me. I'll change my flight. I'll get us both a ticket home."

"I'm not leaving." I can't leave. Like everyone else, why doesn't she get it? "I'm not going anywhere, Alana. I have to find Gabriel and bring him home safe."

"Home?" she questions. Then she cocks her head to the side, her eyes penetrating mine. "And just exactly where is home, Bri?"

"Here." I bite out, challenging her. I'm sick of people thinking I've gotten too close to a child that isn't mine. Okay! So I did. I know this and now everyone else does too. Doesn't change one damn thing. I want him home, with me, or with Drago. I just want him safe and loved.

Is that so wrong?

"Jesus fucking Christ."

THE FOLLOWING MORNING, I'M ON MY WAY TO MEET ERIC. AT ABOUT FOUR o'clock this morning he sent a vague text message with an address that isn't far from my condo, so I'm guessing it's the address for the field office he works out of. Since it's Saturday, he obviously isn't opposed to working weekends. It's a relief too, because while I'm out on leave I don't have any other resources other than Eric to contact for leads on Diaz.

Connie hasn't returned a single call or text message. She's been my partner for two years. Hell, I considered her a friend and thought she felt the same way. So, one would think a simple text asking if I'm okay is the least she could do.

Mike, on the other hand, is another story. He called me last night, but I didn't answer, letting it roll over to voicemail, which he didn't leave a message. I almost called him back, questioning if it could have been about Gabriel, but I know that wasn't it. At this point, I'm not sure if he would even tell me if there was an update.

Eric phoned late last night, telling me he put in a request to his SAIC to get Tom to release Gabriel's kidnapping case to one of his fellow undercover DEA agents. His partner I'm assuming, since he's keeping his mouth shut on who is going to be searching for Gabe while we search for Diaz.

To me, it's all one and the same, but the DEA has a special task force that handles certain things alongside other federal agencies. Apparently, because Sebastian Diaz isn't American, Gabriel's case is considered human trafficking. Just the thought of that makes my stomach roll. He can't be lost forever. He can't, and I don't think that's Diaz's goal. He's just using Gabe as leverage to get D to concede and do what he wants.

My cell rings.

Grabbing it from the cupholder, I do a quick glance at the screen, seeing my brother's name.

"Hey."

"You know, it didn't go unnoticed that you didn't show for Thanksgiving, nor did you bother to call. So, what gives, little sister?"

Is he serious? He sounds nonchalant, like Alana hasn't told him anything that we discussed yesterday, and we talked a lot and late into the night. She kept texting on her cell phone, so I assumed she was talking to my brother.

It was nice having her here. Actually, it was a relief getting everything off my chest. A small part of me felt it was wrong to unload so much on her. Drago crosses my mind for a brief second before I respond to Jackson.

"Do you and your wife not talk?"

"I haven't seen Alana today. I think she's still in New York. What does that have to do with this?"

"New York," I blurt out. "I dropped her off this morning at the airport. She showed up here yesterday."

How does my brother not know that? He thinks his wife was in New York?

The same worry I had a couple of months ago creeps into my head. *Are Jackson and Alana okay?* Their marriage has always been solid. I don't understand this. Suddenly it feels like I don't know what's going on in my own family. Then again, I've kept them in the dark about what's been going on with me, so even though it doesn't feel fair, maybe it is.

"What the fuck was she doing in LA?" His anger cuts through my thoughts.

"She mentioned she had a business meeting, so I'm guessing that." He's silent for a long beat, then he whispers something I can't quite make out. "I'm sorry, what? Jack, I'm driving, so speak up."

"Kincaid and Declan," he whispers. "It's nothing, Bri. So, why no call to say you were working?"

Am I really going to get into this on a phone call? Jackson deserves to know the real reason I've been avoiding them, but I can't seem to get the words to move past my throat.

"It's more than just a case I'm working, Jack." I call my brother by the nickname only his wife and I use. She stole it from me.

He was my Jack before he was hers. When I was really young, I couldn't say his full first name. I could only get the first part right. It only comes out on occasion now that I'm grown.

"I've got time for my little sister."

"Since when does the all-powerful Jackson Andrews have spare time?" I chuckle, hearing his breath vibrating through the line. It warms my heart that my comment made him laugh.

"Only for special people. So," he prompts.

"I need you to ask your wife. It really is a long story, too long, and not one that should be told over the phone. Plus, I just parked. I have a lot to get done today."

"It's Saturday and you don't work weekends unless you're on-call. You aren't on-call for another three weeks."

During mine and Alana's talk, I didn't get into being on admin leave or that my job is hanging in the balance right now. I had already said too much as it was. That would have put her over the edge. She already hates the unit I work for at the PD. She'd flip her shit if she knew I'm currently helping the DEA on a case.

"Since now," I admit. "Jackson, please talk to Alana. She'll fill you in and then if you want to talk, and I know you will, call me. But know that I'm fine. Alana showing up was a really good thing and I should have told you both what was going on."

"Brianna," he draws out. "You're making me worry and I worry enough as is. Man up and tell me yourself."

"Jackson," I whine. He's right. I should, but sitting here hashing out the whole ordeal isn't going to get me one minute closer to nailing Diaz or finding my boy. "You have nothing to worry about. I'm a grown woman that can take care of herself. If I weren't knee-deep in a lot of shit, I'd come home and tell you, but I can't, so talk to your wife."

"Why do I get the feeling I'm going to want to rip someone apart?"

"Because you love me and are way overprotective. You're the helicopter parent no one knows is a helicopter parent. You hide it well."

"I'm not a helicopter parent. What the fuck is a helicopter parent?"

"Ask Alana that too. I have to go. Love you, big brother."

"Love you too, brat."

I press "end" on the call, dropping my cell phone into my purse, then push the door open and get out of my car. I stand, looking over the roof of my Audi, eyeing the unmarked building. I've driven past here multiple times not realizing this was the LA field office for the DEA. There is no signage marking the building. It's a white two-story that's quite inconspicuous. There are windows lining the upper and lower level and a glass door at the front with writing on it that I can't make out from the parking lot.

Walking around my car, I head to the door. Pulling on the metal handle, it doesn't budge. It's locked. It's then I notice the keypad to my right and an intercom system. Eric didn't mention I'd need badge access, so I either call him or press the call button.

Reaching up, I press the white, round button and then wait.

It's at least a full minute before the door opens with Eric peeking his head out.

"You're early." He swings the door open, gesturing for me to enter. "I wasn't expecting you for another fifteen."

"On time"—I do air quotes as I slide past while he holds the door open—"might as well be late. I don't do late, Alders."

"Eric," he corrects. "Just call me Eric. I hear my last name enough. It gets tiring after a while." He steps in front of me, turning to face me while walking backward. "Since we're friends, you can stop all the formal shit."

"Who says we're friends already?" I don't give him a chance to answer. "Took my last partner"—I do air quotes again—"at least a month to become friends, and now I'm not sure we ever were."

"Ah," he says, his voice sounding fake. "Does someone have their panties in a wad because I stole you from the mundane world of the local PD?"

He bypasses the elevator, going to a solid steel door in the corner, pulling on the handle and opening it.

"Wouldn't know." I shake my head, but he's not looking at me as he walks through the door and into a stairwell. I follow him through where he quickly heads up the staircase. "The bitch hasn't called or even text me since I got shot."

Good to know where I stand with her. And maybe I'm better off now that I realize where I stand on her "give a shit" shelf. If your partner lacks care, then they're the last person you need having your back. Chances are, they won't be there to have your back when all hell breaks loose.

"So, you're the one with her panties all twisted." He pauses halfway up the first flight of stairs, looking over his shoulder. "Let's leave that shit down here. Okay?"

I stop just before my foot lands on the first stair, staring at his moving form.

That motherfucker!

He asked. Why ask if he didn't want an honest answer? So, what if I'm a little butt-hurt over the person I would have taken a bullet for without a thought? I get to be mad over this for more than two seconds. Hell, what if it were him? I bet he would care if his "real partner" did the same to him. Bet he'd be a little pissed off too.

IT TAKES ME SEVERAL MINUTES TO COOL MY QUICKLY ESCALATING ANGER before I trot up the stairs, entering the only door at the top, letting it close behind me as I take in the room.

The space is open with a lot of natural lighting coming through the windows that line each side of the building. There are twelve large cubicles with plexiglass windows taking up the top-half of them. There are three sections with four cubicles attached to each one, making it look like there are three teams that take up this floor.

I don't know why that thought comes to me. In the police department, we have one partner and our desks butt up to each other with Mike being the lone one in an actual office since he's the senior detective.

I notice a single office door in the back of the room. The office is solid glass from floor to ceiling with the blinds closed. The room is dark, telling me there isn't anyone lurking inside. I'm guessing that's the SAIC's office. It would only make sense, unless the

Special Agent in Charge is located on the first floor. It could be the copy/printer room for all I know.

"Yo," Eric calls, gaining my attention. "How long does it take you to inspect the place? We got shit to do, Andrews."

"Thought we were friends. Why the formality all of a sudden?"

I start to head toward him when another head pops up over the cubicle that is catty-cornered to Eric's.

"He isn't your friend, Detective. You're just here on a consulting basis." Summers crosses his arms, watching me with narrowed eyes as I make my way to them.

"What's he doing here?"

"Summers is here to help," Eric tells me, taking a seat at his desk, before swiveling in his chair to face me.

I prop my shoulder against the metal edge that connects the top and bottom half of the desks together, my eyes never leaving Summers' deep green emeralds.

He doesn't scare me if that's what he's trying to do. Sure, last week I was a little intimidated at first, but then he called me out for sleeping with Drago and getting pregnant. Maybe he did it on purpose; maybe he didn't. Regardless, it more than stung, and the hurt I wasn't expecting pissed me off.

"How is Internal Affairs supposed to help us find a lead on Diaz or learn if—"

"I guess you don't understand your role here," Summers cuts me off. "You're only here as a consult. Nothing more. Alders and I are going to locate Diaz."

"Again." I drop my eyes to Eric. "Why is IA here?" I cross my arms.

"I thought I told you to check your shit downstairs?"

"I'm here because I'm part of this team," Summers interjects. My eyes flick back up to his. "My IA role comes into play because you, yourself, think Houston is involved with Diaz. And we happen to be in agreement. But just so we're fucking clear, the only reason I'm not hell-bent on nailing your little ass for misconduct of a police officer is because your friend there"—his eyes cut down to Eric's before the disdain in them return to mine—"convinced me that Diaz and Houston are bigger fish to fry."

I grit my teeth together so that I don't open my mouth and say something I might regret.

Something in Detective Summers' eyes soften. I guess he realizes I'm not going to come back at him with a rebuttal. It's not like I can anyway. I am guilty of misconduct. Even I know that.

Doesn't mean I am fully sorry for my actions, though. But it does mean I can shut my mouth and take what he wants to throw at me.

"Look—" Eric starts.

"I'm not finished." Summers lets out a long breath of air. "I turned in my report to Mike, the Deputy Chief, and the Chief of Police late yesterday evening. Your leave ends tomorrow, Andrews, and you can go back to full-duty work starting on Monday. You're welcome."

I wonder if that's why Mike called me last night?

"And what did your report say?" I ask without my earlier attitude interjecting this time. I'm curious; too curious, so I want him to tell me. I wasn't sure if he'd find real evidence that would suggest I wasn't deep undercover like Eric made it sound and like that NDA stated.

Oh, shit. The document both Eric and I signed.

If he did find something that would not only put me but also Eric in a lot of hot water too. Maybe that's why he's allowing me to return to work without any ramifications.

He's silent, staring at me. It's Eric that speaks.

"Basically, that you were doing your job to the fullest extent. There was nothing he found that led him to believe you weren't doing anything unethical or out of line. His recommendation was to reinstate you immediately. And luckily for you, the chief of police agreed."

"And Ramirez?" I ask, directing my question at Summers.

"Is pissed and wants a meeting Monday morning."

"Great." I roll my eyes, fearing this isn't over.

"Worry about him next week. Let's discuss Diaz and Houston. I'm not missing my daughter's t-ball game." Summers flips his wrist, looking at his smartwatch. "I have to be out of here in the next hour if I'm going to make it."

It's then I notice the wedding ring on his ring finger. I hadn't noticed before. It makes me glance down, scanning Eric's finger. Bare. Guess only one of them is married.

I can't help that my mind briefly thinks of Drago.

He came to me yesterday. Maybe that's something; maybe he still cares, but . . . then it makes me wonder how he knew I wasn't okay. Could he have accessed my medical records or gotten someone at the clinic to tell him?

No. I dismiss that right away. I was fine when I left. It was when I got home that day that something happened. So how did he know?

"All right then. Let's get to it," Eric says, pivoting around in his chair to face his computer. "Andrews, grab a chair from that desk." He nods his head in the direction of the one to his right; the one I passed coming to stand at the opening of his cubicle.

Pushing off the metal railing, I grab the chair that's pushed against the desk, noting the cubicle is bare, like no one ever uses it. The chair arms aren't worn like Eric's and the top of the desk is clean of any clutter. No pictures or personal items line the space to tell me this desk belongs to someone.

I don't get a chance to ask though. Eric starts talking and hitting keys on his computer.

"We haven't found anything on Houston's phone, so I doubt we will."

"I'd bet my career Houston is dirty," Summers chimes. "Just because he's a dirty cop doesn't mean he's a stupid-fuck, though. Men like Diaz don't get away with the shit they do by bringing just anyone into their organization that can potentially take them down. Also, he'd be using a burner phone. We all know that, so there is no point in wasting any more valuable time listening to Houston's calls. We need to go at this from a different angle. Who's the weakest? Who do we focus on?"

Chasity's face flashes in my mind.

"What about Gabriel's mother? I've seen Chasity Carlisle and Houston together."

I glide my chair over to the opening at Eric's desk, taking a seat behind him.

"Yeah? You know that how, Detective?" Summers asks.

"I tailed them weeks ago. She's the niece of the Deputy Chief of Staff to our mayor."

Alders and Summers both share a look.

"Care to fill me in on the private convo you two are having?"

"Harper has been trying to get Sam to step down," he tells me, referring to Dylan Harper, Mayor Samuel García's Deputy Chief of Staff. "Retire. Dylan wants the mayoral spot, but he knows running against García isn't going to make that happen. Everyone loves Samuel García. Harper has been trying to get that spot for three years now, but since García took office he's done and continues to do more than any other past mayor combined."

"But what would García leaving office have to do with Harper being elected? What is the connection with our case?" I ask.

"Maybe nothing," Summers says. "Maybe everything. Harper and Alessandro De Luca are brothers." He raises an eyebrow. "You know who he is?"

Chills run up my spine when he says De Luca's name.

"They're half-brothers. Different fathers, but brothers nonetheless. Harper might want into the most powerful seat in the city so that he can have more control over drugs that come and go. It's not a stretch."

"No," I agree. "It's not."

Could Chasity have planned her pregnancy? Could Gabriel have been just a pawn to get D to bend to a drug lord's demand? As I think the words, it sounds so far-fetched, but something tells me it isn't.

I have to find Gabe, and I have to do it soon.

What happens when Diaz finally realizes there isn't anything that would force Drago to do something he doesn't want to do? D told me just that when we were arguing.

"Then she's where we'll start," Eric follows up.

"Andrews," Summers calls, backing out of his cubicle and rounds to where Eric and I are. We both turn to face him. I stand when he nears. "Do you think you can talk to her without Houston getting wind of it?"

"I don't know. I'm sure I can figure out a way, but I thought I was just here to *consult*, Detective."

"Touché." His lips tip up. "By the book." He shakes his head. "You can't be heavily involved. But this isn't a black and white case. To nail a man like Diaz and to take a badge away from a dirty cop, we can't play by normal rules. If I'd thought for a second you were just as dirty as Houston, you wouldn't be here. So, find out what you can on the down-low. If you get caught, it's on you. Got that?"

"Yeah. Loud and clear."

"Good." His grin widens into a knockout smile, and suddenly, I remember why I didn't like him to begin with. His green eyes sparkle when both sides of his mouth tip upward, making it clear as day that smile is a weapon, and he should put it away before he hurts someone. "Call me Justin from here on out."

He whips his head toward Eric while I'm left stunned. Who knew he could go from so mundane to attractive just from changing his demeanor?

"I'm out. Text if anything major happens. If not, I'll catch you Monday, brother." He leaves, making a quick exit.

Damn, how does his wife keep women off him?

"She doesn't. That's why they're separated."

"Wait. What?" *Did I say that out loud?*

By the shit-eating grin on Eric's face, I did. *Oh, fuck me.* Way to make an impression there, Andrews, but hell, it's not like I have a man right now anyway, so there is no harm in admiring a little eye candy.

The detective in me does wonder exactly why they're separated, though. Did he cheat on her? That'd make him less attractive and more unappealing, which may be better for me. Not like anything would ever happen just because he's the first cop I've ever found attractive. I'd never go there, married or not.

It would be impossible, even if I wanted to entertain the idea for half a second. No, there is another man that's stolen my attention and even if he doesn't like me right now, it doesn't stop the way I feel about him.

Why does this have to suck so bad?

CHAPTER FIFTEEN

Monday rolls around and we finally have the green light to take over the kidnapping case. Well, the DEA's special task force does, and I have a feeling the task force includes Alders and Summers, even if Eric hasn't actually told me. Justin's mention of being on this team certainly gives way to that belief, plus Eric told me his partner would be searching for Gabe.

I get it's a conflict of interest and I can't officially be a part of Eric's team, but it still stings a little. As much as I want to scream bullshit, I know it's not. In any other circumstance, I'd readily agree.

I just hope Eric's partner doesn't fuck around and does what needs to be done to find Gabe—since Drago won't.

Gabriel is still my highest priority and I will find him. I have to believe searching for Diaz's inside man will lead me straight to Sebastian himself, and in turn, find the baby I need back in my arms.

The last couple of nights I've scoured known drug places looking for anyone that might have any connection to where Diaz may be hiding out. I've hounded two informants that I've worked with on multiple occasions, but they know nothing. It was a lost cause from the get-go; even they admitted a man like Diaz could spot a narc a mile away. I had to at least try.

This morning I'm at the Pacifica office—my precinct. Eric is meeting with Ramirez and Houston now, informing them he's taking the case. I'm not exactly sure why Lance is in there since he's a homicide detective, and seeing as how I didn't die, there isn't a murder to investigate. Who knows? Apparently, I'm not privy to this information—yet.

When Justin said the chief wanted to meet today, I had expected it to take place at his office downtown, not here on the northeast side of the county. Guess he wasn't too happy about me coming back to work after all.

"DEA, Bri?" Connie says, the disgust evident on her tongue. "You never once mentioned your interest in the DE fucking A. They're brainless cowboys, and you want to be one of them? Others around here might be buying that bullshit, but I'm not. We've been partners for two years."

She has the audacity to be mad at me. It pisses me off, and if she isn't careful, I'm going to tell her exactly how I feel.

Connie has been going off on a childish tangent for the last half hour. I wish Eric would hurry the hell up. I mean, how long does it take to lay down the law and tell a local department a federal agency is taking their case?

"Why, huh?"

"It's been over two weeks and you haven't once come by, or even returned a text or phone call since I've been shot. You weren't at the hospital. If it had been you, I would have been there every second I wasn't out looking for the fucker who shot you. But not you apparently, so I guess we weren't that tight of partners to begin with."

I really want to tell her to fuck off but causing a scene isn't worth it. The one she's causing is enough for those around us to gossip about for weeks.

"I do too care." Her mouth drops open in shock. "How can you say we weren't tight? I tell you things I don't even tell my sister for Pete's sake."

"She was ordered not to talk to you, Bri," Mike chimes in from his perch on the corner of Connie's desk.

"No one asked you to butt in."

"You're both acting like children." He crosses his arms, eyeing me with disapproval. I have to look away, finding something—anything—on my desk to look at instead. His respect matters most to me. His approval is something I've sought since I joined the detective department.

"Who told you I wanted to become a DEA agent? Ever stop to think I'm just helping them out?"

"Houston says you've been playing both sides of the field. Using PD resources to further the DEA's case. What happened to looking out for your own?"

"We're all on the same damn team. We all want the same damn thing."

At least that's what I thought. Isn't being a cop about justice? Serving and protecting? But there are obviously those on the force that aren't abiding by the laws or upholding them—Lance Houston being one.

"Oh, please. Don't give me that BS, *we're all on the same team*," she mocks in a whine.

She acts like it's us versus them. Who knows; maybe it is. I do know one thing, though. If Tom is on the side of the dirty, he's the last person I want to work for.

"Can it, Bristols." Mike scowls at her. Then he unfolds his arms as he lifts his ass off the corner of her desk. Looking down at me, he says, "Bri's right. We are all on the same side; even she is. Right, Andrews?"

The temperature inside my head escalates.

"If your—"

I don't get a chance to finish my thought. Mike rounds behind my desk. Bending down, he stretches his arms out, wrapping his hands around the armrests on each side of me and stalls inches away from my face.

"No," he bites out. And then he lowers his voice so that only Connie and I can hear him. "I don't think for a second you're a bad cop or a bad person, but whatever shit is going on up there"—he jerks his chin up, indicating to my head—"has you so messed up, you haven't been acting like yourself for a while now." He pushes himself away, taking a step back.

"Mike," I call, but he isn't finished.

"I should have never let you take that kid home with you." He sighs, shaking his head. "It all stems from that. I know it does.

Maybe you are helping the DEA on their case, but I can see this is also personal for you. I just don't know if it's because the boy was taken from your home or if it something deeper with Acerbi."

He stands in front of me, inspecting me the same way he would a suspect and I hate it.

"This blows." Connie throws her head back, making her chair recline back. "I don't want a different partner!" The last word is gritted out between her teeth.

Wait a minute. She isn't getting a new partner, so what is she crying about?

"I'm still here. Just because I'm helping Special Agent Alders on a case doesn't mean I'm quitting. We're still partners. I still work here."

"You still work here? Sure," Mike chimes in. "But the chief forced my hand, so I had to assign her to the new detective that started Friday."

"We're full up. We don't even have room for a thirteenth detective. Where is he planning on putting them?" I gesture around the room. There are twelve desks, but one of them belongs to the administrative assistant that's assigned to the detective department since Mike has his own office as senior.

"He's a transfer from the South Park District." Cupping the back of his neck and squeezing, Mike blows out a breath. "Pretty sure he wasn't planning on the guy being a thirteenth member of the team, but more as your replacement."

My mouth drops open in shock. I'm speechless. I have no idea what to say to that information. The bastard was going to fire me no matter what.

"But your boy Summers put a kink in that plan, I guess." Connie sits back up, eyeing me while chewing on her lip. "Look, I'm sorry I didn't show up at the hospital. Well, I did, but the chief said I couldn't see or talk to you because IA was being brought in to investigate your actions. He said I could be subject to the same if he found out I knew anything. I got scared, okay?" she admits.

For a second, I do feel bad. Connie knew certain things because I told her, so if the chief had been privy to that knowledge, she would have been facing the same hot water I had been in with IA. Lucky for me, Eric came to my rescue.

I nod, letting her know I understand. It still sucks, and I believe if our roles had been reversed, I would have found a way to let her know I was at least thinking about her.

"If there's a new guy taking my spot and *my* partner, then where the hell does that leave me?" I look to Mike for answers.

"With me." I snap my head around, seeing Eric walking toward me with a box in his hand. "Snagged this from the mailroom. Grab whatever personal things you have and throw it in here. You can get the rest later. Hurry. I want to get the fuck out of here before I lose my shit."

"I'm sorry. What's going on?" I ask, not sure if I'm questioning him or Mike as I look between them both.

"We'll talk on the way out. But for now, until this case is wrapped up, you're fully with me."

Eric places the box on my desk then takes a step back.

His phone rings, so he digs it out of the pocket of his black BDU tactical pants. He takes one look at the screen and then sighs. Before answering it, he glances up at me. "Meet me outside.

No more than five minutes."

He doesn't give me a chance to reply before he turns, walking back out the way he entered.

"That's who you get assigned to?" Connie raises her brow. "I get some half-wit, and you get a wet dream. How is that fair?"

I laugh, because it's right then I realize Eric is her type to a T.

WALKING OUTSIDE, THE MID-SIXTIES TEMPERATURE IN EARLY DECEMBER does little to cool me off. And from the looks of Eric, it's doing the opposite. I feel the heat rolling off him as I near. He isn't happy about something, that's for sure.

"That call you took," I inquire, coming to a stop in front of where he's leaning against his SUV. "Is that what has you so pissed off?"

"I don't lose my cool, ever, in front of others. I had to get out of there; I felt myself unraveling quickly."

"Why? Did Ramirez say or do something?"

He wants me gone. He could still be pushing that. Hell, he probably is since he's already brought in another body to replace my position. Shit!

"No." He shakes his head. "Hop in. We're going to meet J for lunch."

"It's only ten." I eye him over the hood of his Tahoe as I round the vehicle to get into the passenger side.

"Yeah, but I don't eat breakfast. By the time we grab something, the restaurant will be filling up and it'll be twelve before any food is in front of me. Let's go, Andrews."

Eric was antsy the whole drive. His only words were to inform me that we're meeting Justin at Mint, a trendy restaurant inside The Cove—an upscale luxury hotel downtown. Luckily for me, it's considered a working lunch, so the meal is expensed according to Eric.

With Tom out to ax me, I'm starting to think I was lucky I still got paid while I was out on leave. Something else I might owe thanks to not only Eric but Justin too. He knows the nondisclosure agreement Eric presented to my boss with both of our signatures on it is bullshit, yet he still recommended my reinstatement, putting in his report that he didn't find any foul play on my part of the investigation into any criminal actions on Drago's part; citing I accepted an undercover special assignment where having a personal relationship was part of the plan from the beginning.

I spent the first part of my morning reading every detail he outlined in the report. The phone number Tom gave me for Captain Roy Williams was the wrong number, so even though it was a department-issued cellular number, the number Tom gave me was currently unassigned. But being that it was only off by one digit, Justin cited it as an error on the chief's part.

I'm starting to wonder if it really was an error, or if it was intentional. What if Tom isn't the man and cop I thought he was? It's one thing to be a hard-ass and expect your subordinates to follow your rules to the letter. It's another entirely to break the rules and ethics we all swore to uphold.

"Goddammit," Eric huffs out in frustration.

Looking over, I see him cutting his eyes up and down, looking at his cell phone and then back to the road.

"Problem?"

"Yeah, but nothing I can't handle. Just some shit from another case I'm working." He sighs. "Look, I'm going to drop you off to meet J. He can bring you back to the field office to grab your car afterward. Is that cool?"

"It's fine unless there's something I can help you with?"

I'm not sure I want to be alone with Justin. I don't know him that well, and he may be a part of Eric's task force, but he's still IA. It's a stigma, I know, but it's one I'm not sure I can get past.

"Unfortunately, no." He parks along a curb, not pulling into the valet parking section in front of the hotel. Throwing the gear shift into park, he leans back into his seat and looks over at me. "It wasn't your boss that pissed me off. Well, he did, but that wouldn't have gotten under my skin. He doesn't want you in the detective bureau anymore, yet he doesn't have a viable reason to fire you. So, he's stuck until you fuck up or he still has the option to transfer you to another precinct, which is where he's leaning."

"Ugh," I breathe out, relaxing into the back of the seat. "Fuck me," I whine, because why not. It's not like I can beat the shit out of something to expel all the frustration coursing through me. It's not unusual for me to get angry or upset in my line of work, but I've always had kickboxing and now MMA training to work out all the stress inside me. Now that I haven't been to the gym in over two weeks, I'm tight all over, especially in my neck and shoulders.

"It was Houston." Eric's admission brings me out of my thoughts. "That's who ticked me off and why I told Ramirez I'd take you off his hands while this case is active or until he finds you another home with PD."

"What?!"

Is he serious right now? I never asked or even wanted to be a part of the DEA; not that there's anything wrong with anyone that is. It's just never once crossed my mind. I like my job and where I work. Other than being mad at Connie these last couple of weeks, I enjoy being partners with her.

His head swings toward me and there is something in the way he looks at me that makes me do a double take. It's concern.

"Houston's partner, Travis Hayes, is going out for surgery later this week and is expected to be out for at least six weeks. Houston conveniently volunteered to let you step in and—" Eric looks away from me, blowing air out of his mouth.

"And what?" I demand.

A scowl develops between his brows.

"It was the way he said it and the gleam in his eyes." Eric shakes his head rapidly. "I didn't trust him. I don't trust that motherfucker," he clarifies.

"I'm not afraid of Houston if that's what you're thinking."

"Maybe you should be." He turns his head, training his dark eyes on me again.

"What the hell does that mean?"

"It means Diaz tried to kill you. If you hadn't been wearing a vest, you'd be dead right now. Do you really understand how lucky you are to be sitting there?"

As his words sink in, I realize it hadn't truly hit me until right now. He's right. Not about being afraid of Houston, I'm not, and that's not going to change because Lance may or may not have had something to do with Diaz and his men coming after Gabriel in my home. I could have died on the floor of my condo at the hands of a drug lord. I could have never seen my family or Drago, or even Gabe again.

"Look," Eric says. "Let's drop this for now. It's done, and you're stuck with my ass for the time being." He throws his gearshift into drive without taking his foot off the brake. "Head on in. J should already be inside. I'll catch you later or I'll call you tonight to hash out the plan for where we go from here. Sound good?"

I reach for the door handle, nodding. "See ya, Alders."

AFTER USING THE BATHROOM, I ASKED A HOTEL EMPLOYEE PASSING BY ME where to find the restaurant. It's on the lobby level, so it doesn't take me more than a minute to walk there. It's bustling though, and it's not even noon. I guess Eric was right. This is certainly a busy place.

I've been in this hotel a handful of times. Every time Alana comes to town, it seems we come here for a spa-day together, but I've never eaten at this particular place. My sister-in-law usually likes to dine at the most expensive places and they have a fancy restaurant on the third floor that she and I love.

Looking at the entrance, this place has a laid-back vibe while maintaining the fancy, high-end persona it's known for. There is nothing at The Cove, a luxury hotel, that's lacking, and from what I can tell, the restaurant and bar are unique in what they offer. There's a younger crowd of patrons crowding the entrance, making me think this place is your typical run of the mill everyday food, but Mint is famous for its American-style cuisine with a gourmet twist.

Walking up to the host, I stop in front of him, hoping Justin is already here and we don't have to wait. I'm impatient and waiting for a table is not my strong suit.

Before he lifts his head, I catch sight of Justin sitting on the right side of the restaurant waving me over.

"Can I help you?" the host asks.

"Actually, I see my friend, but thanks anyway."

Once seated, the waiter is in front of me before I can even open the menu.

"If Alders called in a favor to his dad, then he must have thought you were in danger."

"What do you mean?"

"Well, you're supposed to be helping only when we need you, not tagging along with Eric."

"No," I correct. "What do you mean he had to have called in a favor to his dad?"

It dawns on me, Eric mentioned his parents live in Virginia and that's when it hits me. *Holy shit.* Magnum Alders, the director of the DEA is his father. I guess it never crossed my mind that they could be related since Magnum is white, but then Eric could be half African-American or even adopted.

"So, you didn't know he had to clear it with his dad, or you didn't know Eric's father is the director?"

"Both," I admit.

"Fair enough."

Picking up the menu, I flip it open. There are a lot of options and none that I'm skimming look very healthy.

"So, what's semi-healthy at this place?" I ask, assuming he's eaten here before.

"Not much really." He grabs his menu, flipping it open. "Bottom right corner. I usually stick with the grilled chicken Caesar or go for a bun-less burger. Their burgers are pretty good too."

"Bun-less." I laugh. "I never took you for the burger type without all the carbs."

He rolls his eyes while dropping the menu back down in front of him.

"Can't stay this good-looking downing a plate of carbs." He points to himself, chuckling. "I try to follow the Ketogenic diet at least ninety percent of the time. Heard of it?" he asks.

"Yes, I've heard of it."

I've actually wanted to try it for the longest time, but then I'd have to give up my signature Starbucks coffee, the Chinese food I love on occasion, and not to mention the fried cinnamon elephant ears I always get from one of the vendors when I spend a day out at Venice Beach. Not that I've gotten to do any of the things I used to enjoy since Gabriel appeared in my life. He really did turn everything upside down, but I still don't think that was a bad thing. I could give anything up if it meant getting him back.

Needing a change of subject, I take a breath and then ask Justin another question. "So, I guess you and Eric work together often since you're also part of the task force?"

"When I'm needed. I'm based downtown out of the headquarters office, which is where all of IA is located. But I'm sure you already know that."

"It's not a secret where your department is."

"True, but I'm rarely at my office. Too many officer complaints. So between my IA cases and the task force, I barely have time to breathe." He flips his wrist, looking down at his smartwatch. "I have forty-five minutes before I need to be at the Echo Park station for an interview."

"So, order and eat fast then?" I laugh. "Oh, Eric said you would be able to take me back to the field office where my car is."

"Fuck." He shakes his head.

"My dad's office isn't far from here. Could you drop me there and I'll get him to take me?"

"Sure." He nods. "Something to learn about Alders. He can be a hard-ass at times, but generally, he knows what he's doing even if his methods don't always seem the obvious choice. But don't ride with him. Always take your car, because he's going to pawn you off on someone else."

Justin takes a sip of his water.

"Noted," I tell him.

"It's not that he does it on purpose. But he's always going from case to case. He can flip a hat better than any cop I've ever met."

I take Justin's recommendation and mirror what he's ordering when the waiter brings me a glass of water.

"If this isn't ideal for eating, why are we here?"

"The kid's mother." Justin brings the glass of water to his lips again, sipping. "She frequents here. Eric was hoping we'd spot her and you could try to get useful information out of her."

"Why not bring her in for questioning?"

"Remember what I said the other day? This isn't black and white, and we can't play by the rules on this case. If Diaz or anyone connected to him gets wind that we've taken her in for questioning, it'll likely end up with her dead. Even if she is involved, I don't like getting people killed. I'm not overzealous in any way. If I take longer on something, it's so that I don't fuck up. And I don't fuck up, Bri."

"Neither do I," I spit, taking offense.

"You sure about that?" He cocks his head and arches an eyebrow.

"I thought your case against me was behind us?" I narrow my eyes at him.

"It is, luckily for you, but don't think for a second I won't give you hell from here on out about it." He smiles, lighting up his face. It makes my anger turn into annoyance. I don't want to find him attractive, not even a little bit, but I have eyes and he is.

We order our lunch and surprisingly it doesn't take long before it's placed in front of us. For a packed restaurant, service seems spectacular so far. Although, I'm not looking forward to the check even if it will be expensed at a later date. I still have to make money last until I get paid next week.

"So, why IA?" My curiosity gets the better of me as I stir my fork around my salad.

Lifting his eyes, he sets his fork down and steeples his fingers together.

"You can't serve and protect those you're sworn to when your own house is littered with the same criminals we're fighting against."

"Fighting?" I question his use of the word.

"You don't think we live in a world where it's us versus them, do you?"

"Maybe," I concede. Sometimes it feels like the world hates law enforcement, but other times I see the good and the gratitude from people we help.

I turn my head away, only meaning to briefly look elsewhere, but my eye catches sight of Drago sitting at a table on the other side of the restaurant. I can't control the sharp intake of air I pull in, and I'm not quite sure if it was loud enough for Justin to have heard it. Seeing Rebecca De Luca perched next to him with her hand wrapped around the bend in his arm causes my stomach to plummet and my throat to close up.

I vaguely hear Justin call my name, but I can't look away. Drago is having lunch with her and a man. He's older, judging from the gray in his dark hair, but I can't see his face. Could it be D's father I wonder?

Rebecca is smiling so much it actually lightens up her face, making her look like less of a bitch.

My eyes drop, watching her run her palm slowly down his forearm until she reaches the hand Drago has resting on the table. She slides her fingers over the top of Drago's hand, wrapping hers around his.

The air I gasp is involuntary. I couldn't have stopped myself if I'd tried.

"Is something wrong, Bri?" Justin asks.

If the concern in his voice matches his expression, I have no idea. I still can't stop staring at Drago's table. As if feeling someone watching him, D's eyes snap to mine.

"Jesus Christ," Justin draws out. "At least act like you don't have feelings for him. Seriously, Andrews."

Closing my eyes, I shake my head, trying to gain back my composure. It doesn't work; only frustrates me.

I lift my eyelids, taking in Justin's disapproving green gaze. "I need to go to the bathroom."

"You do that." He nods as he brings his napkin to his mouth, wiping.

Once I'm in behind the ladies' room door and out of Drago's sight, I sag and breathe.

Why is he here? And with *her* of all people, letting her touch him. My skin heats with anger while my chest hurts. If I hadn't gotten out of there, I'm not sure if I could have stayed rooted to my seat. I want to go over there and rip her hand off him. She shouldn't get to touch him, not like that, not so intimately.

Pushing off the door, I walk a few steps until I reach the sink where I turn on the faucet and begin splashing cold water on my face to cool off.

It's a rather fancy bathroom, so there are cloth hand towels folded and placed to the side of the sink instead of the standard paper towel dispenser. Grabbing one, I dab it onto my skin, drying up the water.

After staring at myself in the mirror for as long as I can possibly get away with staying in here, I take a deep breath of air and then toss the used towel into the basket underneath the sink and then leave, heading back out to where I left Justin.

Only I don't make it more than a foot out the door before I smack into a hard chest.

Snapping my head back, I look up, seeing Drago staring down at me.

"What are you doing here?"

"You took off to the bathroom so fast I was about to come in to make sure you were okay."

"No," I bite out. "Why are you here with *her*?"

"Why do you care? You said yourself you aren't any of my business, so why am *I* yours?"

"Don't twist my words. I'm not the one that broke up with you." My words exit bitterly.

Stepping around him, I try to seek distance so that I don't lash out—or breakdown. The latter being more likely at this point. I thought I had my emotions in check. I was doing really good. I haven't cried since I released everything on my sister-in-law this past weekend. I had gotten past it all. Or I thought I had. When I realized he was sitting across the room from me, everything came back tenfold, hitting all my senses at once.

Drago snags me around the waist, stopping my escape, then he turns me back around to face him. He waits until I'm looking up at him before he says anything, and it takes me a moment to drag my eyes up his chest. The crisp white dress shirt he's wearing contrasts well with his bronze skin, and I like that he doesn't wear a tie. He looks dressed up and handsome, yet more appealing and maybe a little dangerous.

I still haven't figured out why I like that about him so much. Maybe it's because deep down, I know he's a good man. He's not a criminal like his father or like others perceive him to be because of the last name he was given at birth.

Finally, I raise my eyes, meeting his. I have to swallow the lump in my throat. I want nothing more than to reach up and pull him down to me. I want his lips on mine and his arms around me, securing my body to his. I miss the feel of him. I miss him so much and it hurts more and more with each day, worsening versus getting better.

"I'm not with her," he tells me, and I do want to believe him, but I saw what I saw. She was touching him and he wasn't making her stop.

"You sure about that?"

"Yes," he breathes out. His dark gaze drops down, eyeing my lips.

It only causes more questions to wrack my brain. Does he want to kiss me? Does he still want me? If so, why did he force me away?

Grabbing my hips gently, he guides my body closer to his. With his right hand, he roams up my waist until he reaches my throat where his scorching hot palm lingers. Parting my mouth, I take in air and then exhale on a shaky breath.

The way he's looking at me ignites all of my senses and without thinking, I lean forward, inhaling him through his shirt. His smell, clean and manly with a hint of salt water sends a bolt of electricity to my core. It's calming in all the places I'm plagued with the anxiety I'm not used to. It's shocking in all of the places I've been lonely for what seems like forever, even though it's only been a little over two weeks since we've touched. It's like breathing in air when you're on the brink of suffocating.

"D," I breathe out, mumbling his name through the soft material.

His left hand squeezes my hip, but it's a pain I welcome. With his other hand, he slides up, running his thumb under my chin, forcing me to look up at him once again.

My eyes close briefly when his fingers slide through strands of my hair, but I don't want to miss a second of this moment, so I slowly open my lids to look back into those eyes I love so much. He's staring at my mouth again and before I know it, he's sinking down to my level.

Suddenly, he stops his descent. Drago's eyes jerk up, looking over my head just before someone's hand wraps around my waist, pulling me until I'm flush against another rock-solid chest. The gesture is firm, but not rough. Possessive or protective maybe.

"Excuse us, will you?" Justin doesn't give D a chance to respond. By the fury in Drago's eyes, I'm not certain he's capable of getting words out right now. "I'm going to take my date back now. Perhaps, you should get back to your own date before she comes looking for you."

Justin pulls me away as he takes a step backward. The sudden loss of contact with D brings a whine out of my lips. I needed him and he let Justin take me without a fight.

Staring at Drago, I beg with my eyes, needing and wanting him, yet not able to call out to him. I watch Drago's dark eyes intensify the farther away I get. Then my eyes drop, seeing his hands clenched together in fists at his sides. It's not much, but for a split second, it gives me a little pleasure to know he's affected by seeing another man touch me the same way I am when Rebecca had her hands all over him in the restaurant.

"Let's go, Bri," Justin whispers into my ear.

Grabbing my hand, he squeezes tight, making sure I can't readily escape his hold and drags me behind him until we're outside of the hotel, heading toward the parking lot.

"We didn't pay," I yell, while at the same time yanking to get my hand free from his.

"I took care of it," he barks but doesn't stop.

"Justin, let go," I demand.

Finally, when we're at least twenty yards from the main entrance, he stops, turning around to face me, but he doesn't let me go. It's becoming awkward and strange, him holding my hand. I'm not sure if I feel like a kid right now or what. Either way, he shouldn't be touching me.

"Let go!"

He releases me, the reluctance showing clear in his green eyes.

"What the hell was that?" He shrugs like it wasn't a big deal. Oh, it's a big deal to me. "That back there"—I throw my fist up, stabbing my thumb behind me—"was some territorial shit. So, I'm going to ask again, Summers. What was that?"

I take a step forward, crowding his personal space and place my hands on my hips, waiting for an answer.

Justin's chest expands, filling with air as he looks down at me. His green eyes bore into mine, but I don't cower. It's not in me to do so. When his lungs fill to capacity, he releases them, fanning my face as he exhales. Surprisingly his breath doesn't smell like the meal he just ate. It's minty like he popped a mint or chewed some gum.

"I'm good at getting under people's skin. It's why I close more IA cases faster than any other Internal Affairs detective. I have a hard time turning that skill off."

I shake my head. "What does that even mean? Are you saying you just wanted to get under Drago's skin?"

"I felt he deserved exactly what you felt when you watched him and the woman sitting next to him, right before you escaped to the bathroom, Bri." He blows out another frustrated huff of air. "And I wanted to see if his feelings for you are as real as yours are for him."

"And what did you see?" The sizzle coursing through me dies.

Why do I even want to know? Is it because I want reassurance that I'm not making Drago's feelings for me more than what they actually are?

"Doesn't matter, Andrews. You cannot have a relationship with him. What the fuck is going through your head? Do you want your boss to contest my findings? Do you want to lose your job?"

"No!" I cross my arms, hating where he's taking this conversation.

"So, then it's my turn to ask you. What the hell was that back there?"

I can't answer him because I don't know myself. I know D was going to kiss me and right now I'm pissed at Justin for stopping it. Does he have a valid point? Sure. But I can't control my heart. I want my career and I want the man back there that I love.

Is that really so much to ask?

"Fuck!" Justin scrubs his hand down his face. "I'm going to be late."

Flipping my wrist, I look down at my smartwatch to see what time it is and sure enough, he is going to be late. He has ten minutes before he has to be at his interview.

"My father's office is only a couple of blocks. I'll walk."

He looks at me like I've grown two heads.

"No, you won't. Let's go. I'll still drop you off. If I'm late, I'm late. I'm not that kind of asshole, Bri."

"I never said you were. It's not a big deal, Justin."

He sighs, closing his eyes. for a second, I think he's going to concede and leave me, but he doesn't. My hand is once again locked in his and he's pulling me toward the parking lot. This time I don't grumble. I know it would be of no use. He's set on taking me, so why argue?

CHAPTER SIXTEEN

My dad's office is only five blocks away from where we were, and I could have easily done the trek by foot instead of Justin driving me. Five blocks are nothing compared to what I used to walk when I was first hired on as a rookie. Although, I can say I don't miss it. I love working out. I enjoy the MMA style best. Treadmills, ellipticals, and normal gym equipment, I hate. It bores me; there is no thought process to the workout. It's mundane and not something that engages my mind.

"Hey, Susan," I greet my dad's receptionist.

"Brianna," she greets me, the surprise evident on her face. "What brings you by today?"

For a lady close to my father's age, she is fit, the same as my dad. Susan is taller than me by several inches with styled dark blonde hair. I have a lot of hair myself, but I can never bring myself to trim it above my shoulder blades. Hers sits just under her chin, cut at an angle. The last time I saw her, she had a hairstyle that reminded me of Rachel's from *Friends* back in the day when I used to watch that sitcom as a teenager. The show was nearing its end by the time I started it, but I always found it funny.

Before I have the opportunity to ask if my dad is busy, I hear shouting coming from behind his closed office door.

Tapping my hip on instinct, I double check making sure my weapon is there even though I already know it is. Now that I'm finally wearing it again, my holstered gun is like a second skin. You know it's there but you don't always feel it. It long stopped feeling foreign.

The shouts are loud and don't sound like my father's voice—which has me on high alert.

"Bri," Susan calls, but I don't answer her as I move in the direction of my dad's office.

He's in real estate, corporate and residential, so this may be just another day at the office for him, but I'm a cop and I too often see yelling escalate to violence. My father and I may never see eye-to-eye on most things, but he's still my dad and if I need to protect him, I will.

I open his office door without knocking, expecting to find anyone besides the man I see shouting at my father. The side of his face is filled with more anger than I've ever witnessed.

"Jackson," I holler over his booming voice. The room finally goes silent. "What the hell? Why are you yelling at Dad?" I demand. I've never seen my brother raise his voice. Sure, he's a stern man and I've watched him on numerous occasions correct or discipline one of his kids, but he nor Alana scream at them. He's never yelled at me, even though I've given him plenty of reasons to over the years. It's not that I ever got into a lot of trouble, but I was a teenager and there was more than once that I acted a little too wild for my own good. Parties were fun and they always had alcohol. Back then, I couldn't hold my liquor for shit. What kid can?

"What are you doing here, kiddo?" Dad asks, concern etched on his forehead. "Are you okay?"

I can understand why he fears something may be wrong. It's not like me to pop into his office unannounced. I can probably count the number of times I've been here since moving to LA.

"Bri." Jackson twists around, facing me. He lets out a heavy sigh before stalking over and grabbing me in an aggressive hug. Also unlike my brother. He is a lot larger than me and firmer. Jackson is tall at six-foot-two, the same height as our dad, but he's leaner than Drago. Jackson is a big runner, so even though he's strong, he's leaner than most men. Aggressive, he is not; at least he's never been with me.

"Your brother is upset I didn't tell him what happened to you," my dad says, standing from behind his desk and buttoning his suit jacket.

"You mean pissed off you didn't tell me my sister was shot or that she lost a baby for Christ's sake?" Jackson corrects. He releases me, taking a step back. "Why didn't you call me, Bri? Why keep me in the dark like you did?"

"Jack," I start to whine. I knew when he found out I'd feel like shit. This is much worse than when I told Alana. She got over the hurt quicker than I thought, so my guilt evaporated. With my brother, I don't think that's going to be the case.

"Why wasn't I notified, Brianna?" I really hate when he calls me by my full name. He makes me feel like one of his kids when he does it, and he knows that, which is why he uses it to his advantage.

"Jackson, give your sister some space and let her tell me why she is here." My dad rounds his desk, walking toward us.

"No." Jackson points his finger at our dad, his anger returning. Looking back at me, he says, "I want answers, Bri."

I ignore my brother for a moment to address my dad. "I wanted to see if you had time to run me back to my side of town."

"Where is your car?" Jackson demands. I get that he gave me my car as a gift, but his anger mixed with a demanding tone is getting on my last nerve.

"It's at a field office not far from my condo. The fellow officer I rode with had an emergency, so I said I'd find a way back." I don't bother with telling either of them about Eric or his task force or even the DEA. Too many questions would spark.

"What kind of jackass leaves a woman stranded in LA?" Jackson huffs while shaking his head.

"I wasn't stranded. I was a couple of blocks over. Jeez, Jackson, you do remember I'm an adult and a cop, right?"

"And you should be neither."

I roll my eyes at my brother's unreasonable attitude. At some point, he's going to have to accept I'm grown. If he's still like this with me, I can only imagine what he'll be like when his three kids reach adulthood.

"Brianna is more than capable of taking care of herself,

Jackson," Dad states, crossing his arms over his chest while staring my brother down.

"Don't talk to me right now, Dad. I can't even fathom what you've done."

"Get off Dad's ass," I bark, getting sick of Jackson's tone and the way he's treating our father.

"I don't think so. He lied to me and he kept something from me he had no right to."

"Like hell I don't. She's my daughter." Dad's hands drop to his hip and I swear I see steam coming from his ears that have turned a bright shade of red.

"Oh!" Jackson throws up his hands. "Now you want to play the fucking parent." My father's eyes light with fire after Jackson's words fly out of his mouth, shocking me too. Even if my brother has somewhat of a point, that was uncalled for and he knows it.

"Jackson!" I shout. "Stop this. Dad did what I asked him to. He honored my wishes. If you're pissed off, then be pissed off at me. Not him!"

"I can't be pissed at you, Bri. Don't you understand that by now?" Jackson pinches the bridge of his nose as his eyes go up toward the ceiling.

"Son," my father starts. "I get you're mad, but if you'd done the same and asked me to keep something between us, then I'd have done the same. And so would you."

My brother's jaw locks. He knows our dad is right, but he isn't going to admit it. They are both alike in that way—stubborn.

He blows out a breath of air, letting his head fall until his eyes meet mine. "I'll take you wherever you need to go. I have a rental."

"I'm showing a house at two. I can take her," Dad informs us.

"Jackson," I say, making sure I have his attention. "I am sorry I hurt you and Alana by not telling you, but I'd still make the same choice if the circumstances were the same. A lot happened, and I don't have the time to hash this out. I'm working a case and it requires my full attention."

"There's no way your department would allow you on that case, Bri. What are you doing?"

I eye my father, telling him to shut up with my eyes. If given a crumb, Jackson is like a bloodhound; he won't leave without answers.

I wonder what all his wife told him?

If she had told him about Drago and Gabriel, why isn't he trying to pull that information out of me? I know my brother. If he knew, he would have had a conniption fit. He's mad, but he's only upset that I didn't tell him about being shot or the miscarriage. If he knows I lost a baby, then questions about the father are bound to be asked.

As if hearing my thoughts, Jackson asks the inevitable.

"Since when were you seeing someone? And who is it?"

Why couldn't my sister-in-law have told him everything I told her? It would have made this so much easier. I'm not a pussy though. My problem is I don't have time for this shit. His answers can wait until I locate the baby that needs me. *The baby that I need.*

"She isn't seeing anyone, Jackson. Now leave your sister be. When she is ready to talk to you about it, she'll talk."

"Butt out, Dad."

"No!" The authority in his voice rings clear. Jackson has pushed him too far. "Brianna doesn't need people hounding her. And that's exactly what you're doing. Act like the thirty-six-year-old you are and shut up."

Taking in a long pull of air, my dad cuts his eyes to me.

"Let's go, kiddo. Your brother is finished."

"Goddammit, Dad," Jackson huffs.

"Watch your mouth in front of me."

"Like you said, I'm thirty-six. You don't get a say in how I act or what I say." Jackson faces me again. "This isn't over, Bri. We're going to talk, whether you want to or not. What happened isn't something you can bury with work. Hell, you were shot. Why are you even working in the first place?"

"My gunshot wound isn't bad." My father's eyes tell me I'm full of shit, but I continue. "The bullet grazed my leg. Thankfully, I was still wearing my bulletproof vest. My ribs were bruised, but I didn't break anything. I came out okay. And as far as mentally, I'm okay there too."

Even I know that's a lie, but I need them both to believe it, and when Jackson relaxes his stance for the first time, I think I've convinced him. Looking out of the corner of my eyes, I know I didn't convince my dad. Sadness passes over the eyes that mirror Jackson and mine. I'm guessing he's thinking about my mom. For the first time, I want to console my father, but because Jackson is here I can't. It would raise more questions and I'm not sure if my dad has told Jackson about our mom's miscarriages. It's not my place to do so if he hasn't.

"Are you sure you're okay?"

"I promise I am, big brother. And if that changes, I'll call you."

He grabs my forearm lightly, pulling me to his chest where I'm wrapped in a tight hold.

"You better, Sis. You better."

CHAPTER SEVENTEEN

The next day, Eric and I are at a coffee shop where we know Chasity frequents often. She's also posting selfies with the latest coffee fad. Who knew coffee could be a fad; I didn't. I thought it was just a drink. One I love unconditionally, but still just a drink.

I miss my daily trek to the coffee house across the street from the precinct where either Connie or I would go, or we would meet there when the office got tiresome.

I miss her, but I'm still not over how she acted even if we are back to talking.

"Why does finding Gabriel seem more personal to you now?" I ask, attempting to get my mind back on track as I stir the heavy cream around in my cup.

"It's not," he bites out, the lie evident not only to me. He knows it too.

"Level with me, Alders." I lift my eyes to meet his. "Why are you so hell-bent on helping me find Gabe versus focusing on Vincent Acerbi?"

His eyes drift down to the table as if in thought. Lifting his lids, our gazes lock once again.

"It's you. Your determination to find a kid that isn't yours. You care more than that boy's mother does. You don't just want to save him, Bri. You need to save him. I see it clearly. You love that boy like he's yours when he isn't."

His words stab me square in the chest. I don't like hearing the words "he isn't yours." I know he's not, but I don't like being reminded.

He continues when I don't speak. I can't. My throat locks up, not allowing words to come out.

"It's not DNA that makes a person a parent, Bri. It's not giving birth or holding your child when they're only seconds old that makes a parent either. It's here." He stabs his chest with his pointer finger. "And it's here." He does the same, jabbing his finger into his temple. "Being a parent is about loving someone without conditions. It's about not only wanting but also needing to be in that child's life; doing anything and everything to make sure they are safe and happy. It's a form of true love in a way, because there is no love that compares to that of a parent."

His words penetrate, but there is still doubt that continues to linger in my head. Gabriel isn't mine. He's Drago's. His father should want him. Need him. It doesn't matter the reason or how he came into this world. He's here. He is D's son. Not mine and I hate that. I shouldn't resent the fact that he has a real mother, no matter how much of a piece of shit she is. Gabe is hers too.

"She isn't his real mother," he says as if hearing my thoughts.

"Maybe not," I concede, then down my drink, needing the hot liquid to coat my throat to keep the tears locked away. I'm sick of the tears. I'm sick of crying over what I've lost: Drago, Gabriel, my baby. Life fucking sucks right now, and I don't know how I got here.

"My dad isn't my biological father."

I snap out of my choking thoughts.

"What?" I remember my thought yesterday when Justin revealed the DEA director is Eric's dad. Does that mean he's adopted then?

"My dad, the man I love and look up to the most in this world is not the man that took part in creating me. Doesn't mean he isn't my father. He is and there is no one that will ever take his place. He molded me into the man I am today. He loves my mother so fiercely I wonder if it's even possible to find the kind of love they have. Looking at them and knowing the fucked-up shit that happens day in and day out, it doesn't seem like a possibility. I love my dad even more simply for how he loves my mother and me. So, what I'm saying is you are that boy's mother whether you believe it or not. You love him like no other person does and that makes you his mom."

Does it? Does it really?

I've never admitted to wanting him out loud. I can't want him, because when we do find him, Drago and I won't be together. What good is wanting something I can't have?

"Hey!" We both pop our heads up, seeing Connie stop in front of our booth. After a beat of silence, she cocks her head to the side, eyeing downing at me. "You going to scoot over and let me sit or not?"

I slide over and she lowers down, taking a seat next to me and in front of Eric.

"What are you doing here?" I ask suspiciously.

She smiles, widening her mouth into a grin at Eric before placing her forearms on the table and turning her head to face me. Her smile instantly turns into a scowl. "I hate the douche-prick the chief assigned to me. I had to get out of the office. I knew you were here."

"How?" I question, and then realize my stupidity.

"How do you think? Duh!" She grips her cell phone, flashing it at me. "We are still sharing our location like good partners."

Connie and I met in the academy, but we didn't become close until we were both promoted to detective and assigned to the same precinct two years ago. We decided it was in both of our best interests to continuously share our location with each other using our cellular devices. That way if something happened or we couldn't reach each other, we'd know where to look.

Turning her head, she looks back at Eric.

"So, pretty boy, how do I get in on this DEA thing Bri has going on? She and I are a package deal."

I almost snort my coffee. Just yesterday she was name-calling them and now she wants to be one. Yeah, right! That transferred detective must be a piece of work if she can't deal with him.

"That bad, huh?"

She throws her head back against the cushioned headrest.

"You have no idea."

Connie usually isn't this dramatic. Leaning forward, her blonde hair skims over the table and her eyes land back on Eric. He's observing her, yet he's keeping his expression neutral. I know he's her type, but is she his?

Suddenly, I feel like the third wheel even though I'm the one that's supposed to be here with Eric discussing our next move if Chasity doesn't make an appearance. I'm getting tired of no action. Day by day my hope wanes.

"Sorry, Detective," Eric says, a smirk pulling at the corner of his lips. "I don't think I'm man enough to handle both of you."

She leans forward, her upper abdomen pressing against the edge of the table as her low cut top pulls a little lower down her chest.

Jesus. I shake my head. She isn't subtle at all. And from the way Eric's eyes dilate a little makes me think he's just as interested as she is.

At least the one thing I do know is Connie will only be in it for the pleasure. She doesn't do boyfriends. She loves her independence and freedom. Plus, she's more career-driven than I am. If our roles had been reversed, I'm certain she wouldn't have made any of the decisions I made. She wouldn't have found herself obsessed over a baby that wasn't hers or in love with a man that doesn't want her.

I need to clear my head. My mind keeps wandering between everything, which is exactly what I don't need. I can't focus on finding Drago's son when I allow him to take up too much space in my head and my heart. I keep telling myself to shove him back, but I haven't yet. As impossible as it seems, I have to stop thinking about him.

Why do people fall in love? This sucks!

THAT NIGHT, ERIC AND I HEAD TO THE COVE, THE UPSCALE HOTEL JUSTIN and I ate at yesterday. Eric says there is a quaint little bar inside that the three of us can grab a bite to eat and have a couple of drinks. It's a lot later than I usually eat, but Eric and I were busy all day and Justin was working several of his IA cases. I knew Internal Affairs was a needed function inside the police department, but I had no idea the number of daily complaints that come in that Justin's department has to follow up on.

"What time did Justin say he would meet us here?" I ask, walking through the side door to the hotel that Eric holds open for me.

"I got a text before I got out of my SUV. He said he was leaving headquarters and should be here in fifteen. With traffic, he'll probably be more like twenty."

"Do you think we're wasting too much time and energy waiting for Chasity to show up at one of the places she's known to frequent?"

Unfortunately, we can't ping her cell phone. There isn't one in her name or under her aunt or uncle that aren't their own. Eric hasn't come up with any possible source of cellular contact to track. She has one. Come on; who doesn't these days. Plus, she's young. Of course she would have a cell phone. I've had one since I was thirteen.

"Diaz has plans for that boy. He's not going to harm him until he gets Acerbi to do what he wants," Eric says, sounding confident.

"Unless he gets tired of waiting or realizes Drago isn't going to take his bait."

He eyes me sideways. "What makes you so sure your boy isn't going to do exactly what Diaz wants?"

"You said it yourself, Drago nor his siblings are criminals."

"Young Bri," he chastises me. "Even good people are capable of committing crimes—especially when it comes to the safety of their children."

"D doesn't believe me," I explain. "He's convinced himself there is no possible way Gabriel is his." Eric simply shrugs at my last statement.

When we enter the small, dimly lit bar, I only see a handful of patrons. Some are sitting in booths, talking quietly among themselves. Then I see a group of younger adults cackling to my right. They're taking up every amount of space in a sectional booth.

"Fuck," Eric drawls out, bringing my attention back to him. His body locks, as does his jaw. When I start to turn to see who has pulled this reaction out of him, he clutches my arm by the elbow, pulling. My eyes stop their scan, cutting back to now furious eyes. "Let's hit up another place. There are plenty of restaurants in the area."

"But you wanted somewhere quiet where we could eat and discuss the case."

"We can do that someplace else."

Suspicion gets the better of me, so as he starts to pull me out of the restaurant, I turn my head, looking at the bar. A fury I've never felt before strikes me like a bolt of lightning igniting the summer brush of dead greenery. I see red and don't even remember snatching my arm back from Eric's grasp until I'm standing behind Drago.

It's not him per se I'm fixated on.

"Bri." His voice is surprised and perhaps I hear a twinge of guilt, but it could be my imagination playing tricks on me. I've always thought I could look at any situation, personal or professional, and be objective. See things for what they really are, but ever since I've met Drago, I've been questioning that skill.

My eyes finally snap up, looking away from where her hand is wrapped firmly around D's exposed lower bicep.

"Take your hands off him," I order. Do I have that right? No. But suddenly I find myself not in the right state of mind. It's pissing me off, but she's pissing me off more.

She turns her face, looking over her shoulder. A smirk slowly climbs up her lips. "And why would I do that, *Detective*?"

Shit. I guess she remembers me from the first time I was inside Drago's office on the day we met.

Drago jerks away from her, his body and stool putting several inches between them. *Was it guilt?* He's acting like it is. And the fact that I want to punch him in the balls for allowing her to touch him again doesn't go unnoticed by him either. He visibly swallows.

"Because he isn't yours," I bark at her.

"Please excuse us." Eric's deep voice cuts like a sharp blade as

I'm jerked away from them and I'm hauled out the front entrance of the bar. He doesn't stop pulling on me until he rounds a corner, where my back is pushed against a wall. My head tips up, looking into blazing eyes.

"What the fuck was that?" I cross my arms over my chest, needing the small barrier it places between us. Not that it helps much. He still looms over me. "Do you know how fucking hard I worked to spin your pregnancy when that dick of a boss of yours brought it into question?"

"I don't care!" I yell, fuming mad. That bitch was hanging all over him.

"Well, I do," Eric spits in my face. Placing his hands on my arms, he pushes them apart, taking a step into my personal space, scowling at me. He could be really handsome if he wasn't wearing that "someone pissed in his Cheerios" look all the time. "You can't get spotted acting like the jealous girlfriend. What if—"

Eric is snatched backward, yanking me forward with him. I don't have time to brace myself as my face plants in the center of his chest. Rapidly, he releases my wrists.

"Bri, are you—" he starts to ask me, ignoring the person who dare lay a hand on a cop.

I'm pushing off him when I hear Drago's deep, fire-penetrating voice. Looking up, I see D's mouth inches from Eric's ear. Drago has him in a hold that Eric isn't even trying to get out of.

"Don't ever fucking touch her, E. She's mine."

E?

Where have I heard that before?

I step back, watching them. Eric's body is being forced, held in an arch against Drago's chest.

"D," Eric says in warning through clenched teeth, clearly not likely being immobilized, yet still not making one move to get out of the hold he's in.

A memory from weeks ago flashes before me. *E* was what Drago called a person he was having a telephone conversation with on a day I showed up at the dock unannounced.

They both stumble backward, landing into the wall on the other side of the hallway. Drago's hold loosens enough for Eric to slip out and spins around to face him.

"Good God, look at you. You're piss-poor drunk, you stupid fuck. I can smell it on you like it's seeping out of your pores."

They know each other. That realization hits me in the face, and suddenly, I'm wondering just who I can trust. Eric's acted like— no, he told me he's been investigating Vincent Acerbi for years. He never once mentioned knowing Drago on a personal level.

And now I'm wondering why.

What could possibly be the reason for keeping that major detail from me?

Drago goes to push off the wall and stumbles again, almost falling forward. I'm at his side without thought, gliding my body under his for support.

There is a lot both of them need to explain to me. Detective Justin Summers for one. Is he in on this too, or is Eric so deep into bringing Drago's father to justice that he's found a way to infiltrate Drago's life? Could that a possibility?

I can't and don't even want to think about that right now. I need to get Drago out of here and far away from that slut that clearly doesn't have real feelings for him like I do.

"Let's go, D. You're coming with me."

"Bri," Eric bites out.

"We'll talk tomorrow." He gives me a look like he's about to rip into me, but I beat him to it. "This isn't up for a discussion. I'll call you in the morning."

I pull Drago away, leaving Eric standing there fuming. For a second, I wonder if I'm digging myself into a deeper hole than I already am. What's Eric going to tell Justin? I don't need him to re-open my Internal Affairs case. It would only ruin my chance to find Gabriel. I can't let that happen, but I can't and won't leave Drago here.

Fear is a motherfucker.

CHAPTER EIGHTEEN

At first, I was surprised that someone who drives a Bugatti on a daily basis would be staying in a regular room rather than one of the suites higher up—or even the penthouse. Then I thought, Drago has never come off as over-the-top or someone who cares about materialistic things. He has a nice house and an expensive car, but I haven't seen anything else that gives away he comes from money.

I like that about him. Even though I come from money, I don't rely on my father's wealth, or my brother's. I pride myself on being independent; a woman that can take care of herself. I never wanted to be someone that, years down the road, couldn't land on her own feet no matter the circumstance.

And then my mind wandered over into dangerous territory. Drago had a room at a hotel and Rebecca De Luca was with him tonight. Anger coats my skin and I hate the feeling that's etched inside of me. *Was he going to fuck her in here?*

If he was, do I really want to know about it?

Unlacing his left boot, I pull it off, placing it next to the right at the end of the bed.

"You're so fucking beautiful."

I tip my head up, looking at him as he stares down at me. His hands are braced on either side of him, gripping the comforter he's sitting on, and currently the only thing keeping him in an upright position. He's drunk; really drunk. Like Eric, I can smell the bourbon on him from my kneeled position in front of him.

"Just sleep it off, D."

I stand, taking a step away from him, looking around the room. It's large enough with a full-length couch next to the bed and an oversized reading chair close to the floor-to-ceiling windows. The curtains are drawn open, and although it's pitch black in the sky, the city still bustles below.

I can't leave him here alone; I know that. Not knowing Drago's tolerance for alcohol or even how much he's had, I need to stay to make sure he'll be okay. I can leave before he wakes up in the morning. Maybe he won't even remember I was here. That thought wrecks me. I don't want to be so forgettable to him, but what if I am?

"I haven't had you in so long." His words cut through my negative thoughts, pulling my eyes to him again. "I can remember every detail in my head." He raises his hands in front of him, flipping his palms over, looking at them as if they've offended him. "Yet, the feel of running my hands all over your body is just out of reach like some cruel joke." He clenches his hands, dropping them back to his sides, resting them at the edge of the mattress.

His eyes climb, seeking mine. When our gazes lock, he stands.

"I need to be inside you, or I'm going to continue to die and wither away until there is nothing left of me. I need to feel you again, baby." I gasp, not expecting that admission. D stalks forward, but I step backward. With every step he makes, I retreat until my back meets the wall. "Please, Bri," he begs.

Who knew this large beast in front of me was capable of begging for anything. His sheer need for me is my undoing. I was going to make sure he got into a bed and I was going to stay to make sure he didn't throw up and choke on his vomit, but not once did I think I'd be giving myself so willingly to him again.

After all, he is the one that ended us. He didn't want me, so why does his need for me break down every wall I've put up?

"Don't be gentle," is my only request, because I need him as much as he needs me—maybe more. And although I love gentle Drago, I crave the beast that I know lurks under the surface of his skin, or maybe it's the dragon inked on him that's a part of who he is. Either way, I want it and I need it.

"Get out of those fucking pants before I tear them off your body." Heat scorches my skin, heating me from the inside out. I can literally feel it climbing up my neck. No one's words have ever affected me the way his do; no one else's ever will. I know that as matter of fact as I know my own name.

My dress pants are gone as quickly as I can un-loop the buttons, shucking them down my legs and kicking them off to the side.

He's on me within the next second, pressing my head against

the wall as his lips devour mine. Nothing about his kiss is gentle; it's hard, demanding, and in full control. My head starts to spin as his scent mixed with the whiskey infiltrates my senses.

I vaguely hear his belt coming undone and the zipper of his slacks being pulled down. The next thing I know I'm hoisted up the wall, and on instinct, I wrap my legs around his waist. He's still wearing his dress shirt, but then so am I. He must have pushed his boxer briefs down with his pants, because his thick erection twitches through the material of my panties, causing electrical currents to ripple through my pussy.

I'm wet, I know I am; I have been since the second his tongue swept inside my mouth, dancing with mine. Every single time his teeth bite down on my bottom lip I get a little dizzy. It's one of my favorite things he does to me.

Drago's hand grips the back of my thigh on the side of my body that wasn't shot with such strength I'm certain it'll leave a bruise that will match the blue hue around my wound. But I couldn't care less. I want this kind of pain. It's more pleasurable than not.

I can taste the whiskey on his tongue. It tastes of burnt sweetness and maybe something citrus. As drunk as he seemed only minutes ago, you wouldn't know it with the steadiness of how he holds me exactly where he wants me; where I want to be.

Dropping me an inch, he presses my upper back farther into the wall. And I gasp, taking his breath down my throat when his dick starts running up and down the lips of my pussy.

"I want my panties off," I demand. "I need to feel you skin-to-skin, D."

The satin material is keeping his cock from touching my clit.

The desire, the need to have his dick running through my pussy lips instead of on the surface is strong.

He reaches underneath me, pulling my thong over my ass cheek, giving me exactly what I want. I swallow, closing my eyes when I feel his cock touch my skin for the first time in far too long. Drago keeps ahold of my panties so they stay out of the way as he slides through my folds, rubbing my clit just right.

Jesus, this feels good.

Gripping his shoulders, I dig in with my fingers and press down more so that his dick is a hard rod between me.

"Oh, yes," I moan. It feels so right that emotions take hold, pressing against my chest and threatening to explode.

"I knew the second I laid eyes on you when you stepped out of your car that you'd bring me to my knees. I knew, Bri, and I still couldn't leave you alone." His voice is as steady as his hold on me.

I force my eyes open, looking up to his dark stare. He doesn't seem to blink as he watches me.

"I didn't want you to leave me alone." And I didn't. From the beginning I wanted him. I tried hard to do my job and keep it strictly professional. I failed, but I don't regret it for a second. He's too right for me. We fit together better than puzzle pieces.

"Yeah, but I should have. I knew the whole time I should have left you as just another local cop that I could despise."

"Do you despise me?" God, I hope not. I couldn't take it if he did.

"No," he admits and looking at those beautiful, vulnerable eyes, I know he's telling me the truth. "I never once despised you. I wanted to. I tried to, and it pissed me off that I couldn't."

His cock enters me swiftly, hitting the back of my cervix with a slam. I cry out, the pleasure so unexpected but welcomed all at the same time. Drago's hips piston, connecting to mine over and over. I meet every thrust, chasing my release. This isn't going to last long. I know he's trying. I see the strain in his eyes as he attempts to hold back, waiting for me.

With every exit and entry inside me, our eyes never falter, always staying locked on each other's. And in his, I see what I've been looking for—love. It overwhelms me to the point tears leak from the outer corners of both of my eyes. He loves me. I know he does, and that knowledge fuses something inside me together. I drop my forehead, resting it in the crook of his neck as a whimper escapes my lips.

On his next thrust, hot semen coats my insides, setting off my own orgasm that seems to last longer than any I've ever had before. My body hums with satisfaction as the pulsing inside me continues.

God, I needed that so bad. I hadn't realized how much until right now.

Drago sets me down gently on my feet. My shaking legs prevent me from releasing him.

"That was . . ." I trail off, my words failing me. I can't even verbalize what that was except sheer amazing. I'm not even embarrassed I teared up. It was honest emotions and whether he appreciates it or not, I can respect myself more for not hiding them from him.

"I'm not done with you, baby. Not by a long shot. This is just starting. I'm going to fuck you until I'm sober, and then I'm going to fuck you until I can't move. I'm going to drown that sweet, beautiful pussy in my cum tonight."

His lips come down on mine, devouring me with a kiss and stealing the breath from my throat. He sucks, pulling on my tongue. He nips my bottom lip hard enough that pain and pleasure storms through my body.

Ripping off me, he steps back, pulling me off the wall.

"Ditch the shirt and everything else. I want you bent over that chair." My eyes follow his, seeing the oversized reading chair in the corner of the room next to the window. Pushing me toward it, he smacks my ass, making me gasp. "Now, Detective."

Yes. That's exactly what I want too.

I breathe, steadying myself. Smiling, I raise up onto my tiptoes, smacking my lips with his again. I can't get enough of him and I don't ever want to. I know I'll want him forever. There's nothing that'll change that.

"Yes, sir," I say as my heels land back on the floor. Yes, sir indeed.

He loves me, and I can get through anything that's thrown at me with that feeling settled deep inside me.

CHAPTER NINETEEN

My body is wrecked in the best possible way. I know that before I even open my eyes. The only reason I'm not hesitant, fearing last night was a concoction my mind put together is because our bodies are still tangled around each other's. His strong arms cling to me, wrapped around my back. My front is fused to his muscled chest and his cock is poking me in the stomach.

It's what woke me up. After the marathon of orgasms we both had: bent over the chair, pressed into the cold glass window, face down on the couch, in the shower, and lastly, he made love to me right here in the bed before we both passed out from sated exhaustion.

He sobered a lot quicker than I expected, but I'm pretty certain the soberer he got, the drunker I became.

I ache all over, especially on the outside of my thigh where I'm still healing. He worked me over at least three times as much as he did the first night we slept together. I'm sore, but I'm a little more settled than I have been since I woke up in the hospital a couple of weeks ago. I know all the anxiety won't leave until we have Gabriel back. As much as I feel guilty for doing it, right now I have to shove the thought of him or where he is farther back into my mind or my emotions will surface, which I don't need right now. I just want to enjoy this moment a little longer.

Ah shit!

It's only now that I realize we never once used a condom last night. I doubt he did that on purpose this time. Both of us were too caught up in each other to be responsible. When you go without something you crave every second of every day, logical thinking leaves you once you finally have it back.

For whatever reason, as I lay here thinking about it, I'm not feeling any sort of panic or even remorse. I don't get a chance to analyze my feelings. Drago stirs, pushing his hard-on into me more as his arms tighten their hold on me. His face presses against the top of my head and I hear the pull of air through his nose as he breathes me in. Shudders ripple through his body as he exhales, coating the top of my head with hot air.

Without a word, he rolls away from me and gets out of bed, scooping his clothes off the floor as he walks to the bathroom, closing the door behind him. Missing his touch and suddenly cold, I kick the covers to the bottom of the bed, then scoot out. After I have my bra and panties on, I pull up my pants and search for my shirt.

Drago comes out of the bathroom before I find my top,

stopping me in my tracks. Our gazes lock; my seemingly content eyes land on his wrecked brown ones. It's our silent stare that I know. I know he's already pulled away from me. The love I felt last night is gone—vanished.

"Oh, hell no!" I shake my head, not believing this right now.

"Bri," he calls out.

"Fuck you, D!" I shout, not holding back.

"Bri, please hear me out. I—"

"No!" I yell, unable to contain my anger and hurt. "Just no. You aren't doing this to me again, so I'm doing it to you first." Like hell he'll kick me out, breaking my heart all over again. I'm not going through that again. I can't.

"Bri." My name sounds like painful guilt on his tongue. Too fucking bad. I don't want his guilt. I wanted him, but he apparently doesn't want me.

"Shut up! Fuck you, Acerbi. Get out. Leave," I demand. This may technically be his room, but I don't care. I'm not allowing him to be the one doing the kicking out this time around.

After a few seconds of a stare down, he turns, walking away from me instead of to me. And it hurts. It hurts so much I think my chest is going to cave in on itself.

How could he do this?

I thought for sure I'd gotten through to him last night. I thought he felt the same. He told me over and over how much he wanted and needed me.

I shake my head, not believing how stupid I really am. Sex. It was just the raw fucking he needed—not me. He fed me all those lies to get me back into bed one last time. Multiple last fucks, I guess.

The door to the hotel room closes with so much ease it pisses me off even more.

How could he?

How does he not feel what I feel? This can't be one-sided. It just can't be. It's too strong.

Spotting my shirt, I yank it off the couch and finish getting dressed. I need out of this room before I choke to death on the smell of us that remains.

My cell phone rings and I almost don't answer it. The only reason I do is because there is always the smallest chance it could be about Gabriel. Grabbing it off the nightstand, I flip the screen to face me, seeing a California number I don't recognize and don't have programmed into my contacts.

"Hello," I greet.

"How much is the boy's life worth to you?"

The voice that's continuously replayed since the day he shot me registers, heating my skin like someone has lit me on fire. Hatred. Disgust. Anger. Every emotion I hold for Sebastian Diaz surfaces at the sound of his thick Spanish accent.

"Anything," I answer without hesitation. He's a monster, even he'd admit that. He's not going to return Gabriel for some minuscule price. He called me, not Drago, or if he did call him first, D might have told him to fuck off. Why can't he believe me? Gabe is his son. That I'm certain of. I should have brought it back up again last night, but I was too consumed by him to even think to do so.

Diaz snickers into the phone, bringing my thoughts back to

the present. Dread washes over me, making me regret my haste words. What if he wants something I can't give him? Money I don't have, although, I'm not above asking my dad in this case. If Sebastian was after cash, he could have just called my father himself. He may be a criminal, but he isn't stupid. He would know by now who my father is and probably who my brother and sister-in-law are. Oh shit, why didn't I think of them before? He could so easily hurt someone I love. No matter how much Jackson thinks he knows where his family is at all times, you can't always protect them from people dead set on harming them.

"Perhaps," he starts, drawing out his words for show. "I wasn't meant to have killed you. After all, you really do have a sweet fucking ass."

Me.

He wants me. Bile rushes up my esophagus, but I take a deep breath, pushing it back down. Not now. I have to hold my shit together and be the strong independent woman I profess to be.

"Nothing to say, cop?" I'm silent, but not because I'm not going to agree to whatever it is he wants. That was decided the minute he implied the offer.

Me for Gabriel.

Is it a hefty price to pay? Sure. But is that going to make me cower? Hell no. His safety is worth my life, or my body in this case—maybe both. I'm not stupid enough to think Diaz will keep me around forever. He'll grow tired of me and then my life will be dispensable.

Once Gabriel is back safe, D will see and eventually accept him as his son. Deep down, Drago is a good man. And family, his father aside, means the world to him. I've seen him with his brother and sister, his niece, Mona, hell even his dogs. Drago has a big heart and a lot of love to give. And love is exactly what Gabriel needs.

"You know I shouldn't want you, you being a pig and all. You people fucking disgust me."

"We disgust you?" I cough.

"Ironic isn't it." He sighs. "So, about that generous offer I've put on the table . . ."

"When and where?"

"Not so fast my soon-to-be little pet." My nose wrinkles at the words that penetrate my ear. "Don't go telling any of your pig buddies, including that DEA fucker you've been tagging along with, or Drago for that matter. That is unless you want me to slit Acerbi's little bastard kid's throat."

I gasp, pulling in air and giving myself away. The images played out so vividly in my mind, I couldn't control my mouth. I want to slap myself for allowing him to hear just how much I'm affected by the thought of harm coming to Gabe.

"So, then it's settled. I tell you where to be and when, you come alone, right, my soon to be personal fucking property?"

I'm going to enjoy putting a bullet through him. And. I. Will. It may not be today or tomorrow, but soon he's going to wish he'd never walked into my apartment.

"I'll come alone," I bite out.

"And you won't say jack-shit to anybody about our deal, or when and where you're going."

"How are we going to make a trade if no one is there to take Drago's son?" I ask, even though I know all of this could go very wrong if I don't tell Eric. I need backup. It's the only way I can ensure Gabriel is released and given to safe arms.

"I'll arrange someone reliable to transport the boy to his father."

"I don't trust you."

"You shouldn't, but in this case, the boy isn't what I want anymore." A faux moan comes through the phone. "My desire to bend a certain cop to my every demand outweighs my use for the kid."

"Just tell me where. I'll come now." I want this over with. I want Gabriel in safe hands, and if that can't be mine, then Drago's it is. It's only right for him to be with his dad, not me.

"Not so fast, whore." I bite the inside of my cheek so that my anger at his word doesn't cause me to ruin any chances of Gabe being rescued. "I have to make sure you'll keep your end of our deal. I'll be in touch."

The call ends before I'm able to press him further.

"Fuck!" I yell, releasing the pent-up frustration and hatred coursing through me.

Closing my eyes, I pull in as much air as my lungs can hold, attempting to gain control. Just a little longer and Gabe will be safe. I force myself to believe my thoughts. I have to, or else I'll break, and that's the last thing I can afford to do. Gabriel needs all of my strength right now and that's exactly what I'll give him.

CHAPTER TWENTY

I sit on the floor of my bedroom only wearing a black bra and matching bikini panties. The sun from the sheer curtains beats down on my back, heating my skin, but it doesn't penetrate past the surface. On the inside, I'm freezing cold—and empty.

It feels like I'm at war with everyone—Drago, my dad, Jackson, my department, Diaz, and myself.

Drago wants me, yet he really doesn't. I won't be a ping-pong ball, bouncing to him when it's convenient for him and then be tossed away when he's done with me. My dad is wrong. Drago didn't give me up to protect me. I'm capable of taking care of myself; I always have been. I can take whatever is thrown at me. If D wanted us together, we'd be together and fight through anything that comes at us. But that isn't the case.

My father admires Drago now. A dry laugh bubbles from my lips as tears simultaneously drop, sliding down my cheeks and onto my thighs where the others have landed since I've been sitting here. My dad despised Drago not that long ago, but now he thinks D did the right thing by walking away from me. Dad doesn't want me to be a part of the Acerbi world or what even being friends with D would bring into my life.

What he doesn't understand, or realize, is that I'm already a part of it. Even if Drago and I never come back together as one, I'm a part of his dangerous life. I deal with the gangs and drugs daily, or at least I did. Now it seems my department is working against me to take that away. Even if I get to keep my job, Tom wants to transfer me. If that happens, it's unlikely I'll land in the same or similar unit.

Maybe I do need to give this mock DEA interview process with Eric consideration. If I become a DEA agent, I'll still be working to help rid our streets of drugs that kill too many kids every year. It's why my role means so much to me. Being a homicide detective helps bring justice to the family of a murdered person. Being in my unit, I'm able to affect the lives of living people.

The image of my brother when he left the other day won't stop plaguing my mind. He's mad and hurt that I didn't turn to him; that I didn't call him when I woke up. And I get it, but at the same time, I had Gabriel's whereabouts front and center to worry about. I couldn't allow what happened to me to step in front of that, so pushing it to the back of my mind was a necessity.

A shudder runs through me. More tears fall, dropping and sliding down my thighs.

More and more it's getting harder to ignore the baby I lost. Why didn't I know? There was a life growing inside of me. Isn't that something a woman should have instincts about? I rely on my instincts daily, so why did they fail me this time? And why does this hurt that lives deep inside me only grow? I thought loss was supposed to ease with each day, not fester.

When does it stop? I want it to stop. I didn't know I was pregnant. I never experienced the shock or joy, so what right do I have to feel this way? Why do I feel lost and messed up in the head over something I didn't know existed until it was stolen from me?

Maybe it doesn't go away. That thought wracks me even more. Maybe this is a hurt that you never recover from. God, I hope not. I don't want to forget. I'm not asking for that, but I do want the holes in my chest to fill. The only way I know to achieve that is to find Gabriel. I'll do anything to find him—anything.

Last night I stalked Chasity's Facebook page. She's a sociable one. Bitter seeps in as I picture her face in my mind.

Connie confirmed for me last night that Chasity was informed of Gabriel's kidnapping the day it happened and she told the officer that Gabe was our problem now. We took him, so he's ours.

I grit my teeth, balling my fists. How did she give birth to him and not feel a thing? I never knew my baby and I'm wracked with too many emotions at once. Sorrow and guilt trumping all of them.

Pushing up from the floor, I force myself to be done with the pity party I'm having. This does nothing to help find Gabriel.

Chasity posted she would be spending the day pampering herself at Serenity, the spa located inside The Cove hotel. So, that's where I plan on being too.

Eric arranged it earlier this morning, ensuring I would be getting a pedicure the exact same time she would. I can't even enjoy the thought of a free Pedi when my mind is focused on pulling information out of her—and I will. If I have to use threats, then so be it. If I have to get physical with her, I will. I meant what I said. I will do anything at this point to find Gabriel.

I have to.

His life is important. He matters and doesn't deserve what was placed on his shoulders. Diaz will go down for using him as a pawn, for kidnapping him. No one has ever been able to pin a drug charge on him, but we can charge him with kidnapping. If found guilty, he would serve time. Although, prison is too good for him, and in my eyes, not justice.

It's hard to come to terms with that thought. I don't believe in the death penalty or killing a person outside of self-defense. Yet, all the anger I hold for Sebastian Diaz that's exactly what I want. But even so, justified murder in one's mind is still murder nonetheless.

I have doubts that I could pull the trigger, ending his life, even if it is what he deserves.

Am I that person?

Can I do it?

Only time will tell.

THUMBING THROUGH A FASHION MAGAZINE, MY TOES SOAK IN THE HOT bubbly water in front of my reclined chair. Supposedly, it's some kind of coconut scent, but I don't smell anything over the heavy chemicals wafting through the air. I usually paint my own toes, not allowing myself to spend money on this luxury. When Alana and I do this, at her treat, I'm able to relax and enjoy the experience.

Today I'm not afforded that familiarity. There will be no relaxation until I've apprehended Sebastian Diaz and I know Gabriel is safe. God, I pray I find him safe and sound. I really don't know how much more of this worry and anxiety I can handle.

If it's this bad and I'm not even his parent, I can't imagine what it must feel like for a real mom or dad to lose their child. Briefly, my mind thinks about the child I did lose, but I keep shoving those thoughts as far back and away from my conscious thought as possible. Now isn't the time, and I'm not sure I want to face those feelings.

Movement to my right gains my attention as someone takes a seat in the chair next to me. I don't need to look at her to know it's Chasity Carlisle. It's already been arranged that she would be seated next to me.

I wait until her feet are soaking in the bubbly water and mine are resting on the platform outside the soaking tub where the pedicurist is filing the bottom of my foot. She's carrying on a conversation with one of her coworkers, not paying their clients any mind. That works out better for me anyway. I don't need or want them to be chatty or hear me speak to Gabriel's mother.

Glancing over, I pretend to be interested in the shade of nail polish Miss Carlisle places down next to the pedicurist station.

"That's a pretty shade. What is it, if you don't mind me asking?"

I smile, keeping half of my face out of her line of sight by letting my dark hair cover the right side of my face.

"We both know you aren't interested in the color of the week I'm getting."

"I'm sorry, what?" She's managed to catch me off guard, and that doesn't settle well with me.

"I'm not that naive. I know who you are, Detective. They'd never allow me to roam the city on my own if I didn't know what you looked like, so I could dodge you should I see you." I see she hasn't lost her condescending voice. Can't say that I've missed it either.

"So then why are you sitting here next to me?" Since she wants to cut to the chase, I see no point in holding back my interrogation. Time is of the essence. If I don't find Gabriel soon, Drago may never see his son again.

"Because I'm tired of being played like some dumb little blonde that doesn't know shit about shit."

"Then tell me where I can find Sebastian Diaz and I'll get out of here and no one will know you've said a word to me."

"You want him or Acerbi's spawn?"

"Did you just refer to your son as a spawn?" The instinct to punch her in the mouth is so natural I don't even feel bad for the thought crossing my mind. I won't do it. I can't afford to. Not only could she press charges for assault. More importantly, she's just let on that she may know where Gabriel is, and if that is the case, I have to remain calm—no matter how hard that is.

"Both," I tell her.

"Which is worth more to you?"

"Miss Carlisle, I'm not here to play games with you. If you know where either or both are, please tell me. I promise to keep you out of it if it leads me to find either one of them."

"Oh!" She laughs, finally cutting her eyes over to me. "You don't actually think I'm scared of you, do you?"

"Frankly, I don't care, but I'd be willing to bet everything I have that you're scared of Diaz. Only someone dumb wouldn't be, and since you've already professed that you *aren't* dumb . . ."

"But," she drawls out, "if you take him out, you'll be solving both of our problems."

"You don't think there is someone waiting to take Diaz's spot once he's arrested?"

"You don't arrest a man like Sebastian Diaz, Detective. You put as many rounds in him as you can and end the problem once and for all. Aren't our prisons overly populated as is? You'd be doing our system a favor by killing Sebastian. Don't you agree?"

"I agree with justice, so unless he does something to warrant being taken down with a bullet, that isn't my plan." The lie comes out smooth on my tongue. I don't need anybody thinking I want to kill the man that's stolen precious things from me. An eye for an eye. That's the way I see it.

"We both know he won't go down without a fight. But I don't know exactly where he is. He isn't exactly known for broadcasting his whereabouts."

I thought she wanted to cut the bullshit and tell me what she knows. But she's toying with me and it's pissing me off.

"If you don't know anything then you aren't of use to me." The first coat of polish is applied to my toes and it's likely when she confirms she's useless, I'll be getting out of here even if the pedicurist is half done. Guilt already eats at me for being in a place like this, getting somewhat pampered when there is a life in danger somewhere out there.

"I never said I didn't know anything. Didn't anyone ever tell you not to assume?"

"Then give me something I can use. Or would you rather me drag you down to the station. You know, Diaz would probably get wind of that before I had you in the back of my car." I'm not above scaring her if it gets me information.

"Sebastian has a fake customs broker where he brings his product in."

"That's impossible. Customs and Border Protection would be all over that."

"Okay," she huffs. "Maybe it's a legit person or business, but it's still a facade for what he uses it for. I've been there. The only people there are the ones that work for Sebastian and that other guy, Brandon, I think."

"Where?" I'm not going to get into the logistics of this. Maybe he's using the spot as entry into the U.S., but it's still farfetched.

"Same place as your boyfriend's shipping company. Just on the opposite side. Port 124 to be exact. Are we done now?"

"You've known where your baby is this whole time and you've allowed him to stay in danger? How do you live with yourself?" I really want to know. I can't fathom being in her shoes and not caring about a life I helped create.

"He's not my baby. I never wanted him. I'm twenty, and at nineteen I was pregnant, because the man I love told me to do so. Only now, I know he doesn't love me back."

"Diaz?"

"No." Her nose scrunches up as her head shakes. "Dylan."

"Your uncle?" I ask for clarification.

She rolls her eyes. "He's my uncle through marriage. There is no DNA connecting us. As if," she adds.

I should leave. She's already told me where Gabriel is. That's exactly what I wanted, so why aren't I out of this chair and on my way to rescue my sweet boy?

Curiosity and a need to know something else.

Drago doesn't know how he created that beautiful boy and she is my only way to find out. I need to get her to tell me for Drago's sake—and maybe mine too.

"Drago doesn't remember sleeping with you? So, tell me. How did you get pregnant by him?"

"Your lover boy was out drinking with that hottie brother of his. He *just* so happened to spot a chick he once dated in high school. Only"—Chasity giggles like what she is telling is funny—"she didn't just so happen to be there. Sebastian arranged it. The piece of trash was so desperate for cash she would have had Drago's baby if she wasn't such a weak little bitch. No way was Sebastian letting someone like her pull off his plan."

Is she fucking kidding me right now? Nothing coming out of her mouth is funny.

"Let me get this straight. You tricked a man into having sex with you in hopes of getting pregnant?"

"Do you know how hard that was to pull off? For a minute, I thought I was going to have to take the sperm in his used condom and figure out a way to get it inside me. I mean, eww, gross. Thank God the drug finally took effect."

"Drug? You drugged Drago?"

"Not me. I just sat on his cock and let him do all the work. It was the other chick he was fucking first that spiked his drink when he wasn't looking. Then when he was going in and out of consciousness, she slid off him, taking the condom with her. And then I took her place. He never knew the difference."

"That's rape," I blurt out. This disgusting piece of garbage raped him.

"Oh, don't give me that self-righteous bullshit. It was me that had to carry a person inside my body for months. More like a lifetime is what it felt like, and my poor body still isn't right. Worst thing I ever did was agreeing to that ordeal."

It's taking everything in me not to hop out of this chair and beat the shit out of her. An ordeal? She calls Gabriel, my sweet boy, an ordeal.

"This has nothing to do with self-righteousness. You took part in drugging someone and then had sex with him without his consent. In what world do you live in to think that isn't rape?"

"Whatever," she says, growing bored. There isn't an ounce of remorse other than the pregnancy she feels screwed up her life. "Good luck proving that. My uncle will squash you before that story sees the light of day."

I have to get out of here before I lose it on her. I should arrest her for her admission, but it would be inadmissible. In this case, it's best that I can't. Her arrest would get to Diaz quicker than I can get to him. And that's not in Gabriel's best interest. So, I summon every ounce of strength I have, slip on the sandals I wore in here and bolt as fast as I can without drawing attention to myself. For all I know, Diaz, or even her uncle, could have her being tailed.

I call Eric as soon as I'm on the road heading toward Gabriel. I know this is it; my one chance to get him back safe and sound. I feel it from somewhere deep inside. I know he'll be there and I won't leave that place alive without him.

No matter what happens, I'll do anything to ensure his safety. I wasn't bluffing when I told Diaz that. I meant it then and I still mean it now.

"I know where Diaz is."

"What?!" I shout, not taking my eyes off the road even though I want to look at my cell phone like it'll show me Eric's face. "How? So do I. I'm heading there now."

"A source just tipped me off. I'm en route too. Where are you?"

"Leaving The Cove. I'm maybe fifteen minutes from there."

"Fuck!" A horn blows, telling me Eric took out his frustration on his steering wheel. "I'm thirty minutes out. You'll beat me there. Wait, Bri. I need you to wait for me. You need backup. I can't allow you to go in there alone."

"Eric, you can't ask me to do that. Gabriel is there. I have to get to him before Diaz finds out I know. Chasity could tell him or anyone connected to him about our conversation. He'll disappear and so will Gabe."

"Don't you fucking disobey an order, Andrews. I'm telling you to wait for me and you'll wait."

"You better drive fast." I hang up, not waiting for his outburst that was sure to follow.

I don't know how I lucked out. Maybe it's God or some other powers that be, but traffic is almost nonexistent and that's unheard of in Los Angeles. I get to the shipping port within ten minutes of squealing my tires out of the hotel parking lot.

I silence my phone before lifting my ass to shove it down into my back pocket. Then I reach behind the passenger seat, grabbing my thigh holster with the Kimber 1911 secured along with the two extra magazines. My .380 is already strapped to my chest, the holster secured to the middle of my bra. Getting out of my car, I shove the spare magazines into the opposite back pocket that my phone is in.

I have no idea what I'm walking into. It's better to be over-prepared than run out of ammo and get myself killed.

CHAPTER TWENTY-ONE

Unlike Drago's shipping warehouse that only has one other business on the same stretch as his, Port 124 is surrounded by five other companies with three on the entrance side and two past Nelson Imports.

Like most businesses here, there is at least one building with bay doors on the front for loading and bay doors on the back for unloading the ships. Bigger companies are spaced out with freight containers. The ones on this stretch, same as Drago's, are smaller with only minimal space. Although there are freight containers, they are all small, creating limited spots to hide. Luckily for me, the business next to Nelson's is bustling today. Hopefully, I can use that to my advantage and go unnoticed while I sneak between the two buildings around the back.

Once I've rounded the back, there is one bay door and it's rolled all the way open, only I don't see any workers—or hear any noise. It's odd, even for lunchtime, as most go in shifts so there are always a handful of workers ready to load and unload. That's the first flag that I'm in the right place and this isn't a legit business. Maybe Chasity's information was accurate. I hope so.

Not wanting to risk getting caught, I don't take any chances by walking inside without a plan. I sneak a peek around the corner inside the large warehouse still seeing no one or hearing anything. There are stacked pallets all over the place. Not wanting to hang around outside and get noticed on camera, I duck in and position myself behind a tall pallet of merchandise.

I wait two minutes, making sure there aren't any noises, but then my heart jumps into my throat and I suck in a breath. *Gabriel.* It has to be him. The sound of a baby crying both thrills me and punches me in the gut at the same time. The what-ifs start flooding my head again—and now isn't the time for them.

I look up, seeing a similar office like Drago's on the second level. And now that I'm taking in the interior more, I realize it's the exact same set up as Acerbi Imports. This could be a good sign. Knowing the layout will help me navigate, but that thought goes to shit when I feel the distinct round metal barrel jab into the back of my skull.

A gun.

Someone has a gun aimed at me—at my head. A normal person would probably shit themselves at this point. I remain calm, straightening my spine. Nothing good ever comes of getting scared.

"You're right on time, cop." Diaz's thick accent assaults my left ear, sickening my stomach when his breath hits my ear. "Hands up. You're a cop, so you should know this drill already."

I raise them slowly, holding them parallel to my head.

How did he see me or know I was here? I saw the cameras outside, every building has them, but I doubt many of them have a person sitting in a room eyeing cameras all day. Maybe Diaz does in case local PD or the Feds get wind of this place and decide to raid it. I should have thought of that. I should have waited for Eric like he instructed. Instead, I have a weapon pointed at the back of my head and a dangerous man with his finger on the trigger.

How am I going to get myself out of this and save Gabriel? He's my first priority.

"You said you wanted me."

"But I hadn't told you when or where, yet." He lowers his face, his nose connecting with my tense skin on my neck. He smells me, making my stomach roll again. "You are mine now, and you're about to get a lesson on what happens when you disobey me," he hammers out. Then teeth sink into my skin between my shoulder and neck. It hurts like a son of a bitch. I don't dare move or breathe, but I have to clench my jaw.

"Walk," he demands.

Moving, I slowly come out from behind the pallet, looking around with my eyes without moving my head. Where was he hiding? How did I not hear his steps?

I drop my arms, contemplating going for my weapon. So many things could go wrong if I do, but then there is a chance I could get it and fire off a shot before he kills me. Either way, the chances are higher I'll die at his hands if I do.

If that happens, where does that leave Gabriel? Diaz could get out of here before Eric arrives.

Fuck, I hope he's bringing backup with him.

He grabs me by the waist, pulling me into his hard chest. "Don't even think about it." He removes his hand from my belly and then presses the gun harder into the base of my skull as he maneuvers his other hand, releasing my holstered weapon and taking it from me.

Thank God he didn't wrap his arm around my chest, or he would have discovered the smaller gun I have concealed under my bra. Even with the fitted shirt I'm wearing, it's still hidden. I just need to make sure it stays that way.

"I don't want to put a bullet in that sexy head of yours before I have the chance to wear out this pussy." He cups me from around my front. I rise up on my tiptoes, trying to get my body away from his filthy hand.

Shoving me with his gun, I'm pushed a step forward, thankfully more inches away from him.

"Over there," he says. My eyes see the metal chair, even though I didn't know where *over there* was. "Go make yourself comfortable."

The cuffs that are already attached to both sides are the first things I notice. This isn't going to be good if I allow myself to be restrained. But then what choice do I have?

So stupid, Bri, is all that keeps going through my mind. I couldn't just wait for Eric like he ordered. I had my eyes on the facility. I could have easily kept a safe distance and waited.

Hurry the hell up, Eric.

I sit, placing my hands in my lap.

"Cuff her," he says over my head.

I don't dare turn my head. The look in his eyes is telling me that's the last move I want to make right now.

It's when the person behind me grabs my second arm, yanking it down and locking the cuff tightly around my wrist that I smell the heavy perfume. The same scent I smelled less than an hour ago when Chasity sat next to me at the nail salon. It was brief, but I remember it.

Shit. I'm a fucking idiot. I fell for her bullshit and look where I am now.

"So much for you being tired of people thinking you're dumb."

"Oh, no." She snickers and then stands. "That part was true. It's just that I'm not dumb enough to cross Sebastian."

"Go handle that crying little bastard. I'm sick of hearing that noise," Diaz orders.

"Why do I have to do it? Don't you pay people to deal with him?" Chasity whines.

I have to bite the inside of my cheek to remain silent.

"Because he's yours. Deal with the problem or I will." She huffs, stalking off.

"I'm curious," I mention, needing to draw him into a conversation to give Eric more time to get here. Hopefully, he already is here and he's out there working out a plan to take Diaz down. At this point, I don't care if it's me or someone else that takes the shot as long as the end result is the same.

I should feel guilty for that thought, but I don't. All I see is hatred and an aching need to end the life of the scumbag that took from Drago and me.

"Fine." He lets out a heavy breath, staring down at me. The gun in his hand hangs down at his side, pointing at the ground. Mine isn't in sight, so it must be tucked into his pants at the back. "I'll entertain one question, cop, but only one."

"If you have access to this port then why do you need Drago?"

Why go to all the trouble with a man that wants nothing to do with this life? If anything, forcing a man like Drago could get him caught or killed. So, why bother?

"Redundancy, of course. And well, even I'm not dumb enough to cross Vincent like your man is."

Vincent Acerbi scares him. I didn't think it was possible to frighten a man like Sebastian Diaz, but apparently it is. What does that say about Drago's father then? Is he still running things from Italy? Drago mentioned those discrepancies in his logs, but with all that's happened, and not happened between us, I don't know if he ever found out what they were. It's possible it could be his father.

"How did Drago cross his father?"

"You talk too much. From here on out, you need to realize that mouth of yours is only for sucking my dick—or screaming." He smiles, but instead of it making him look more appealing, it has the opposite effect. All I see is the evil that resides within those dark eyes. "And there will be a lot of screaming; probably not the good kind you're used to, though."

I picture Drago and me in my mind. He made me scream a lot the other night, all of it so very good. But for whatever his reason, it must not have meant as much to him as our time together did to me. I shove the longing back, not needing it to surface now, or ever, if I can help it.

"What the hell is she doing here?" I turn my head. Houston stands stock still thirty feet away from us. "She's seen me now."

"Calm your shit, or I'll put a bullet through your mouth and do it for you. She"—he steps forward, yanking on my hair and jerking my head backward—"won't ever see the light of day again. She's mine now." Diaz's sardonic laugh rings through my ear. "You get to take credit for finding the kidnapped Acerbi baby. I'm making you a fucking hero, so shut the fuck up, Houston. You should thank me." Diaz steps several feet away from me, taking a tall stance.

He's on guard. Does that mean he doesn't trust Houston? He shouldn't. Dirty cops don't have loyalty. They are only out for themselves.

"I'll thank you when she's dead."

Houston moves forward, walking toward me with purpose. Dread washes over me, knowing he's about to do something I can't do anything to stop.

And I'm right. He smiles down, showing his "I've just won" look before bending and running his hand up my thigh, and then he forces my legs apart. He's stronger than I am, so no matter how hard I try to keep them together, it's no use. He cups me between the legs, squeezing to the point of sheer pain. I gasp, baring my teeth at him.

"Get your hand—" My words are interrupted by the blast of a gunshot. I'm startled at first, not knowing where it came from. Then I see blood pouring out of Lance's shoulder.

"Arghhh," Houston yells out in pain. He turns, facing away from me and revealing another hole with blood streaming out of it. It's the entry wound, making the one on his front side the exit wound. Houston was towering over me, so that shot could have easily hit me in the face had it been a few inches to his left. "What the . . . You shot me, motherfucker," he hisses through his teeth, grabbing his shoulder.

"You, nor anyone else, is allowed to touch my property. She"— he swings the gun, pointing it at me—"is mine. Only I get to touch her unless I want someone else to lay a hand on her. And I can assure you, cop, that isn't you. Touch my shit again and it'll be a bullet between your eyes."

Another blast goes off, but it doesn't come from the gun Sebastian Diaz is waving around. The shot pierces Houston's side, taking him down to the ground. He curses, yelling in pain and agony with an ashen look on his face.

Diaz stills, looking at me for a split second before muttering a curse of his own. Then he turns, running toward the open bay door, escaping

Noooo! He can't get away.

Out of the corner of my eye, I see someone running toward me. That's when I see Drago. He's the one that shot Houston. What is he doing here? How is he here?

Did Diaz set him up to come here too, to walk into a trap like I did?

"Drago?" I yell.

Without saying anything, he falls to his knees beside me. Moments later, both of my wrists are free of restraints and I hop out of the chair, nearly falling over Lance to get away from the spot I was being held captive.

Drago grabs me, pulling me away from Houston's still body.

"What are you doing here?" I can't help but ask.

His fingers thread my hair, cupping the back of my head. Then his lips crash down on mine, taking them in a rushed and panicked state.

"I fucking lost it when that motherfucker touched you. Then when that shot was fired, I thought—"

"D, I'm okay. I'll think about that later. I have to get Diaz before he gets away."

"We," he corrects. "Here. Take this." He produces a Glock from behind his back.

I grab it out of his hand as I step up on my toes, stealing a quick kiss from his lips. I need it like I need air to breathe.

"Come on." The time for questions can wait. I have to stop Diaz before he's gone forever.

I FIND DIAZ HEADING TOWARD THE PIER. DRAGO RACES PAST ME, RUNNING faster with his longer legs.

At first glance, I'm confused. Sebastian stops at the end, but there is nothing there. Is he planning on jumping in? If so, we can't let that happen. Him drowning isn't the way I want to see him die. He deserves so much worse and a lot more pain. I want him to experience the same pain and agony I have.

Yet, I doubt it's possible for a man like Sebastian Diaz to feel any sense of loss or despair. I doubt he even knows the meaning of either of those. He's so used to taking from people that I can't fathom Diaz has had much stripped from him.

Drago is gaining on him when I see him pull out what I'm guessing is a cell phone from the pocket of his pants. Whoever he was contacting, or was doing on the device, is interrupted as D tackles him. They both crash to the ground, but it's Sebastian that's on his feet first.

Diaz produces a handgun, raising it and firing before I can stop in my tracks to aim at him. Without looking, I know Drago's been hit. I'm about to pull the trigger when he turns, sneering at me. A second later he jumps off the pier.

Drago is off the ground in an instant, jumping off after Diaz.

When I get to the end, ready to jump into the water after them, I come to an abrupt stop. It's then it registers that I didn't hear a splash when either of them would have hit the water. Just above the surface of the water is a submarine with the top opened. The opening is large, telling me the vessel below the water isn't a small watercraft, but at the same time can't be huge or even close to the size of military grade.

I have no idea what the depth of the water underneath me is, but in all my time on the police force, I've never seen a submarine up close or even this close to the shore.

Was that what Diaz was doing on his phone? Was he bringing it to the surface to use as his getaway?

Time for questions is later. I have to find them. Drago was shot. Injured, Diaz would have the upper hand, making it easier to kill D.

I hop off the pier, landing four feet below and quickly climb over the open lid and down the ladder. It's dark inside with minimal lighting, but the space is large and filled with things wrapped in plastic wrap. My first thought: drugs. But inspection will have to wait.

I run past the stacked merchandise, or dope, and see Drago and Diaz in a scuffle. They are both taking fists to their faces and ribs, each landing blow after blow to one another. Taking a stance, I aim my weapon, waiting until I'm able to get a clear shot on Diaz before firing. I won't chance hitting D.

"Freeze," I yell, commanding Diaz to stop. Even as I say the words I've been trained to say, I know he's not going to obey my order.

I finally get my opening when a punch to Drago's jaw knocks him to the ground. I pull the trigger as Diaz raises his gun to shoot D. He's already shot him once and I have no idea how bad his wound is; I won't let him get another round off.

My aim is steady, so when I pull my finger slowly back, releasing the round, Diaz goes down before he's able to fire his gun.

I race over to where they both lay on the ground and first kick Diaz's weapon away from him. The pussy is too busy grabbing his leg to have enough sense to go for it. The gun he stole from me is laying closer to Drago, so it must have fallen out of his back pocket during their hand-to-hand combat.

Stepping left, I crouch down, immediately pulling Drago into my arms and guide him as gently as possible until his back is against a wall.

"Please tell me you're okay." I start looking for his gunshot wound to inspect it myself.

"I'm fine," he says through gritted teeth, a hiss following.

"You've been shot. You're not fine." He grabs my hand, squeezing before I can lift his T-shirt.

"It's not as bad as it looks."

"I doubt that. You're covered in blood and you're in a hell of a lot of pain."

"Didn't say it didn't hurt like a motherfucker. But it's just a graze. I'll be fine. Don't you need to call for backup or something?"

"Fuck backup. You need an ambulance."

"You better get backup, bitch," Diaz yells. "Because you're dead. Fucking dead, you hear me."

I jump to my feet, walking back over to where he's lying.

"I'm dead?" I question. "From the looks of it, you're the one that should be worrying."

Without thought, I raise my handgun, aiming it at his head. Just a pull of my finger and he'd be no more. Prison is too good for him. This vile human doesn't deserve the breath he's taking right now. He tried to kill me. He stole Drago's son. He murdered my unborn child. It's only fair I send him to Hell, where if there is justice, he'll burn in sheer agony for the rest of eternity.

"Bri," Drago calls out my name, halting me. "Don't. This isn't you. You're a good cop. You can't shoot him."

"He deserves to die."

"I know. And I agree with you, but that still doesn't make it right. You'd lose your job and face criminal action for shooting him like that."

"You going to listen to him?" Diaz laughs. "You don't have it in you to pull that trigger, pig."

"No one else has to know," I say to Drago, ignoring Diaz.

"You would know, and it would eat at you. You know I'm right, baby. Lower your gun."

"He killed—" I can't even say it without getting choked up. My father is right. I have to face this eventually or it could very well break me like it did my mom. I think I'm starting to understand that now. It doesn't matter how strong I am physically or mentally; there are still things that can bring down the strongest person.

"And he'll pay." Drago's words are a promise. "He did, but Gabriel is here. Please go find my son, Bri. Save him."

That stops me. I lower my weapon to my side, cutting my eyes to see D is holding his side. Worry seeps into my bones at the sight of slick liquid coating his entire hand in red.

"You believe he's yours?"

"That's for a later discussion, just please go find him."

As much as I don't want to leave Drago hurt, I do need to find Gabriel. Chasity has likely heard all the shots fired, so who knows if she and Gabriel are even still here. Knowing her though, she probably left him scared and alone and hightailed it out of here.

I'm coming for you sweet, boy. I will find you. God help anyone that gets in my way.

SIRENS ARE THE FIRST THING I HEAR WHEN I CLIMB BACK ONTO THE PIER. I hope like hell one of them is an ambulance. No matter what Drago said, he's badly injured and needs emergency medical attention. Gabriel first, and then I'll get him the help he requires.

I take off running faster than I've ever run before. I haul ass like a life depends on it, and it does—more than one depends on me.

Entering the warehouse, I scan the interior, noting Lance isn't where he had laid motionless when I left. *No Houston.* He could have possibly got away. No matter what, I saw him. If he isn't dead, a warrant for his arrest will be issued before the day is out. I'll make sure of it one way or another. Plus, he'll need medical attention after being shot, so either way, I'll get him. I know I will.

I run up the metal stairs, entering the only office on this level to stop dead in my tracks.

Eric is holding Gabriel, bundled into his arms and is staring intently down at the boy in his arms. A boy I feared I'd never see again. Eric's head lifts, his intense eyes meeting mine.

"You found him."

"No," I counter. "Apparently you did."

His lips tip up. "You got here first. Disobeyed my orders and got yourself caught. You could have—"

"How did you know that?" I step forward, not able to remain at a distance now that I have my sights finally on Gabe.

"Doesn't matter," he breathes, meeting me as he takes a step toward me. "You want him?"

I don't argue. I've waited long enough for this moment. My anxiety won't be uncoiled until he's safe in my arms. When I take him, it's like I can finally fill my lungs once again.

"Where's his mother? She was here. She set me up."

"She isn't his mother, but that bitch is currently in a patrol car being carted off to jail as we speak."

"Drago's been hurt. Diaz shot him."

Before I can tell Eric to call for help, he sidesteps me. The metal stairs clank at the force of his feet running down the stairs. I know I should be following him. I need to make sure D is okay and Diaz is cuffed. I don't care that he's injured. Cuffs will be around his wrists before he leaves here if I have to put them on him myself.

He has people everywhere. Once he's carted off in an ambulance, he could disappear before he ever reaches the hospital. No. I can't allow that to happen. I have to see him there and stay until he's taken and booked. But I don't want to hand this little guy over to anyone. I don't want him to leave my arms.

His eyes flutter, as if he's trying so hard not to fall asleep. My mind runs away for the millionth time, wondering how he's been cared for in the last few weeks. He doesn't look malnourished, but looks can always be deceiving.

Connie. I'll call my partner. Even if she isn't technically still my partner, that's the place she'll always have in my mind. She can make sure he's checked over at the hospital while I'm ensuring Diaz stays under arrest.

I take the stairs slower than Eric, not wanting to jar Gabriel.

Once I walk out the bay door, I see Drago limping toward me with Eric beside him. I quicken my pace until I reach D.

Drago eyes Gabriel before taking his son into his arms, bringing him to his chest, fusing the little guy to his own body. Looking down, he watches his son as I stand frozen in place watching D's eyes. Emotions, too many to decipher between, pass through him.

He really does believe Gabriel is his. I see it clearly, but then I see so much more than just the recognition in Drago's eyes.

"D," I whisper. "He's safe now."

Drago's dark gaze snaps to mine. It's then my chest is pierced yet again with a shattering ache. Liquid pools in D's lower lids, threatening to spill over.

I'm about to step forward to embrace him, to comfort him, to love him—but that attempt is killed before I'm able to make a move. Gabriel is thrust back into my arms so abruptly I stagger backward with him.

"Take him." There is a strain in Drago's voice and I know from looking at him that he's barely holding himself together.

But why?

His son is safe now.

Gabe whimpers from the sudden movements, so I quickly tighten my hold on him, not taking my eyes off his dad as he retreats away from us.

"D," I call out, not understanding why he's slowly stepping away.

His eyes are on Gabe and with each step, worry starts to seep into my skin, taking root in my bones. When his head starts to turn from side to side even slower than his steps, alarms start to sound off in my head.

"Drago," I say a little louder, hoping to get his attention. It doesn't work. "Drago," I bark, making the baby wail. Anger starts to present itself in my chest.

"No." He holds up his palm, stopping me when I start in his direction. "No, Bri. Stay where you are."

"What are you doing?"

Where is he going? He can't possibly be leaving after his son has just been found. We don't even know if he's okay. He's been gone almost three weeks. Anything could have been done to him in that time.

Gabriel starts crying and I know he's sensing something is wrong.

I might not have killed Diaz like I thought I wanted to, but at this rate, I'm going to murder D before all of this is said and done.

"It's okay, little man. You're safe now." I pull him tighter against my chest. I'll have to worry about his father later. I need to get Gabriel to the ER and have him checked over. Until that's done, I can't think about anything else. I thought I could let Connie do it, but now that he's back in my arms, I'm not releasing him unless I'm forced to do so. And even then, it'll be a fight to pry him from my arms.

"Diaz is dead." Eric's words penetrate my ears as he steps in front of me.

It was only a shot to the leg. No way he had time to bleed out so . . . *Drago*. His promise that Diaz would pay pierces my thoughts. He killed him. All that talk about it being wrong if I had done it, and what did he do?

"I can't deal with that right now, Alders." I shake my head. "He's more important," I say matter of fact before stepping around him, leaving the scene.

CHAPTER TWENTY-TWO

Where the hell is he?

I eye the back of the courtroom for the twentieth time in the last ten minutes. Gabriel's case is up next on the judge's docket and Drago should have been here by now. It's been five long weeks since I've seen either of them—and every second has been hell.

After Drago left, I took Gabriel straight to the Emergency Room where he was deemed in good health. It was a welcomed surprise and a relief until Judy Hearn showed up with a judge signed court order issuing custody to her department.

I almost lost my shit right there in the hospital. There is nowhere safer for Gabriel to be than with me. Apparently, she felt differently after he'd been kidnapped from my care, and now that any threats have been squashed, she was okay assigning his care to a real foster family.

From a dependable source inside her department, I know he's already been moved twice because the families couldn't deal with his excessive crying. Can you blame him? He's been tossed around like a sack of potatoes without anyone doing what was in his best interest.

I know I'm not his biological parent; I don't pretend to be. If it were anything like those first few nights in my care, I know it was hard, but I'd finally got him settled into a routine when I had him. With my sister-in-law's help, I found a routine that worked, and I spent time with him, getting him used to me. I miss how he used to fall asleep so easily when his little bare chest would be snuggled against mine. He was at ease, and so was I. I didn't realize that until he was taken.

Jackson and Alana don't understand why I'm here today. It was necessary. There was no way in hell I wouldn't be seated where I am right now. Which was why I didn't ask them to help with my backup plan. My dad, on the other hand, came through for me big time, and I can't thank him enough for seeing this through my eyes even if he doesn't agree with me.

No matter how much I'd love to be Gabriel's mother, I'm still rooting for Drago to walk in here and accept responsibility for him as he would if Gabriel had been planned all along.

Speaking of . . .

I suck in air the moment he pushes through the double doors of the courtroom. Our eyes lock almost immediately. For a split second, my heart soars—only to come crashing down to the ground when he diverts his stare. He goes so far out of his way not to look at me that he turns, walking around the last pew to the other side of the wall before finding a seat in the first row.

Does he not even want to be near me?

I shouldn't be surprised. He hasn't accepted any of my calls, and not wanting to make a fool of myself, I haven't shown up at his work or house to confront him, even though that's exactly what I've wanted to do since he walked away from us. I want answers. I deserve them.

"Docket number 20045," the judge reads from the piece of paper he's holding before looking up. "The custody of Gabriel Acerbi is to be determined. Are all parties here?"

A man seated next to Drago rises, buttoning his suit jacket. "Everyone is here, your honor."

His head twists, eyeing me as if to ensure I'm still here. I'm guessing he's Drago's attorney. I did catch him looking at me a couple of times before D showed up, but I hadn't thought anything of it. It's not like I'm foreign to this court. I've been in this room plenty of times previous to today when I had to testify against the defense.

"From my understanding, the child's mother is out on bail pending trial for accessory to kidnapping?" The judge looks to the lady sitting at a table off to the side. I recognize her but hadn't noticed her sitting there before. She must have slipped in the side door when I was watching Drago enter. She works for Judy Hearn; one of her caseworkers and must be the one assigned to Gabe.

"That's correct, your honor."

"And the child's father?" The judge looks directly at D or his attorney.

"He's here. My client wishes to waive all rights to the child."

I gasp, not actually expecting that declaration. No! He can't. He wouldn't. *Would he?*

"Mr. Acerbi," the judge says. "Please rise and tell me why it is that you do not want to take responsibility for a child you helped create. Explain that to me," he orders. The judge crosses his arms over his chest, leaning back into his seat as he waits.

Drago stands, but there are several beats before he starts to speak.

"Your honor," he addresses the judge. "I'm sure you know where I got my last name from."

My eyes cut back to the judge who remains expressionless. He's not denying or confirming. He's probably questioning how that is relevant, same as I'm doing.

"One could say bearing the same last name as me, could very well put him in more danger than he was when he was kidnapped. I don't think it's in his best interest to come home with me."

"Have you thought this over fully, Mr. Acerbi?"

"Yes, your honor, I have."

"Do you want to think it over some more?" the judge asks, giving Drago another chance to take his request back.

Take it back, D, I will him, my eyes boring into the back of his head. Take it the fuck back! It was a mistake, even the judge knows that, so why is he remaining silent. Take it back, dammit.

"No, your honor." Drago's words come out harsh and I know he said them through clenched teeth.

"Mr. Lawrence, is your client of sound mind in your opinion?"

Drago's lawyer looks to his right. I can't see his face to know what he's saying, if anything, and it pisses me off.

Don't do this, Drago. Don't give up on Gabriel like this. Just don't, my thoughts silently plea, begging him even though he's not looking in my direction.

"Yes, your honor, he is."

It's then that Drago turns his head, looking behind his lawyer's head, finding my gaze. I want to punch him in the face until our eyes lock and I see devastation staring back at me. It's the plea in them that I don't understand at first. He's silently begging something of me, but what?

Instincts are urging me to go to him, and then I remember he's just given up all of his rights to his son and the same anger that manifested when Drago walked away from us reappears.

"It seems neither parent is fit or doesn't want the hardship of raising a child, so where does that leave us?" he addresses the social worker again, and I'm not surprised at the judge's brass jab at D's expense. Although Drago doesn't seem to be paying him any attention, his eyes are still locked on mine, begging me.

My thoughts and gaze are cut off when my father's lawyer stands, stealing my attention. Patrick places one hand over his wrist on his opposite arm. "Your honor, if I may have the floor?"

"Mr. Camden," the judge draws out. "What business do you have with this case?"

"My client, here"—he turns slightly, nodding his head down in my direction—"wishes to petition the court for sole custody of Gabriel Acerbi, seeing how he doesn't have another relative here requesting custody."

I take a steady breath, trying to calm myself.

That's it? Drago isn't going to fight for his son. He doesn't want him.

I watch him leave, my eyes never leaving his body until he's slipped out the door.

How can this be happening right now?

HE'S MINE. MAYBE NOT OFFICIALLY YET, BUT LEGALLY GABRIEL HAS NOW been awarded to me, pending my petition. The judge wants to make sure I'm a good fit and there aren't any relatives hiding in the woodwork that would be better than me.

No one is better qualified than me. That's not being presumptuous. I know in my heart of hearts that I can care for him better than anyone. I didn't believe that when I had hopes that he would leave the courthouse with Drago, but being how the cards fell, I do now.

Petitioning the court for custody was only my backup plan if Drago didn't step up to his role as Gabriel's father. Hearing him denounce his rights to his son broke something inside my chest loose.

How could he do it? How could those words leave his mouth? How could he not want Gabriel no matter the cost?

I know he wasn't conceived out of love. He wasn't planned, yet, even I realize sometimes the paths we don't see for ourselves are often the best things that can come along. I never planned to fall in love with a child whose genetic makeup wasn't part of my own, but I did, and I don't regret one single second of it.

I call bullshit that Drago isn't better equipped at protecting him. He's kept his brother and sister out of their father's world. I have no doubt that he could do the same where Gabe is concerned.

"So, why didn't he?"

That question dies on my tongue when the alarm app on my cell phone goes off.

The social worker, apprehensive that it would be me leaving here with Gabriel instead of his father, told me to meet her on the steps outside the courthouse in fifteen minutes and Gabriel would be waiting. That was ten minutes ago and I won't be late to get him.

I close my eyes and breathe a long breath of air inside the bathroom stall I've been in for over five minutes.

Upon opening them back up, I pick up the stick that's been sitting on top of the used sanitary trash bin hanging on the wall.

Positive.

CHAPTER TWENTY-THREE

I'm pissed.

Beyond pissed off at him.

So pissed off I could rip off the muscle between his legs that I like so much and beat him black and blue with it. I can't fucking believe he showed up, denouncing his rights to Gabriel. Who the fuck does that? Shitty fucking people—that's who.

I really thought I knew him. I thought he cared for his family. Fuck, he acted like Luca and Caprice mean everything to him. *But not Gabriel?* Not his son?

I'm at a loss here. I don't understand, and because I don't get it, anger sweeps in, violently pelting my chest. I want to scream at the top of my lungs. I want to hit something—or someone preferably.

Turning into the driveway, I catch a glimpse of an SUV heading my way. Since I've been in it more than my own car lately,

I recognize it immediately. A strange sensation washes over the top of my head and down the back of my neck.

Eric.

What's he doing here?

I slow, watching his eyes track mine as he passes me, leaving Drago's house.

He has no reason to be here. Diaz is dead. Houston will eventually go to trial for his part in all of it. Lance was the first person Eric found when he arrived. Houston hadn't gotten away, but he was injured pretty badly. For weeks, we didn't know if he would pull through. Guess the bastard is tough and, in this case, I'm glad he didn't die. I look forward to seeing him tried and convicted, knowing the things that happen to cops in prison. That'll be sweet, dirty justice in itself.

Alder's said it himself, the case is done, ended with Diaz and Houston. We don't have anything substantial on Vincent, D's father, and with him not on U.S. soil, we're dead in the water, so why was Eric here?

Pulling my car in directly behind Drago's Bugatti, I stop abruptly, shutting the engine off, and then I hop out without grabbing my keys. I doubt I'll be here long. I only came to give him a piece of my mind. He disappeared just as quickly as he showed up in that courtroom.

Standing next to my car, I inhale, taking a calming breath before opening the rear door.

Reaching inside, I press the release on Gabe's car seat and lug it and him out. He's sleeping, thank God. I've had the hardest twelve hours of my life since the judge awarded him to my care. I hate it's not official and who knows how long it'll take to officially adopt him.

It's something I don't want to think about right now.

I'm here for one reason and one reason only. Although, he is going to tell me why Eric was here before I leave.

With the garage door open, I decide to enter through there, rounding D's car instead of going to the front of the house. Chances are, the door will be unlocked here versus going to the front. Catching him off guard is my plan. I won't be turned away before I'm inside. I won't give him the chance or the choice not to hear me out.

We're over. Fine.

Eventually, I'll accept that and move on. But not before he acknowledges his son and gives me an explanation as to why he doesn't want him. Not all babies are conceived out of love. That doesn't mean they don't deserve just as much love as the one that was planned and wanted from the beginning. All babies are precious and a gift to be cherished.

So why doesn't he?! That question makes my blood boil just beneath the surface of my skin.

I wrap my fingers around the knob and twist. I luck out, finding the door unlocked, so I push it open, entering through the mudroom. The kitchen is just past the utility room and that's where I place Gabriel down on the dark, hardwood flooring next to the stools.

When I exit the open kitchen, I see Drago slumped back into the couch with a glass in his hand.

"Are you kidding me?" The words fall from my lips. *He's*

drinking? He's seriously drinking right now? I can't believe this, but I guess I shouldn't be surprised. Give up your son—let's celebrate. Why the fuck not!

"Why are you here?" His voice is laced with surprise as his wide eyes take me in.

"You're getting drunk. That's just perfect. Way to end the day on a high note."

"I'm not drunk. I wish I were fucking drunk. Drunk would be better than the state I'm in now."

He looks like hell. As I step closer, I drink in his appearance. His hair is even longer on top and disheveled like he's been yanking on it out of frustration. Maybe giving up his son wasn't a walk in the park for him like I thought. Still . . .

"You killed Diaz, I didn't say shit. I let it go because he deserved that bullet in his head. You don't want to be with me, okay fine, I'll even deal with that. But giving up your son, no, Drago, I won't let that go. I won't deal with that." I throw my hands into the air. "I saw you today. It killed you to say those words to the judge. So why? Why did you do it?" I implore him to give me an answer— any answer.

"Because I had to," he bites out.

He blows out a breath. Sitting up, he places his glass of whiskey on the coffee table in front of him, shoving it away.

I expect him to say something more, to explain, but he doesn't. He just sits there with his elbows on his knees staring off into space.

I came here for answers and answers I intend to get.

My eyes cut down, looking at the mess strewn out everywhere.

Manila folders are open with papers spilling out; some almost falling off the coffee table.

Before I start to question the mess laying in front of Drago, Gabe makes a sound from where I left him on the floor in the kitchen.

"He's here?" Drago jumps to his feet. He doesn't wait for a response.

I turn, watching him walk over to where he's strapped into his car seat carrier.

"Well, I didn't exactly have anyone to leave him with, you know. My friends and family aren't thrilled with me right now."

I can't ask Connie. Even though she's tried to be supportive in theory, she doesn't like that I took on the responsibility of another person when he isn't mine. She doesn't get it. Alana and Jackson don't get it. My father will probably never understand, even if he's the reason I was able to get temporary custody of Gabriel today. As much as he dislikes the idea, he's been the most supportive person about this. No way in hell I would have asked him though.

Gabriel and I may not share DNA like he and Drago, but I do love him, fiercely, like he is my son. *Why doesn't D feel this way too?* I don't get it. I need him to make me understand.

Looking down again, I see something that I hadn't noticed before. A chain, half-hidden under papers. I reach for it, picking it up, and when I open my hand, I find myself staring at a neck-chain badge holder with an unmistakable gold piece that reads: Department of Justice on the top and then Drug Enforcement Administration US Special Agent.

Why would Drago have someone's DEA badge in his

possession?

Chills roll down my spine as I flip it over.

I gasp, seeing Drago's picture and badge number.

It's his?

"Bri," he calls my name from behind me.

Turning around slowly, I face him, and if it were any other time, I might swoon at the sight of Gabriel clutched to his chest with his arms wrapped tightly around his son.

"Is this real?" I hold out my palm, opening it for him to see. I already knew it was before I even asked. I know a real badge when I see one.

Drago's eyes leave mine to look down. He's silent, not saying a word—not confirming or denying anything. He's in deep thought, though. I can see the wheels turning as I look at him.

I'll be damned if he gives me some bullshit explanation, so before he speaks, I open my mouth, demanding the truth. "Answer me. Answer me now!"

He bypasses me, taking Gabriel to the couch where he sits down with him. Drago keeps his eyes downcast, watching the baby whose eyes are closed, sleeping.

"I've been undercover for seven years." He keeps looking at Gabriel, not once lifting his eyes. "I've had enough to take down Diaz and his whole crew for a long time—but he wasn't the one I wanted. I want my father. I wanted to be the one to put that son of a bitch away. And I want to look him in the eyes so he knows it is me that took him down."

He finally looks up. Sighing, he relaxes his back into the couch. "Why didn't you tell me?"

"Same reason you didn't tell me about him," he nods. "I couldn't. I couldn't risk fucking up. But I did. I still managed to fuck up and I don't even know how it happened. How he happened."

"You were drugged. Chasity admitted her uncle told her to do it. Someone wanted this to happen to use him over your head. Diaz, I guess. She isn't speaking from what I'm told."

"Fucking bitch." He shakes his head. "Who goes along with something like that?"

"Someone who thinks she's in love with Dylan Harper, apparently." I don't want to talk about Chasity. If I never heard her name again, I wouldn't complain.

A grunt comes from D's lips.

"You're really a cop?" I question him, even though he's already confirmed it. Drago nods, watching his son, running his fingers over his smooth baby skin. "Is that why Eric was here? Did he know?"

If that bastard knew and kept it from me, I swear to God—

"E is my best friend . . . and partner." He lifts his head, eyeing me wearily.

I huff out a breath of air. *That motherfucker* I scream in my head. He's going to hear it from me the next time I see him. I bet Justin knew too. Who else knew I wonder? Who else was laughing at me?

"You still haven't explained why you did what you did today." I am dead set on answers. He's not getting out of this, cop or not.

"I had no choice. I can't risk my father finding out about him."

"Who's to say he doesn't already know?" Hell, who's to say he wasn't a part of it all along? He has the most to gain from trapping

Drago.

"I can't. But if I make it look like I don't care and don't want him, then he's safe. You're safe if my father thinks I don't want you. At least until I can bring him down for the crimes I know he masterminded."

"That's your excuse!" I berate. "You think walking out of our lives somehow keeps us safe?" I give him time to formulate another answer. "How dare you. How fucking dare you decide that without me! Did it ever occur to you that I'd rather chance you in my life than spend a minute without you?"

I'm beyond mad at him right now. This is so much worse than thinking he didn't want me as his girlfriend. This is worse than thinking he didn't want his son. This is downright stupid. Sure, maybe someone else would see the nobleness in it, but I don't. Anything that keeps him away isn't noble. Maybe it's harder having us both in his life, but I'd like to think it would be worth it. It would be worth it to me.

"Well, I guess it doesn't matter now. Does it?"

"Yeah?" I bite out. "Why is that?"

"Because I don't think I can do it again." His voice breaks and then he turns his head. Red-rimmed eyes meet mine and I almost choke. "I don't think I can give either of you up ever again."

I'd laugh if his words weren't damn near bringing me to tears with false hope.

"Why should I believe you? You've walked away more than once already. How do I know you won't do it again when you think one of us is in danger?"

"Because it broke me a little more each time I did it. Because

I can't go through that again. And . . ." He swallows, anxiety thick in his eyes. "Because I love you, Bri."

"You what?"

Did I hear him right? Did he just admit he loves me?

"I love you."

I lose it. Tears tip over my eyelids, running down my face. I'd blame it on the pregnancy hormones, but I've cried more in the last three weeks than I have in my life combined.

"Baby, we need to talk more. There is a lot I have to say and make up for, but let's put him in bed first. I'm sure he's had a long day. I know I have. It's not right to keep him up when he should be resting."

"Where is he going to sleep?"

"Mia has always stayed here off and on. The crib she used to sleep in is still in Luca's old room. He can sleep there."

I nod, agreeing, because Drago's right about one thing: we do have something to talk about. *A big something to talk about.*

"WHERE ARE THE DOGS?" I ASK WHEN HE WALKS INTO HIS BEDROOM.

"At Luca's. I asked him to take them earlier. I wasn't up for taking care of them. I'd just given my son up and knew you'd never forgive me. I just wanted to be alone."

"You can't leave me again, D. I won't go through that hell again. If you aren't completely sure, tell me now."

I'm pulled into his arms before that last sentence is completely off my tongue.

"I'm done walking this path without you. I'm done keeping you in the dark. I won't ever make a decision that'll affect the three of us without you ever again."

"The four of us," I correct, and then bite my lip as I anxiously peer up at him.

"Four? What are you—" his question comes to an abrupt stop.

"I'm pregnant."

It's as if all the air left the room. It's deathly silent, and then a tear leaks out of Drago's eye, cascading down his cheek before his lips crash into mine, uniting us in a way that tells me he does want us—all three of us.

With both of his hands, he cups my ass, hoisting me up his front until my legs are wrapped around his waist. My mind protests, urging me to make him sign a blood oath or something drastic so that I'm certain he'll never put me through that hell again. But my heart wants this; needs this. And my instincts tell me he was truthful when he told me he loves me and won't walk away again. I do believe him, but it's hard to trust someone when you feel so betrayed by their actions.

He carries me over to the bed, not releasing me as he lays me down with himself on top of me. Drago is so much bigger than me, yet his weight is a blessed welcome. The covers smell like him, which I love, but my soul yearns for them to smell like us. I want to be here with him, yet I know if this is going to work, we have to take things slow.

"D," I say breathlessly as I tear my lips away from his. "We need to—"

It's as if he already knows where my mind is going.

"Slow has never been our strong suit, Bri. I had you in bed within a week of meeting you. I wanted to fuck you in my office that first day. Hell, I wanted to shove my dick in you the minute you stepped out of your car. Slow isn't us, baby."

My heart knows he's right, but my brain isn't on the same page, which is why I turn my head, looking away from him. Those deep brown eyes cloud up my thinking. They have the power to bend me to his will and I don't think he realizes that yet.

"You're fighting yourself," he says, calling it out like it is. His fingers gently press into my jaw on both sides, pulling my eyes back to meet his. "We're a foregone conclusion. Neither of us could stop this from happening. We weren't meant to, Bri. Tell me you love me or I'm going to fuck my love into you."

He smiles that infectious, playful grin that always makes me tip my lips up.

"I do love you, D." A laugh escapes my mouth, fanning his face. "But maybe I want you to fuck your love into me anyway."

He's off my chest in an instant, pushing to his knees where he sheds his dress shirt and pants. I go to unbutton mine, but he pushes my hands out of the way, taking the reins.

"Ditch the shirt, baby. This is going to be hard and fast. I'll make love to you later to make up for it, because right now I need inside this sexy-as-fuck body."

"You have a lot to repent for, Acerbi," I tell him as I pull my blouse over my head. "But fucking me wildly isn't one of them. I want this just as much as you do."

He yanks the cups of my bra down, exposing my breasts. My

panties are pulled from my body and in the next second, he's sliding inside my slick opening. I'm so ready for him, for us, that there's no need to prime me. It seems I'm always ready to accept him and that's the way it should be. We're meant to be. Drago was right about that. Nothing short of death could keep us apart.

"Jesus," he breathes out as he comes back down to my level on the bed. "I love your pussy, baby. Have I ever told you that?"

"I've never questioned that, D. Now move."

He bruises my lips with his, owning them. Rising off me, he pulls my legs up parallel to his chest and wraps an arm around them. Then slowly he retreats out of me, but he's back inside in an instant. The brute force yanks a moan from my lips.

"Yes," I cry out. This is exactly what I need. He's exactly what I need; the only man I'll ever need. Tiring of him is impossible. "Again," I demand.

"How much do you love my dick?" He pulls out slowly again and it's maddening torture on my psyche and my body.

"I love your dick so much, now move!"

His smile is wicked, but I love that too. That smile is a promise of a fast orgasm and one I need right now.

Tightening his grip around my legs, he reaches down with his free hand, where his thumb finds my clit. In the next instant, he's moving so fast inside me I'm clueless where he ends and I begin. We're one and it's the best feeling in the world.

Like lightning, my orgasm explodes at the first crack of thunder that is his cock and I ride shock after shock that attacks me, welcoming every sizzle. Drago squeezes my legs, following me as his cum coats my insides.

"Fuck," he finally says, dropping my legs. "That didn't last long, but it sure felt fucking great."

He falls down onto his forearms, caging me before rolling off and taking me with him.

"Babe," I call out after the hum inside me settles a few minutes later.

"Yeah?"

"Logically, how is this going to work? I'm guessing you're still hell-bent on taking your dad down."

"I'll never be able to stop until he's behind bars, Bri. I want this, us, our family, but he has to be brought down, or you and our kids will never be safe."

I smile against his chest. *Our kids.* I love the way that sounds coming off his tongue. It both soothes my heart and ignites my soul. We are a family. And one way or another, we will make this work and be happy.

"Then we take him down together."

His body tenses and I know his first instincts are to object, but Drago surprises me. "Okay, Detective. We do it together."

"Just right after I beat Eric's ass."

D bellows, laughing so loud Gabriel's cries from down the hall ring out the next second.

"Whatever you need, baby."

He slides out from under me and gets up to get Gabe without me having to ask. He does want this. That I'm sure of and my heart soars higher than it ever has. I want this too; every single second we're given.

Tomorrow we can make a plan that'll bring Vincent Acerbi to

his knees for all his past and present sins. Tonight, we're going to enjoy our newly fused family.

When D returns, I've cleaned myself the best I can for now, stole a T-shirt from his closet and slid my panties back on. The bed dips as he brings Gabriel to lay between us. The last thing I remember before sleep overtakes me is thinking this is what bliss feels like.

THANK YOU FOR READING.

Bri and Drago's story concludes in DIRTY SIN, which is available . *Continue reading for a bonus scene from Drago's POV!*

BONUS SCENE

DRAGO

I wait until Bri's footsteps fade, and when the only sound that remains is Sebastian Diaz's heavy breaths masking my own labored breathes, I'm certain she's climbed out of the submarine. A submarine for fuck's sake.

It's something I never would have expected—but should have. I'd like to think I'm a smart man. Everything I've done since I was nineteen-years-old has been calculated. Every move I've made was for a purpose: to bring my father to his knees.

So how the fuck did I miss this detail? How did I not know Diaz was bringing his product in through another source here at the same shipping port I'm at day after day?

Looking across from me, I train my eyes on Diaz. He's slumped against the wall of the vessel he fell against when my girl shot him in the thigh. Motherfucker is lucky she didn't hit an artery—lucky for her and I. She doesn't need his death on her conscience. Regardless of how she thinks she feels now, I know from experience that shit will eat at your soul and leave you branded with nightmares night after night.

I could never allow that darkness to seep into her pure heart. Seeing her wrestling with that demon would be worse than the guilt that has swamped me since the day I took an innocent life. The day my father turned me into a murderer just like him.

I cup my hand over my abdomen on my right side. It's more than a flesh wound like I told Bri. I won't die though—at least not yet.

I had to get her to leave. If she had known I'm hurt worse than I led her to believe—or that there is a possibility I could die—she wouldn't have left my side. She doesn't think clearly when it comes to those she cares about; those she loves. I needed her to save my son. Gabriel. It's still surreal that I have a kid and he's as much Bri's as he is my flesh and blood.

When Eric told me the DNA test was legit, I had a hard time believing it. I have no recollection how it's even feasible. Could the bitch have stolen my jizz? Is that even possible? I guess if I have a child with a woman I've never fucked then anything is possible.

Even though Bri kept Gabriel's real identify from me, I get it. I'm a cop and only four other people aside from me knows my secret. I understand she didn't have a choice, even though I felt betrayed when the truth came out.

Staying away from her these last few weeks have been agony, but it also gave me clarity in more ways than I've yet to admit out loud.

She isn't perfect, but she is perfect for me. I think I've known that from the moment I laid eyes on her through the surveillance camera I have attached to the building across from mine. She's shit at undercover work. I don't know if she knows that, but it's the truth. Still, there has never been a more beautiful, intelligent woman I've met that's captured my attention like she has.

She would have been a good mother to the baby that was stolen from us at the hands of Diaz, and she will be a great mother to Gabriel. That is if he's okay. Bri will find him, that I'm sure of. She's fierce and my boy needs her more than he needs me.

Bri needs him too. I know that like I know what I have to do right here, right now.

It has to be done.

It will be done.

"Fuck you, Acerbi." Blood pools around him from the hole Bri left in his body. It's not even a bad wound. The bastard won't die from it. There's blood oozing out of his nose and from his busted lip from our fight. "You let that bitch cop fuck everything up."

I need to speed my role if I'm going to finish this. No doubt my woman not only called in backup to arrest Diaz but also an ambulance for me.

Planting my palms on the concrete floor under me, I force myself to stand, gritting my teeth through the pain slashing through my system with every move I make. Burning fire licks at the entry and exit points where Diaz's bullet went through me.

My eyes blur for a brief second or maybe more. I've never felt weakness like this before.

Bracing my bloody hand on the wall to my left, I steady myself.

Finally, when my equilibrium returns, I push off, taking a step toward Diaz, but not so close that he could easily reach out and grab me. I stare down at him, allowing the hate I feel for this sick, twisted fuck to surface. Reaching underneath my T-shirt, I pull out the holstered gun I have secured to my hip.

"You stole my son. A son I didn't partake in making. A son you made sure I had for your own sick itinerary." My voice is eerily calm, not matching the heat boiling inside me. "You tried to kill my woman. You knew she was mine, yet you were going to take her too," I voice louder, raising the weapon in my hand, aiming it at Diaz's head.

"You chose that filthy cop over duty. Over family." He spits blood in my direction, but it doesn't reach me. "Over business," he snarls. "Which is why Vincent wanted to teach you a lesson."

My eyes widen, caught off guard to school my features before he notices my reaction.

"That's right, motherfucker. It was your own blood that ordered the hit on your bitch and to take that bastard kid. I was just following orders. Unlike you, I know when to give them and when to follow them. Vincent never could drill that into that stupid head of yours."

My father is having me watched. That's the only plausible way he could know about Bri. It's not like we were out in the open dating like a regular couple. Then again, I was stupid enough to bring her to that football game where my entire staff was present. I guess there's a chance some employees could still be loyal to him. Can't see how, though. Vincent Acerbi is the definition of cruel. He worked the staff at Acerbi Imports, as well as the staff employed at his house on Manhattan Beach, to the bone. Nothing was ever good enough for him. No one was ever loyal enough to him. Since day one of taking over, I've treated every person employed with respect.

My siblings wouldn't have told him. CC fears my father and Luca hates him as much as I do.

Mona despises him. I'm certain she thinks he's responsible for my mother's death. I've never told anyone what Caprice saw when she was little, not even Eric, and certainly not Luca. My sister witnessed my father push our mother down the stairs during an argument they were having. She's been terrified of him ever since and didn't tell me about it until several years later. By then, I had already passed basic training at the DEA Academy and everything was being set into motion to bring my father's organization down.

Had I found out sooner I would have killed him. And maybe I should have, but I thought attacking him the right way—the legal way—would be better for my family. I made a promise to my mother well before she was killed that I would protect Luca and CC from Vincent's way of life. It's a promise I intend to keep, only now I have Bri and Gabriel to protect too.

Ignoring everything Diaz has revealed, I continue with my plan.

"When you hurt my woman, you took something from me I can never get back. You killed my unborn child." My face distorts as the anger, hatred, and despair sinks deeper inside me. Now it's his turn for realization to dawn as his black eyes grow large. "I think it's only fair I take yours from you. An eye for an eye— right?"

His eyes flash, but he recovers quickly, masking his true expression.

"I don't have a kid." He laughs but there is no humor behind it.

"No?" I smile, cocking my head to the side, twisting the weapon in my hand.

Diaz is silent, waiting for me to play my hand—which I intend to do.

"Just because you're only fifteen-years older than him doesn't mean you didn't father him." His lips thin into a firm line. "Just because he was raised by another man, bearing another man's last name, doesn't mean Brandon Marino isn't your son."

I have him exactly where I want him. His last thoughts will be thinking I plan to murder his only son. And that's exactly what I want.

"You fucking touch—"

I pull the trigger. The bullet penetrates his head, and in an instant Sebastian Diaz is dead, blasted to Hell, exactly where he deserves to be. I only wish I could watch him burn over and over and who knows, maybe when my turn comes that's exactly where I'll end up for the things I've done, too.

Diaz's life is the second life I've taken, but this time I feel nothing.

No guilt.

No shame.

No regret.

He tried to make me play by his rules, just as my father tried years ago. Diaz tried to hold the people I love against me to put me back in line.

Too bad for him that line was severed the day I decided to join the DEA nine years ago. I have my father to thank for making that decision easy. Had he not thrown me face first into his dirty world, showed me exactly what "our family" would do to stay two steps ahead of the law, I might not be standing where I am today.

It was a shock—at nineteen—to learn my best friend's father was a DEA agent. An agent that wanted his son to follow in his footsteps. It was an even bigger shock to learn my mother had been working with Eric's dad the last year of her life to bring my father and his organization down.

The kicker was Eric wouldn't join if they didn't recruit me too. E hadn't known about his own father's assignment to bring the Acerbis to the ground. Eric just wanted me away from my father. He knew my dad was bad—didn't know how bad—but he knew he didn't want me on the other side of the law with my father. We couldn't have been friends anymore. We shouldn't have been friends to begin with.

My brother nor my sister know anything about my undercover job. Eric and our SAIC are the only two people I communicate with. Justin Summers knows, but he and I already have enough bad blood between us that we try to stay out of each other's way. Everyone including my father thinks E and I stopped being friends when he left for basic training.

My family will never know. My duty has and will always be to protect the people I love. Not my father. Any love I had for that bastard vanished the moment he forced me to pull the trigger, ending an innocent man's life.

I made a promise to a dead woman that I'd never let my little brother or sister be touched by our father's evil. I wouldn't let them see his true colors or ever get close to Vincent's criminal activities or be tarnished by his alliances.

I just never factored in Bri or a child.

Bri is my biggest weakness. And if I get to know my son, he will be too.

Weaknesses are dangerous.

Weaknesses get people killed.

I love them all: Bri, Gabe, Luca, CC, my niece, and Mona too fucking much to let any harm come to them over what I chose to do with my life.

The hardest thing I'll ever have to do is walk away from my love and my kid.

But it has to be done.

Fuck.

I hope I have the strength to do this, because if I don't and something happens to either of them, it'll be worse than death to live knowing one or both got caught in the crossfire.

I HOPE YOU ENJOYED DIRTY WAR AND THE BONUS SCENE. DIRTY SIN IS NOW AVAILABLE AND THE CONCLUSION TO THEIR STORY!

ALSO BY N. E. HENDERSON

ACKNOWLEDGMENTS

To my loyal readers and new ones—thank you for reading this story and my other books. Thank you for supporting me, loving my stories and characters, and for being a friend. Thank you for the honest reviews for leave.

To Tesha—I love you my friend and thank you for being on my team. You are the perfect beta reader and first editing my books get. We were meant to be brought together. I know I can count on you to give me honest feedback. To tell me when you love something and when you hate it or it isn't working. You are great friend and I'm so very thankful for your help.

To Ellie, my editor—you'll never get rid of me now. Not after having to search and search for the editor that was right for me and my books. I finally found you! Thank you for polishing and making my words pretty. Thank you for not killing me when I missed my deadline and then the next one too. I'm beyond happy to have you as part of my team.

To Charisse, my best friend—I love you. I've said it before and I'll probably continue saying it, you save me when I needed it the most. You brought me back from self-doubt when I almost gave up writing. What a shame that would have been. Thank you for being a third set of eyes on my books even when you have your own books to write.

To Shannon, my cover designer—OMG! I don't know whart to say. The re-design of this series is amazing and beautiful and I'm so in love. This cover especially, it's my favorite.

To Melissa, thank you for being a fourth set of eyes on this book. One person can't catch anything and I'm so happy you fell in love with Dirty Blue and wanted to proofread this one too.

To my friends in my Reader Group—thank you for supporting me. Thank you for your friendship and thank you for your feedback on my books.

ABOUT THE AUTHOR

N. E. Henderson is the author of sexy, contemporary romance. When she isn't writing, you can find her reading some form of romance or in her Maverick playing in the dirt. This is Nancy's sixth book.

For more information:
www.nehenderson.com
nancy@nehenderson.com
facebook.com/authornehenderson
instagram.com/nehenderson
tiktok.com/nehenderson.author

Manufactured by Amazon.ca
Bolton, ON